Sicilian Carousel

by Lawrence Durrell

TRAVEL

Bitter Lemons
Reflections on a Marine Venus
Prospero's Cell

—

NOVELS

Monsieur, or The Prince of Darkness
The Revolt of Aphrodite: Tunc, Nunquam
The Alexandria Quartet:
Justine, Balthazar, Mountolive, Clea
Justine
Balthazar
Mountolive
Clea
The Black Book
The Dark Labyrinth

—

LETTERS AND ESSAYS

Spirit of Place, edited by Alan G. Thomas
Lawrence Durrell and Henry Miller:
A Private Correspondence, edited by George Wickes

—

POETRY

Selected Poems (*new edition*)
Vega
The Ikons
The Tree of Idleness

—

DRAMA

Sappho

—

HUMOUR

Sauve Qui Peut
Stiff Upper Lip
Esprit de Corps
The Best of Antrobus

—

FOR YOUNG PEOPLE

White Eagles Over Serbia

View of Messina before the earthquake

LAWRENCE DURRELL

THE VIKING PRESS
NEW YORK

Published in 1977 by The Viking Press
625 Madison Avenue, New York, N.Y. 10022

LIBRARY OF CONGRESS CATALOGING IN PUBLICATION DATA
Durrell, Lawrence.
Sicilian carousel.
Includes index.
1. Sicily—Description and travel. 2. Durrell,
Lawrence—Journeys—Italy—Sicily. I. Title.
DG864.2.D87 914.58'04'920924 77-4170
ISBN 0-670-64362-9

Printed in the United States of America
Set in Monotype Garamond

For Diana and Yehudi, fixed stars

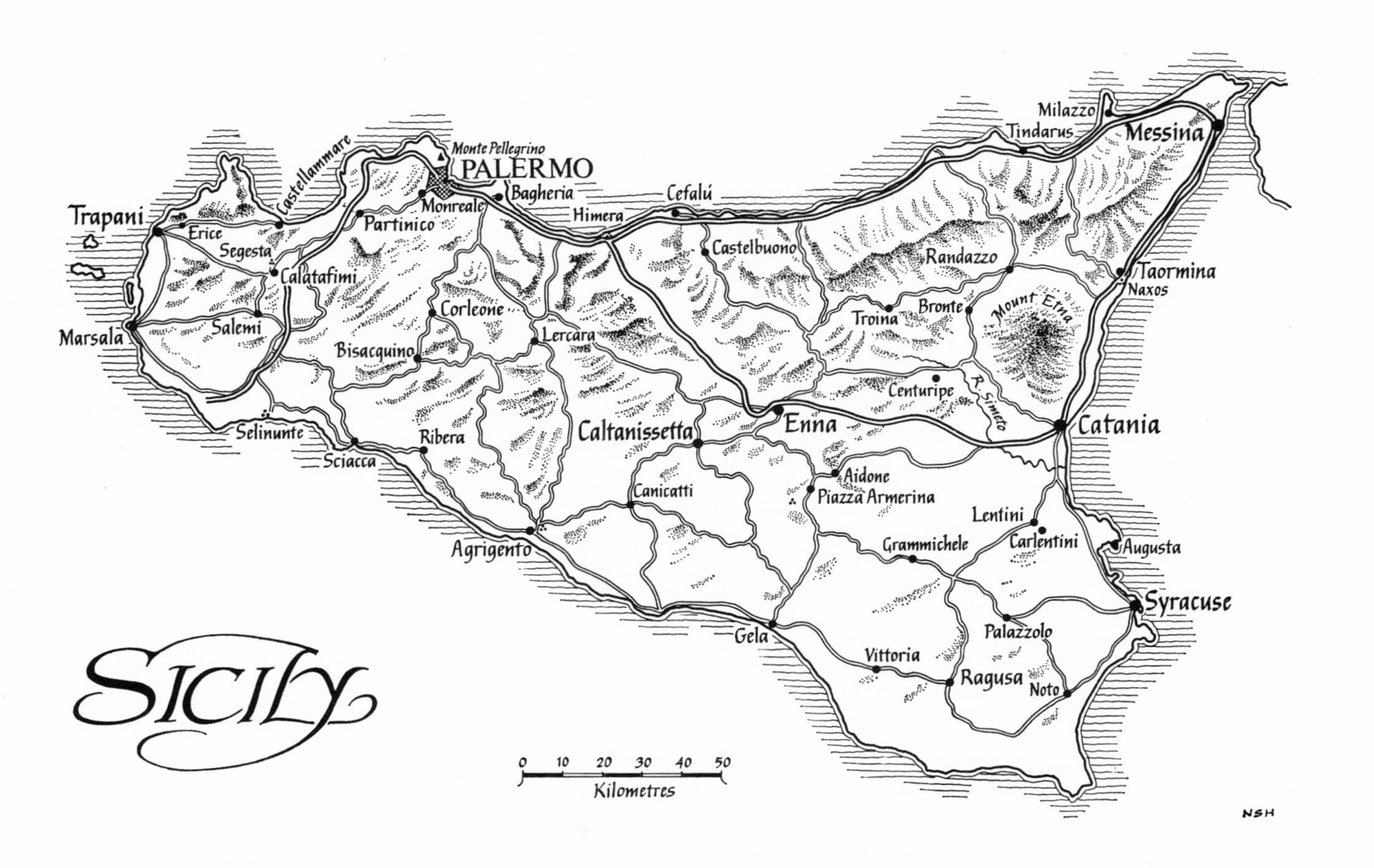
SICILY
Trapani
Erice
Segesta
Castellammare
Calatafimi
Salemi
Marsala
Selinunte
Sciacca
Partinico
Monreale
Monte Pellegrino
PALERMO
Bagheria
Himera
Cefalú
Corleone
Bisacquino
Ribera
Lercara
Agrigento
Caltanissetta
Canicatti
Castelbuono
Enna
Troina
Bronte
Randazzo
Centuripe
R. Simeto
Mount Etna
Tindarus
Milazzo
Messina
Taormina
Naxos
Catania
Aidone
Piazza Armerina
Gela
Grammichele
Lentini
Carlentini
Augusta
Syracuse
Palazzolo
Vittoria
Ragusa
Noto
0 10 20 30 40 50
Kilometres
NSH

Acknowledgements

Though all the characters in this book are imaginary I would like to thank some real people who made it possible as well as pleasurable. M. Pages and Madame Robert of Nîmes-Voyages for their itinerary and Simone Lestoquard for hunting up the illustrations in Paris.

L.D.

Contents

Poems

Illustrations

Arrival

Arrival

As I explained to Deeds more than once during the course of our breakneck journey round Sicily in the little red coach, nobody has ever had better reasons than I for not visiting the island. I had let my visit go by default for many a year, and now with increasing age and laziness and the overriding fact—no, Fact in upper case—of Martine's death, what on earth was the point? I could surely spare myself the kind of sentimental journey which would be quite out of place and out of context? Yes or no? Deeds only shook his head and tapped out his pipe against a wall. "If you say so," he said politely, "but you seem to be enjoying it very much." I was.

The bare fact of my arrival in Martine's own private island had in some way exorcised the dismal fact of her disappearance from the scene—so much had it impoverished life in general, and not for me alone. Moreover the luck was that I was able to talk a little about her, for though Deeds had not known her he had actually seen her quite often driving about Cairo and Alexandria, and lastly about Cyprus where I had helped her to build the ambitiously beautiful house which Piers had designed for her around a cruciform central room which both vowed was based on a Templar motif. But now they were both dead! In some of those long telephone conversations which somehow never succeeded in fully repairing our long-relinquished attachment to the Cyprus past, I could hear, or thought I could hear, the chatter of waves upon the beach of Naxos, the Sicilian Naxos where she had at last come to roost like a seabird, secure at last from politics and civil strife alike. Happy, too, in the possession of the Man That Never Was and her "blithe and beautiful" children.

Unexpected and fateful is the trajectory which life traces out for our individual destinies to follow. I could not have predicted her

Sicilian life and death in Cyprus, years ago. In fact, the Sicilian invitation was one of long standing, and the project of a visit to Naxos was one which had hung fire for many years. But it had always been there. I must, I simply must, she insisted, visit her on her home ground, see her children, meet her husband. And once or twice we almost did meet, the very last time in Rome. Yet never here, for each time something suddenly came up to prevent it. I think neither of us had seriously reflected on the intervention of something as unusual as death—though my wife, Claude, among her warmest friends, had suddenly surprised and saddened everyone by falling ill of a cancer and disappearing. Lesson enough, you would think; but no, I delayed and procrastinated on the Sicilian issue until suddenly one day Martine herself had floated out of reach. That last long incoherent letter—no, absolutely indecipherable—had not alarmed me unduly. An impulsive girl, she was accustomed to write in letters a foot high on airmail paper, and so terribly fast that the ink ran, the pages stuck together, and the total result even under a magnifying glass was pure cuneiform; say, an abstract drawing done in wet clay by the feet of a pigeon. But now the plane hovered and tilted and the green evening, darkening over the planes of coloured fields girdling Catania, swam up at us. The island was there, below us.

Thrown down almost in mid-channel like a concert grand, it had a sort of minatory, defensive air. From so high one could see the lateral tug of the maindeep furling and unfurling its waters along those indomitable flanks of the island. And all below lay bathed in a calm green afterglow of dusk. It looked huge and sad and slightly frustrated, like a Minoan bull—and at once the thought clicked home. Crete! Cyprus! It was, like them, an island of the mid-channel—the front line of defence against the huge seas combing up from Africa. Perhaps even the vegetation echoed this, as it does in Crete? I felt at once reassured; as if I had managed to situate the island more clearly in my mind. Magna Graecia!

But it wasn't only Martine I had come to see. I had other pressures and temptations—inevitable when half my living came from travel-journalism. Yet it was she who placed her darts most cunningly in spots where they cost me most pangs of guilt. For example: "You are supposed to be somewhat of an authority on Mediterranean islands—yet you neglect the biggest and most beautiful! Why? Is it because I am here?" A question which must remain forever unanswered. "After all," the letter continued, "fifteen years is a long time. . . ." It wasn't that either. It was just my old slavish habit of procrastination. The invitation had always been accepted in the depths of my own mind. But circumstances were against it—though I made several false beginnings. And of course we missed each other elsewhere—Paris, New York, Athens; it was extremely vexatious yet it could not be helped. And of course there would always be time to repair this omission and repair the fifteen-year-old breach in our friendship. . . .

In Cyprus, during those two magnetic summers we had discussed at great length the meaning of the word I had invented for people stricken by the same disease as ourselves: islomanes. I had even written a trilogy of books about Greek islands in a vain attempt to isolate the virus of islomania—with the result that later, in an age of proliferating tourism, the Club Méditerranée had even adopted the phrase as a *cri de guerre*—blessed by the French glossies. I had the impression that it had all but made the *Medical Encyclopaedia*. And now?

Well, I had brought with me a few of those long amusing and tender letters to look over as we voyaged; almost all that I knew of Sicily today came from them. In Cyprus she had been a fledgling writer and I had tried to help her tidy an overgrown manuscript about Indonesia called *The Bamboo Flute*. Somewhere it must still be knocking about. It had moments of good insight and some metaphors vivid enough to incite cupidity for I borrowed one for *Bitter Lemons*, but *con permesso* so to speak, that is to say, honestly.

There were of course other strands woven into the skein, like the repeated invitations from an editor in New York to consider some long travel articles on the island. I visited my travel agent in the nearby town of Nîmes where, like an old stork, he nested in a mass of travel-brochures and train-tickets. He was rather a cultivated old man, an ex-schoolmaster who had a tendency to think of himself as a cross between a psychiatrist and the Grand Inquisitor himself. "The thing for you," he said pointing a long tobacco-stained finger at me, "is the Sicilian Carousel—every advantage from your point of view. You will have Roberto as guide and a fine bus." My soul contracted. But truth to tell, the invitation from New York had in some queer way settled the matter. It was also as if Martine had given me a nudge from beyond the grave: had summoned me. But the thought of facing up to the chance adventures of the road made me uneasy. I had become a bit spoiled with too much seclusion in my old bat-haunted house in Provence. My friend must have divined my train of thought for he at once said, "You need a change—I feel it. And the Sicilian Carousel will give you what you need." He handed me a clutch of tomato-coloured brochures which did nothing to allay my misgivings at all. The beauties of Taormina—I knew of them. Who does not? I did not need French commercial prose to excite me. Yet as I drove homeward across the dry garrigues of the Languedoc I was in some obscure way rather happy—as if I had taken a decision which was, at that particular stage, appropriate and necessary. So be it, I thought. So be it.

On arriving home I switched on the lights and took a perfunctory look at Sicily in the encyclopaedia. They made it sound like the Isle of Wight. Then the evening papers arrived with their talk of strikes and lock-outs and so on, and my resolve faltered at the thought of spending days and nights asleep on my suitcase at Nice or Rome or Catania. But somehow I could not draw back now. I lit a log fire and put on a touch of Mozart to console me against these dark doubts. Tomorrow my friend would ring me with the reservations. I cannot pretend that my sleep was untroubled that night. I regressed in my dreams and found myself in the middle of the war in Cairo or Rhodes, missing planes or waiting for planes which never came. Martine was inexplicably there, behaving with perfect decorum, dressed in long white gloves, and subtly smiling. It was the airport but in the dream it was also Lord's and we were waiting for the emergence of the cricketers. I slept late and indeed it was my friend's call which shook me awake. "I have the whole *dossier* lined up," he said. He liked to make everything sound official and legal. "When do I leave?" I quavered. He told me the dates. Technically the Carousel started from Catania; my fellow-travellers were converging on that town from many different points in Europe.

So it was that I began to land-hop sideways across France on a strikeless fifth of July with the pleasant feel of thunder in the air and perhaps the promise of a night storm to come and refresh the Midi. And there was no sign of that old devil the mistral, which was a good omen indeed. It is always sad leaving home, however, and in the early dawn, after a spot of yoga, I took a dip in the pool followed by a hot shower and wandered aimlessly about for a bit in the garden. Everything was silent, the morning was windless. The tall pines and chestnuts in the park did not stir. In the old water-tower the brood of white barn-owls snoozed away the daylight after their night's hunting. The old car eased itself lingeringly away across the dry garrigues with their scent of thyme and rosemary and sage. The Sicilian Carousel was on. All my journeys start with a kind of anxious pang of doubt—you feel suddenly an orphan. You hang over the rail watching the land dip out of sight on the circumference of the earth—than you shake yourself like a dog and address yourself to reality once more. You point your mind towards an invisible landfall. Sicily!

Nice was clothed in a fragile brightness; wind furrowed the waters of the bay making the yachts dance and bow. Light clouds, washed whiter than white, passed smoothly against the summer sky. Coloured awnings, strips of Raoul Dufy—it was all brilliantly there. Yes, but the airport was a ferment of police and militia armed to the eyes with automatic weapons. We had been having an epidemic of aimless kidnappings and slayings during the past few weeks—the new patriotism. Hence all these precautions. The two Arab gentlemen up front hid something in their shoes—a permit to work or shirk I suppose? It could not have been a gun. Hashish? But I had to hurry to make my connection with Rome and I passed through all the X-raying in a rage of impatience. The travel-plan was, as always, brilliantly conceived down to the last detail, but no travel-agent can make allowances for such weird contingencies as a tommy-gun attack or a police search. Nevertheless I did it, but only just. We skated off the end of the Nice runway and out over the sea once more, rising steadily until the regatta below us became a bare scatter of pinpoints on the hazy blue veil. I had now become quite detached, quite resigned in my feelings; the sort of pleasant travel-numbness had set in. Consigning my soul to the gods of change and adventure I had a short sleep in which I had a particularly vivid dream of Martine—but it was Cyprus, not Sicily. There were problems about her land which I was helping to settle in my limping Greek. And then, superimposed on this scene was the troublesome poem about Van Gogh which, like an equation, had refused to come out over the months. I had become so fed up with it—it was almost very good—that I had tried publishing it in its unfinished state in order to provoke it to complete itself. In vain. It needed both pruning and clinching up in a number of places. It was a charity to suppose that Sicily might do the trick, yet why not? A jolt was in order.

Rome airport was no consolation—for it was being literally riven apart, torn up, bulldozed into heaps, smashed. Red dust rose from it as if from a sacrificial pyre. To the roar of planes was added the squirming and snarling of tractors wrestling with the stumps of trees. It was for all the world like the battles of mammoths in the Pleistocene epoch. Improvised footpaths and bridges across this battlefield awaited the visitors on the international lines. As for the internal and domestic flights a whole new airport had been constructed for them—but transport was lacking. Nor were there any taxis, it seemed. Glad that I had packed so lightly I humped my effects and jogged along like the half-witted Sherpa I was towards the new buildings, following clusters of green arrows. I had a good hour and a half in hand for the Catania plane which was a relief, but when I reached my objective I found that once again all passengers were being X-rayed for guns and then passed through the long smugglers' tunnel. On the whole a bad ambience in which to start on a holiday journey, but my spirits rose slightly for I saw ahead of me what seemed to be the whole cast of "Porgy and Bess", or some other big musical, being processed with operatic dignity by weary policemen. It was complicated by the fact that the only bar lay outside the clearance area and some of the cast kept slipping out of the cordon to buy a drink or a sandwich, to the annoyance of the officials. There were some cries and expostulation. One tipsy member of the party broke into a soft-shoe routine which won all hearts but did nothing to settle the problems of the police. At last all was in order and the company assembled in a waiting-room for their plane—alas, they were not to be on ours.

I was turned aside into another enclosure where the Catania passengers were submitting resignedly to the same processing. Immediately ahead of me was a huge Sicilian mother who had, as far as I could make out, won a fertility competition and had come up to Rome to receive her prize and make television history by explaining how she had won the trophy. She had her supporting evidence with her in the persons of six large and lugubrious sons with heavy moustaches. They caused quite a fuss in spite of their good nature and had to be pushed and pulled and shoved like cattle. And volubility! How delicious and infantile Italian sounded after a long absence, how full of warmth and good humour. The policemen conducted, so to speak, their swelling emotions with the bunched tips of their fingers—all so *molto agitato*. The Sicilian version of ox-eyed Hera did her own act back; then all swept into the waiting lounge and sank sighing into seats where the men fell into a prolonged brooding examination of their airtickets. They were on the plane but not of our party. We had been given little distinguishing rosettes for the Carousel. It was about time I pinned mine up. Immediately next to me was an aggrieved French couple with a small child who looked around with a rat-like malevolence. He had the same face as his father. They looked like very cheap microscopes. To my horror the mother wore a Carousel rosette. I bowed and they inclined their heads with coolness.

Then I saw Deeds sitting in a corner also with a distinguishing badge, bowed over his *Times*. I can't say I "recognised" him for I did not know him; but what gave me an instant shock of recognition was the clan to which he belonged. The desert boots, the trench-coat hiding a faded bush-jacket, the silk scarf knotted at his throat, the worn and weathered grip on the floor at his feet. . . . Had he appeared in a quiz I would have had no hesitation in writing out his *curriculum vitae*. Colonel Deeds, D.S.O., late Indian Army, later still, Desert Rat. Nowadays I suppose they have broken the mould of that most recognisable of species, the Eighth Army veteran. The clipped moustache, the short back and sides haircut. . . . "I see you are on this jaunt," he said mildly, to break the ice. And I said I was. His blue eyes had a pleasant twinkle. He said, "I have just come down from Austria. I don't suppose there'll be many of us on this flight." It was at Catania that we were to join the rest of the Carousel group—though the very word "group" gave me a twinge of resigned horror. If they were all like the two Microscopes in the corner I could just imagine the level of the conversation.

But Deeds was quite a find. He had, he said (somewhat apologetically), managed to secure one of the "plum" jobs on the Allied Graves Commission which entitled him to have a regular "swan" every two years, notably in Sicily his favourite island. ("You can have the whole Med, but leave me Sicily.") The jargon was heart-warmingly familiar—it was Cairo 1940. It was the lingo of El Alamein, of the Long Range Desert Group. We had done everything together, it seemed, except meet; and, I might add, fight, for I had spent those years safely in the Embassy at Cairo and later on in Alexandria. But it was a mystery how we had not contrived to meet. We were both, for example, at the fateful party given by Baron the photographer in a tethered Nile house-boat where he lived. Our chief entertainment was provided by a huge belly-dancer like a humming-top who, as she rotated, kept altering the axis of the overcrowded boat; once, twice, it shivered and righted itself again. But just as the orchestra swept into a climax the whole thing suddenly turned over with its hundred guests and we were all of us in the Nile. Deeds like myself had waded ashore, but a shadow was cast over what was a hilarious evening by the death of one of the guests, who had grabbed the landline of electric wire which fed the lights on the house-boat. He was instantly electrocuted. We remembered many other occasions at which we had both been present, both in Cairo and then later in Cyprus. Yet we had never met! It was bizarre. He even remembered Martine, "Rich society girl wasn't she? Good dancer." But I did not feature in these memories. Where had I been, he wanted to know?

As for Martine he remembered her, indeed had known old Sir Felix, her father. "A good-looking blonde? Yes, I do remember. She looked rather spoiled." Martine would not have forgiven him the description, for when I first met her it was only too true; and curiously enough when first we found ourselves alone on the deserted beaches beyond Famagusta, it was roughly her own estimate of herself. She had just come back from a trip to Indonesia and Bali and proposed to try her hand at a travel-book about the experience. "I found," she said somewhat disarmingly, "that I was becoming hopelessly spoiled by money, birth and upbringing. I decided to stop being a society fashion-plate and start trying to realise myself. But how, when you haven't much talent? I started with this journey, which I did entirely by bus and train. I avoided all the Embassies and all my compatriots. Now I want to settle in this island and live quite alone. But I'd like to write."

She was forthright and without vainglory and consequently very touching. I was terribly glad that chance had made us friends as I too had decided to settle in the island and was experiencing numberless difficulties in shaping up my little house in Bellapais, in the shadow of the Tree of Idleness which was for two marvellous summers our point of rendezvous. . . .

The Catania lounge had filled up now and I delayed expatiating on Martine to Deeds; I simply said that it gave me pleasure to recall her memory and that in venturing into Sicily I felt that I was accepting too late an invitation which I should have taken up years before. And also I expressed my misgivings about this way of doing it. I had begun to think that my decision to join the Carousel was utterly mad. "I shall loathe the group, I feel it. I was not made for group travel." Deeds looked at me with a quizzical air and said, after a pause: "Yes, one always does at first. It's just like joining a new battalion. You think: God, what horrible people, what ghastly faces and prognathous jaws, what badly aspected Saturns! Jesus, save me! But then after a time it wears off. You get to know them and respect them. And after a couple of battles you don't want to part with them. You see, you'll be sorry when it comes time to say goodbye." I didn't believe a word of it, but the presence of this quiet reserved Army officer was comforting, simply because we had a good deal in common and had lived through the same momentous epoch. "Remains to be seen," I said warily and Deeds unfolded his *Times* and scrutinised the cricket scores with the air of a priest concentrating on Holy Writ. I was tempted to ask him how Hampshire was doing, but it would have been false to do so; I had been out of touch with cricket for more than fifteen years and it was possible that Hampshire no longer existed as a county eleven. I turned and watched the sea unrolling beneath us, and the distant smudges of the island printing themselves on the hazy trembling horizon. Deeds grunted from time to time. In his mind's eye he could see green grass, hear the clicking of cricket balls. . . .

The evening had begun to fall softly and the grey-green theatrical light of the approaching sunset had begun to colour everything. The dusk seemed to be rising from the ground like a faint grey smoke. From this height the sea looked motionless and the relief-map of the island's southern slopes had attained a fixity of tone which made it look fabricated, unreal. Indeed, to be sincere, it was not vastly different from flying over Crete or Rhodes—at least not yet. I murmured something like this to Deeds who agreed but said, "Wait till we reach Etna—that's an individual sort of feature." So wait I did, drinking a bitter blush of Campari. We were slowly descending now in a carefully graduated descent: this could only be judged by the fact that the minutiae below us began suddenly to come into focus, to become coherent forms like farms and lakes and valleys. "There!" said my companion at long last and Etna took the centre of the stage to capture our admiring vision. It was very close indeed—for we had come down low to prepare the run in on Catania airport. It looked like a toy—but a rather dangerous one. Moreover it gave a small puff of dark smoke—a languid gesture of welcome, as if it had heard we were coming. Though we were flying not directly over it (I presumed because of the hot currents which it siphoned off), we were not too far to the side to avoid looking down into the charred crater—a black pit in the recesses of which something obscure boiled and bubbled. Then, as the range spread out a little I saw that it was not simply one crater but a whole network of volcanoes of which Etna was the most considerable in size and beauty. But everywhere there were other little holes in the earth-crust, for all the world as if the whole pie had burst out because of the heat in minor geysers. It was beautiful in its toy-like way, this range, and yet I could not avoid a slight feeling of menace about it. There was really no reason, in spite of the occasional severity of an outburst of lava. Etna had become an almost domesticated showpiece, and we were promised an "optional" ascent to the crater in the last week of the tour.

I was reminded, too, that the volcanic crack which here traversed the southern tip of Sicily passed also through the Ionian Sea, under Xante and a part of Greece near Corinth, and finally through Cyprus where it usually tore Paphos apart. Twice during my years there I had been woken by its passing during the night—with the mad roar of an underground train, seeming to pass under my very bed, while the dust rose in clouds and the timbers of my old house groaned in their sleep. Earthquakes, I have experienced quite a number! The premonitory signs too are strange if you are on the sea coast. The water becomes still and lifeless and almost opaque; a few little involuntary waves spin up, as if the sea was trying to be sick. And then the dead leaden hue of the horizon! Birds stop singing suddenly and dogs lope back to their kennels full of an inexplicable uneasiness. And then, when it does come, at first one only notices the eccentric behaviour of solid objects, like an electric wire swinging like a pendulum or an armchair mysteriously airborne. Then comes the roar like a thousand avalanches. And the small birds in the orchard fall to the ground and chirp. . . . "If you drew a line along the earth-crack, the long fault which ends somewhere in Persia I suppose.... Could one find similarities of temperament and outlook in the inhabitants who live along it?" Deeds shook his head; "The sort of question I distrust," he said, "unless you would say that they were all a little cracked. Revolutionary secessionists—Sicily is as much that as Crete and Cyprus."

The islands of the mid-channel are the earthquake ones, and they tend to be somewhat boisterous. Never accuse a Sicilian of being a Roman, nor a Cretan of being from anywhere else. It was true; but somehow this kind of argument never led far enough. Deeds went on, as we started to swoop down on to the airstrip: "My troops were convinced for some weird reason that one's toenails grow faster in Sicily than anywhere else on earth. It was a strange thing to believe, but they did. They didn't believe in circumcision or the Ten Commandments. All their faith went into toenails and their rate of growth in Sicily. I had a toenail inspection once in my battalion just to test the matter out. There were a lot of misshapen toes and ingrowing nails and bunions, but nothing really definitive emerged except that I got ticked off by the general for not occupying myself more with the enemy."

"Perhaps it was German propaganda?"

We were prevented from pursuing this congenial theme by the fastening of safety-belts and the smooth run in. The small and chaotic airport of Catania was rather reassuring after the ruins of the Roman one. It was homely and provincial and it was clear that when any Sicilian arrived or departed from the island the entire family, down to the sixth degree of consanguinity, felt obliged to come and see him off or meet him coming in. It was just like Corfu where people would walk right across the island as a pure courtesy to shed a farewell tear with one. And here they all were eating ice-cream and shrieking at each other in the strange Italian they affect which is somehow heavy and almost guttural. The airy-fairy lilt of the Roman line had given place to something which reminded one faintly of the dialect of Trieste or the Ticino. But the air was fine, everything had a candid and fresh smell and feel. Landscape-addicts can in the space of this first sniff—not at the actual odour but at the spiritual whiff—detect the fruitful and blessed spot instantly. Unfruitful places, however superficially beautiful, smell either dead or simply odourless and without character. Sicily smelt fine, though a purist might have said it was only the smell of floor-polish which the cleaners were rubbing into the lounge floors.

But the struggle to claim our bags and disentangle ourselves from the airport authorities took a bit of time. I could see why; it was the arrival and departure complex of the Sicilian soul. Everyone had brought along six relations for the ride and each insisted on holding his suitcase. Consequently a tremendous snatch and grab scene ensued at every exit—people trying to outvie each other in family warmth. Even greybeards treated the whole thing as a rugger scrum, plunging in with arms flailing. The result was that we were expelled in and out of swing doors, hemmed in by the press, with the speed of toothpaste out of a tube. But it was good-natured shoving. And pretty soon we discovered our bags and slung them into a taxi as instructed by a man with a hat reading "Guide".

The French Microscopes showed some reluctance joining us, clearly hating our general appearance. But here Deeds' compassion proved fruitful. He did what I should have done. He addressed them in correct but rather wooden Britannic French. The result was astonishing; their faces bloomed like watered flowers. Their relaxation transformed them into rather a decent-looking couple with a nervous child who would make his way one day as a chartered accountant. It is funny how one can sometimes read situations like one reads a newspaper. We now saw written on their faces the fact that this was the first time they had ever left France for a foreign trip and that they were terrified because they knew no other language and could not communicate with the barbarous tribes through whose countries they would have to pass. The result was a panic almost equivalent to a stricture. Even their faces became constipated by mere fear. Now, in the knowledge that Deeds knew a few French nouns and verbs they were transformed and inundated him with friendly chat. I was delighted with my friend—as I dared to consider him—for he had neutralised their horror and transformed them into ordinary middle-class people like ourselves. It was a step forward.

But Catania was hot and sultry that evening and it was the

moment when the offices were emptying and everyone was rushing home to dinner. The suburbs looked cavernous and dirty and overgrown and our taxi made hardly better time than a rickshaw with a drunken driver. However, progress we did, and I spent my time gazing out at the strange box-like squares. Here and there we passed a pleasant airy square and breathed a little bit of space. The one which contains the insignia of the town, in the form of a charming operatic elephant and a lava obelisk, had great charm and we promised ourselves a longer prowl about it in the evening after dinner when we had met our fellow-travellers.

Catania

Catania

Our fellow-travellers! Oh God, what was in store for us? But the hotel to which we repaired was all right in its gloomy way, and at least there was plenty of hot water. So we repaired the damage to our beauty and then held up the bar for a calamitously expensive Scotch, feeling that it might help us to overcome the horrors in store for us. But as time wore on and the pangs of hunger began to twinge at us we moved into the ghastly white light of the long dining-room and took up an emplacement at one of the tables (the group held a strategic corner of the place to itself) marked *Carousello Siciliano*. Indeed wherever we went our reserved seats were thus marked. It was engaging enough, but on this first evening while we waited with impatience for our fellow-travellers to arrive (would it be rude to start?) it sounded ghoulish.

However the Scotch was so expensive we simply couldn't keep on ordering it. We decided therefore to begin, and to hell with the rest of the Carousel. But in that glaring white light with its bevy of indolent waiters everything was indecision. We had taken up positions at the first reserved table and to steady our nerves Deeds tried to be facetious in a reassuring way, telling me that these marked tables had a tang of opera about them, and that he felt he would like to burst into song like a gondolier. But it was heavy stuff and he knew it. Well, boldly we started in on the dinner at last, a disappointing little offering of spaghetti or rice with gravy. It was honest enough fare I suppose but it had clearly been blessed by British Railways. Moreover the waiter who served us was suffering either from a terrible bereavement or a deep Sicilian Slight. He could hardly contain his sobs; his head hung low and waved about; his eye rolled. He mastered himself for serving, yes, but only just and when it came to wavering the cheese over the plate his repressed fury almost got the better of him and Deeds mildly took his wrist to help him scatter his Parmesan.

We were well embarked on this introduction to the joys of the island cuisine when there came the noise of a bus and voices of foreign tang—and we knew that our fellows of the Carousel had arrived. They stacked their baggage in the hall and then like ravenous wolves made a bee line for the dining-room where we sat, gazing bravely through our tears at them. "God! They do look ghastly," admitted Deeds, and so they did. And so, I suppose, did we, for when they saw us sitting at a Carousel table their beseeching looks turned heavenward and their lips moved, no doubt in prayer, at the thought of being locked up in a bus with us for two weeks. . . . It was mutual, this first appraising glance. They straggled in in twos and threes until about fifteen to seventeen hungry people were seated around us being served by the sobster waiter and his colleagues. The white light poured down on us turning us all to the colour of tallow. But Deeds had found a very pleasant dry white wine and this helped. In gingerly fashion we started passing the salt and pepper, picking up dropped napkins, and generally showing a leg.

Later of course our companions developed distinct identities but on that first evening in the dismal light it was impossible to distinguish accurately between the Anglican Bishop who had developed Doubts, the timid young archaeologist, the American dentist who had eloped with his most glamorous patient, the French couple of a vaguely diplomatic persuasion and all those others who hung about on the outskirts of our table like unrealised wraiths. Later their characters printed themselves more clearly. Tonight we gathered a few random impressions, that was all. The Bishop was testy and opinionated and had been airsick. He kept sticking his forefinger in his ears and shaking vigorously to clear the canals, as he put it. His wife was both tired and somewhat cowed. We knew nothing then about his nervous breakdown in the pulpit. His name was Arthur. The dentist was shy and hung his head when spoken to in a strong British accent while his partner looked pleasantly saucy. I sympathised with him. The Bishop spoke English as if he had a hot potato in his mouth. The rest of the table was made up by the rather distinguished French couple who could not, I decided, be diplomatic for they spoke no English and were glad to lean on us as translators.

And then Roberto made his relaxed appearance, shaking hands all round and moving smilingly from table to table, slipping from one language to another with smooth skill and checking off our names on the tourist list. He combined charm and kindness; later we discovered that he was efficient as well. He knew Deeds quite well from a previous trip and their greeting was most cordial. My friend explained when he had left us that Don Roberto came of a noble but penniless family and had been a university lecturer in history; but the boredom of academic life with its endless intrigues had sent him in search of something more suitable to a lively nature. He had found it in becoming guide, philosopher and friend to the travellers on the Carousel. His calm friendliness had an immediately reassuring effect; it acted as a catalyst.

We dug deeper into our charmless food and poured out more stoups of wine. It would have been a pity, after spending so much money on the trip, not to enjoy it a little. The French diplomat had a head which came straight off a Roman coin—the benign features of one of the better emperors. His wife was fearfully pale and looked very ill; she was clearly convalescent after some obscure illness and looked all the time as if she were on the point of fainting. The concern of her husband was very evident. The dentist ate his food with a sort of soundtrack; he was clearly a great masticator, and probably a health-food addict. The French Microscopes were far off; they had found another microscope to talk to.

"When I was young," said Deeds, to nobody in particular, "there was a great Victorian moustache-cup among the family heirlooms, out of which my father drank his Christmas punch. On this object the family had had engraved the motto DEEDS NOT WORDS which is perhaps why I am so dashed taciturn."

Though it was relatively late when our dinner was concluded with a pungent *grappa* we were disinclined to turn in straight away A few of our fellow-travellers took refuge in the lounge where coffee was available and where there was light enough to write postcards, sort papers, count up currency. Roberto was talking to the pretty German girl about archaeology. There were two striking but severe-looking French ladies sending views of the town to their relations. They were very finely turned out and would obviously be destined to match up with the proconsular gentleman and his distinguished but pale wife. We were to be a group speaking three languages—which offered no problems for Roberto. He smiled and waved to us as we passed through the swing doors into the warm and fragrant darkness outside. It was pleasant to stretch one's legs once more, and the hot night was full of flower scents. Quite soon, however, Deeds steered us into the little Bellini garden I had hoped to see before we left—for it was here that Martine in high summer had sat to write me a letter and mend the broken thong of a sandal.

It was a good letter, and I had brought it with me to Sicily in order to try and re-experience it here. It had come after a silence of nearly two years and after several long journeys. "We have been brought up to believe that facts are not dreams—and of course they are." It was strange to think of her penning the words as she sat here among all this greenery. And there were other little touches of observation too, which proved that the writer in her had gone on maturing long after the ambition to write had become dispersed by her domestic concerns. A note about the curious volcanic stone which gave a feeling of weightlessness and insubstantiality, and altered the sound of heels upon it. Then, too, of the marvellous vulgarity of Bellini's "Puritani" as played in Sicily—its appropriateness to the place and mood. Smoking a cigarette I pondered these matters beside a silent Deeds. The air was rich with the smell of invisible flowers. I wondered where people went when they died. Right back into the painting I suppose.

"Bedtime," said Deeds, looking at his watch and I rose to follow him through the dark streets to the hotel. Here we elected to turn in right away for the call on the morrow was to be a relatively early one and I had to rearrange my affairs against a week of hard travelling. The words "hard travelling" were a joke when one thought of the luxury of the Carousel. Nevertheless.

But before I put out my light I could not resist opening the little green file of her letters in order to re-read the two she had sent me from here while she had been touring the island in her little car. There were good things there, things which connected. . . . "I always remember the way you pronounce the word 'Impossible!' But Larry dear the impossible has always been just within man's grasp—happiness and justice and love. You feel it so strongly among these battered vestiges. It is always such a near miss. O why can't man reach for the apple instead of waiting for Eve?" Why indeed? "The universe is always bliss side up if only he knew it."

To sleep. To dream. Light airs, ever so faintly sulphurous seemed to drift into the room through the curtains. Does lava have any smell—or am I imagining things?

I had an extraordinarily vivid dream of our long-lost selves reliving a short sequence of our Cyprus lives. The house had been built on a promontory hard by a little Turkish mosque. Underneath was a tiny beach where we bathed half the night. Though the island had plunged into an insurrection against our rule there were pockets of emptiness where one could still find a moment of ordinary peace in which to swim and talk—yet never be too far from a pistol. By that time I was working in Nicosia but I used to slip over the Kyrenia range as often as possible to meet her. As a matter of fact I had got her into bad habits—for we often drove outside the sectors under army control and deep into enemy country, so to speak, in order to see a particular church or bathe at a special beach I knew. How dangerous was it? Not very, but the thing was problematic and depended upon a chance meeting with a platoon of resistance fighters armed with automatic weapons. It salted the whole operation with a fitful uneasiness. One never knew.

And then, too, one had a bad conscience like naughty children who know they are disobeying their parents. But these sallies brought us very close together. She sat beside me with my pistol lying in her lap—just to have it handy in case we were overtaken on some country road by some youthful band of hotheads. More than once a car had been overtaken and shot up by the EOKA youth. Through all the beautiful hills and dales of the island we travelled thus, with our lunch in a hamper and our towels beside us. Nothing ever happened, thank God. But once I had a glimpse of the courage of Martine. We had climbed a hill to visit a church and left the car along the olive groves. Having stayed rather longer than usual we came down at dusk to find three darkly clad men in the middle foreground advancing towards the grove where our car lay.

It looked suspiciously like a reception committee which had finally made contact—perhaps signalled by one of the villages through which we had passed. My heart sank as I measured our distance from the car. I cursed myself for taking such risks, specially with the precious lives of others. How foolhardy to imagine that just by staggering our times and places for excursions we could in the long run escape the vigilance of the terrorists! But there was no time for breast-beating, for they had seen us coming. At all costs we must recover our car. They had something in their hands, perhaps weapons. It was still too far to see clearly. My hand sought the little pistol which lay under a napkin in the food haversack. We advanced arm-in-arm with a simulated nonchalance.

I could have imagined a slightly tremulous Martine in the circumstances, but not at all. The hand on my arm was firm and untrembling and her step was light and confident. It was a moment of tension which did not last long however. We saw that they were forest-guards making some sort of inventory of the trees—forest-guards and tax-collectors no doubt. The only weapons they carried were pens and ink and writing blocks. They talked in preoccupied tones, and looked up idly to see us pass in front of them and regain the car. It was irritating to have been scared by such a meeting; and Martine, divining my pique, smiled and pinched my arm affectionately. "Not this time," she said, as I let in the clutch and eased the car out of the olive shadow on to the tarmac. The sunny glades smelt of rosemary and dust even in the dream; a blessed wind rose with our movement and cooled our foreheads. Martine was deeply thoughtful—that beautiful face with its snow-brown skin held sideways against the flying olive-groves, deeply thinking. No one could look like that and not be thinking very deep thoughts. I offered her a penny. "I was wondering what we will have for dinner," she replied with the same Socratic air. And then slept like a white Sphinx.

The dream faded into an untroubled sleep, and when I woke it was almost seven on a cloudless morning. Time for a dip in the hotel pool before breakfast. And here I found the gallant Bishop performing feats of youthful athleticism while his wife sat in a deck chair holding his towel. His morning boom of greeting proved that he had become acclimatised by now and was ready for anything. He swung about on elastic calves and even was so bold as to go off the top board—at which his wife covered, not her eyes, but her ears. I hoped he would not become too hearty and decide to hold Protestant services in the lounge as is the way of bishops travelling in heathen countries. I returned to pack and dress and then descended to find Deeds eating a slow breakfast and picking his way through the local Italian paper while Roberto guided him with an occasional bit of free translation. The French proconsular couple shared our table and seemed rested and refreshed.

I thought, however, that they eyed me a trifle curiously, as if they too were busy speculating as to what I did in life. The German girl was reading Goethe's enthusiastic account of his own trip round Italy. I hoped to find the text in English or French as I knew no German. The Microscopes were wolfing their food and calling for refills of coffee with the air of people who knew that it was all paid for in advance. They were determined to leave no crumb unturned. Pretty soon, I could see, complaints would start. The British would revolt over the tea and the absence of fish-knives. The French would utter scathing condemnation of the cuisine. Poor Roberto! For the moment, however, all was harmony and peace. The novelty of our situation kept us intrigued and good-tempered. The brilliance of the Sicilian sun was enthralling after the northern variety. And then there was the little red bus which we had not as yet met, and which was at this moment drawing up outside the hotel to await us. It was a beautiful little camionette of a deep crimson-lake colour and apparently quite new. It was richly upholstered and smelt deliciously of fresh leather. It was also painstakingly polished and as clean inside as a new whistle. It gave a low throaty chuckle—the Italians specialise in operatic horns—and at the signal the chasseurs humped our baggage and started to stow.

We were introduced to its driver, a stocky and severe-looking young man, who might have been a prizefighter or a fisherman from his dark scowling countenance. His habitual expression was sombre and depressive, and it took me some time to find out why. Mario was a peasant from the foothills of Etna and understood no language save his own dialect version of Sicilian. He also distrusted nobs who spoke upper class—and of course Roberto spoke upper class and was a nob, being a university man. But from time to time when a word or a phrase became intelligible to Mario the most astonishing change came about in that black scowling face. It was suddenly split (as if with an axe-blow or a sabre-cut) by the most wonderful artless smile of a kindly youth. It was only lack of understanding that cast the shadow; the minute light penetrated he was absolutely transformed. But he was grim about his job, and would not touch a drop of drink throughout the trip; it made Roberto, who was a convivial soul, a trifle plaintive to see such devotion to duty. Well, on the sunny morning we gathered around the little bus and eagerly appraised it, for we would be virtually living in it for a week. It looked pretty good to me—the luxury of not having to drive myself. Mario shook hands darkly with us all, the proconsulars, the Microscopes, ourselves, the German girl, the two smart French ladies and the half dozen or so others who as yet swam in a sort of unidentifiable blur, waiting to develop their pictures, so to speak. Among them, as yet unidentified by science, were the egregious fellow called Beddoes, a Miss Lobb of London, and a rapturous Japanese couple, moon-struck in allure and wearing purple shoes.

Deeds and I settled ourselves modestly in the last two seats in the back row, enjoying therefore a little extra leg-room and a small lunette window of our own. The others took up dispositions no less thoughtful, realising that we would need space to stretch and smoke and doze. Across the aisle from us, however, there was an empty row and this was suddenly occupied by a passenger to whom we hadn't paid attention before. He was a somewhat raffish-looking individual of medium height clad in veteran tweeds with dirty turn-ups; also old-fashioned boots with hooks and eyes and scarlet socks. On his head he wore a beret at a rakish angle from under which effervesced a tangled mop of dirty curls worthy of Dylan Thomas. To everyone's discomfort he smoked shag in a small and noisome French briar. He talked to himself in a low undertone and smiled frequently, exposing very yellow canines. "A rather rum chap," whispered Deeds confidentially, and I could bet that after a pause he would sigh and add resignedly, "O well, it takes all sorts. . . ." The nice thing about Deeds was not only his kindness but his predictability. I felt I already knew him so well by now that I could guess the name of his wife—Phyllis. And so it proved to be. But the chap over the way had started to make conversation—a sort of sharp and knowing line of talk. He said his name was Beddoes and that he was a prep-school master. "Just been hurled out of a prep school near Dungeness for behaviour unbecoming to an officer and a hypocrite." He gave a brief cachinnation and sucked on his noisome dottle. Deeds looked thoughtful. Well, I could almost hear him think, if one goes abroad it is to meet new faces in new places.

Yet, at the moment all was harmony, all was beatific calm and indulgence. Even Beddoes seemed all right in his rather sharp-edged way. Later of course we were to ask God plaintively in our prayers what we had done to merit such a travelling companion. But not today, not on this serene and cloudless morning with its smiling promise of hot sunshine and a sea-bathe along the road. The little heartsblood-coloured bus edged off with its cargo into the traffic, feeling its way circumspectly about the town, while Roberto sat down beside the driver and conducted a voice test on the microphone through which he was to keep us intellectually stimulated throughout the Carousel. His own ordeal was just beginning, of course. At breakfast he had bemoaned a guide's fate to Deeds, saying that one was always telling people something they already knew or something they did not wish to know. One could never win. Sometimes, attacked by hysteria, he had tried telling people false facts at breakneck speed just to see if anyone was awake enough to contradict him: but nobody ever did. But today he ran a certain risk with the Bishop as a passenger, for the latter sat forward eagerly, on the *qui vive* like a gundog, all set to ingest Roberto's information. A trifle patronising as well, for it was clear from his manner that he already knew a good deal. Yes, it was as if he were doing a *viva voce* in school catechism. Roberto began somewhat defensively by saying that we would not have time to do everything as there was much which merited our judicious attention. "But we will do the two essential things so that you can tell your friends if they ask that you have seen the Duomo and St. Nicolo." It wasn't too bad as a ration, Deeds told me; but he had spent a delightful hour in the Bellini Museum and the Fish Market, both of which we should be missing on this trip. No matter. Sicily smelt good in a confused sort of way. I was anxious too to get a first glimpse of that curious architectural bastard Sicilian baroque which had so enraptured Martine. "You expect it to be hell, but you find it heavenly—sort of fervently itself like the Sicilians themselves." At that moment our bus passed under a balcony from which apparently Garibaldi had prefaced a famous oration with the words "*O Roma, O morte*".

Beddoes made some opprobrious comment about demagogues which earned him a glare from the sensitive Roberto. At the site of the no longer extant Greek theatre the guide uttered some wise words about Alcibiades, a name which made the Bishop frown. "A dreadful homo," said Beddoes audibly. Deeds looked rather shocked and moved three points east, as if to dissociate himself from this troublesome commentator. I hoped he wasn't going to go on like this throughout the journey. But he was. "Dreadful feller," said Deeds under his breath. Beddoes proved unquenchable and totally snubproof. Moreover he had very irritating conversational mannerisms like laying his forefinger along his nose when he was about to say something which he thought very knowing; or sticking his tongue out briefly before launching what he considered a witticism. Now he stuck it out to say, apropos Aeschylus, that his play *Women of Etna* was based on reality. "The women of Etna," he went on with a winning air of frankness, "were known in antiquity for their enormous arses. The whole play, or rather the chorus, revolves around them, if I may put it like that. The women . . ." But Roberto was wearing a little thin, at least his superb patience was markedly strained. "The play is lost," he hissed, and repeated the observation in French and German, lest there should be any mistake about it. But this remark of Beddoes was not lost on the German girl who was I later discovered called Renata and came from Heidelberg. She turned hot and cold. Beddoes winked at her and she turned her back.

The parent Microscopes held hands and yawned deeply. I wasn't shocked by this, though Roberto looked downcast. The reaction was at least honest and simple. The proconsulars had the air of having read up the stuff before coming on the trip, as of course anyone with any sense would have done. But I prefer to experience the thing first without trimmings and read it up when I get back home. I know that it is not the right way round, for inevitably one finds that one has missed a great deal; but it gives me the illusion of keeping my first impressions fresh and pristine. Besides, in the case of Sicily, I had my guide in Martine whose tastes, as I knew from long ago, coincided very closely with mine. Consequently I was not unprepared for the mixture of styles which she found so delightful. The little hint of austerity from the north housed the profuse and exuberant Sicilian mode, which itself glittered with variegated foreign influences—Moorish, Spanish, Roman. . . . But even Catanian baroque managed to convey a kind of dialect version of the Sicilian one, though its elements, fused as they were into several successive bouts of building after natural catastrophes, gave off a touching warmth of line and proportion which argued well for the rest. We paid our respects to Saint Agatha, the patron saint, in the cathedral dedicated to her, which wasn't, however, quite as thrilling as Roberto tried to make it sound—there seemed little about it except the good proportions which we might appreciate. As for

Agatha. . . . "I had an aunt called Agatha," said Deeds, "who was all vinegar. Consequently the name gives me a fearfully uneasy feeling."

But St. Nicolo was a different kettle of fish on its queer hill; it had a very strange atmosphere, apparently having been abandoned in the middle of its life to wear out in the sunshine, fronting one of the most elegant and sophisticated piazzas bearing the name of Dante. Apparently they ran out of funds to finish it off in the traditional elated style—and in a way it is all the better for it. The largest church in Sicily according to Roberto, it needs a lot of space-clearance to show off its admirable proportions; just like a large but beautifully proportioned girl might. We draggled dutifully round it, with a vast expenditure of colour film by the German girl and the Microscopes. Beddoes, too, seemed to admire it for he forebore to comment, but walked about and thoughtfully smoked his dreadful shag. Roberto tactfully sat in a stall for a good ten minutes to let us admire, and then launched into a succinct little vignette about the church and the site which, I am ashamed to say, interested nobody. It is not that culture and sunlight are mutually exclusive, far from it; but the day was fine, the voyage was only beginning, and the whole of the undiscovered island lay ahead of us. The little red coach whiffled its horn to mark its position and we climbed aboard with a pleasant sense of familiarity, as if we had been travelling in it for weeks. I was sure that among our party there would be someone who would prove an anthropomorphic soul (like my brother with his animals) and end by christening it Fido the Faithful. I was equally sure that when the time came to part from it Deeds would recite verses from "The Arab's Farewell to His Steed". These sentiments I was rash enough to confide to him, whereupon he looked amused but ever so slightly pained.

But by now we had bisected the town and nosed about the older parts, a journey which involved nothing very spectacular except perhaps a closer look at the little Catanian emblem—the Elephant Fountain with its pretty animal obelisk motif. And now it was time to turn the little bus towards the coastal roads which might bear us away in the direction of Syracuse where we would spend a night and a day in search of the past. But first we had to drag our slow way across the network of dispiriting suburbs which smother Catania as a liana smothers a tree. The sudden appearance of Etna at the end of one vista after another—she seems to provide a backcloth for all the main boulevards—reminded one how often the town had been overwhelmed by the volcano, which made its present size and affluence rather a mystery; for Etna is far from finished yet and Catania lies in its field of fire. But the suburbs . . . one might have been anywhere; the squalor was not even picturesquely Middle Eastern, just Middle Class. With the same problems as any other urbanised town in the world—devoured like them by the petrol engine, that scourge of our age.

But Roberto was well pleased with us for people had begun to unlimber; the Bishop chatted to the two smart ladies from Paris, who spoke English with the delightful accent of the capital which makes the English heart miss a beat. The proconsul made notes in the margin of his *Guide Bleu.* The Americans became more talkative after a long period of shyness, and the lady remarked loudly, "Yes, Judy is flexible, but not *that* flexible." The rest of her discourse was lost in the whiffle of the horn and the clash of changing gears—Mario was scowling and muttering under his breath at some traffic problem; he was the only one of us who seemed out of sorts. Roberto performed his task dutifully, describing everything through the loudspeaker with elegance. A distinct thaw had set in, however, and our voices rose; we spoke naturally to one another instead of whispering. This is how I came to overhear those tantalising fragments of talk, a phrase here or there, which, divorced from context, were to haunt my sleep. I was to wonder and wonder about the flexibility of Judy, mysterious as a Japanese Koan, until a merciful sleep liberated me from the appalling problem. Then one of the French ladies remarked on a clear note, "*Pour moi les Italiens du nord sont des hommes décaféinés*", a sentiment which made the Sicilian blood of Roberto throb with joy. But at last the coast road came in sight and we opened throttle and started to hare along upon winding roads above a fine blue sea. Never have I felt safer than when

Mario drove; his timing was perfect, his speeds nicely calculated not to awaken his drowsing or even sleeping charges, should they have been snoozing by any chance.

The opening stages of our journey were sensibly enough planned; this first day was an easy one in terms of time and distance. We wove across the vast and verdant Catanian Plain eagerly watching the skyline for the appearance of a stray Laestrygonian—the terrible ogres of the Homeric legend; I had a feeling that Ulysses had a brush with them but wasn't sure and made a note in my little schoolchild's *calpin* to look them up in more detail. I did not dare to ask the Bishop or Roberto. The Simeto, a sturdy little river, together with two smaller tributaries waters the plain, and it is celebrated for an occasional piece of choice amber floating in it, which it has quarried somewhere on its journey. But where? Nobody knows.

The old road turns inwards upon itself and slopes away towards Lentini and Carlentini whence a brutally dusty and bumpy road leads us onwards into the hills to draw rein at our first Greek site—a resurrected city not unlike Cameirus in Rhodes, but nowhere near as beautiful; yet a little redeemed by the site and the old necropolis. What landscape-tasters the ancient Greeks were! They chose sites like a soldier chooses cover. The basic elements were always the same, southern exposure, cover from the prevailing wind, height for coolness and to defeat the humidity of the littoral. They had none of our (albeit very recent) passion for sea-bathing; the sea was a mysterious something else pitched between a goddess of luck and a highway. It is not hard to imagine how they were—with their combination of poetry and practicality. There was no barrier, it seems, between the notions of the sacred and the profane either.

After a short briefing we were turned loose among the ruins like a flock of sheep—hardly more intelligent either, you might have thought, to watch us mooching about. The Microscopes had begun to feel hungry, and the pile of box lunches and flasks of Chianti were being unloaded and placed in the shade of a tree against the moment when culture had been paid its due. In the bright sunlight the blonde German girl reminded me a little of

Martine for she had the same thick buttercup hair and white-rose colouring which had made my friend such a striking beauty. But not the slow rather urchin smile with the two swift dimples that greeted the lightest, the briefest jest. Nor the blue eyes which in certain lights reminded one of Parma violets. But I was sure that here she had sat upon a tomb while her children played about among the ruins, smoking and pondering, or perhaps reading a page or two of the very same Goethe—as unconditional an addict of Sicily as she herself had become.

It was, however, a well-calculated shift of accent, of rhythm—I meant to spend the first day in the open air, lively with bees in the dazing heat, and where the shade of the trees rested like a damp cloth on the back of the neck. Little did it matter that the pizzas were a trifle soggy—but I am wrong: for the first faint murmurs of protest came from the French camp about precisely this factor. And the two graceful Parisians added that the paper napkins had been forgotten. Roberto swallowed this with resignation. Far away down the mildly rolling hillocks glittered the sea on rather a sad little bit of sandy littoral, and here we were promised an afternoon swim when we had digested our lunch, a prospect which invigorated me and raised the spirits of my companion. But some of us looked rather discountenanced by the thought, and Beddoes swore roundly that he wasn't going to swim in the sea with all its sharks; he wanted a pool, a hotel pool. He had paid for a pool and he was damn well going to insist on a pool or else. . . . So it went on.

Deeds, on the contrary, declared that things were not so bad after all; that we were all quite decent chaps and that no great calamities or internal battles need be expected. It was true. Even the Bishop, who in my own mind might be the one to inflict deep irritations on us because of his knowledgeability and insularity and patronising air—even he went out of his way to humour Roberto in terms which almost made him a fellow-scholar. I could see that he was a pleasant and conscientious man underneath an evident Pauline-type neurosis which is almost endemic in the Church of England, and usually comes from reading *Lady Chatterley's Lover* in paperback. Deeds had got quite a selection of guides to the island in English and French and these we riffled while we ate. He professed himself extremely dissatisfied by them all.

"It took me some time to analyse why—it's the sheer multiplicity of the subject matter. The damned island overflows with examples of the same type of thing—you have six cathedrals where in other places you would save up your admiration for the one or two prime examples. How can a guide book do justice to them all? It just can't, old man. Here you get six for the price of one, and the very excellence of what it has ends by fatiguing you." I wondered if he was right. The illustrations, however, to his books seemed to bear him out to a certain extent. Perhaps that is why Martine had remarked more than once in her letters, "What we lack here is a 'pocket' Sicily; there hasn't been one since Goethe. The present guides lack poetry, and the existing star-system devised for ruins is rather unsatisfactory. Please hurry up." But it was not a task that could be undertaken on such brief acquaintance with the place; I would never manage more than a journal of voyage with a brief snapshot of her from time to time—the absentee landlord of Naxos. Nor did I dare so much as to regret her death—I could hear the chuckle which would certainly have greeted such a sentiment. On many domains Martine might have been deficient and lacking in human experience; but on what I considered prime matters like death and love she was wise beyond experience. She would frequently disappear to India without leaving me a word; there was some Indian princeling there who was as attached to her as I was. When she returned it was always with carpets and shawls and screens to deck out her house on the promontory. But this was not all, for her Prince sent her back laden with issues of the Pali texts, annotated in a spidery hand by his father, and bearing a royal bookplate. These we would read together and discuss at great length, lying in the deep grass of the ruined Abbey of Bellapais, or among the shattered pillars of Salamis. The range and prolixity of Indian thought haunted her with its promises of a serenity at the heart of self-realisation; but there was no way to advance in this direction without self-discipline. She had quite defeated tobacco and only drank very modestly, out of mere politeness, and indeed with something approaching distaste. At least she eyed my heroic potations with an expression which might be described as compassion bordering on scorn!

Her Prince encouraged these fragile aspirations which were (so she hoped) going to transform the spoiled society girl, anaesthetised by too many parties, into someone very valuable to herself and to others. No, the aspirations did not go as far as sainthood. But she planned for calm, balance, and a personal freedom in her solitude. She, like me, had wanted to settle in Greece, but the vagaries of the Control Exchange had defeated these intentions. But Cyprus was a sterling-area Greece, and that decided us. . . . Though I had not actually met her for about six months—during which we were both taken up with buying a house, or land, and in general feeling our way towards an island residence—I had seen her about the little harbour of Kyrenia, always alone, and usually reading a book. She wore a Wren's white mess jacket with brass buttons and a dark swimsuit which showed off to perfection not only her line but also the blonde skin which the sun turned to brown-sugar. Nobody could tell me who she was—indeed I knew nobody to ask. But once or twice a week I passed her as she lay asleep on the mole, myself also with a towel and a book. Then one day we found ourselves sitting together at a lunch-party and felt the tug of a familiarity which we had been too polite to profit by; we already knew each other so well by sight. She was amused and pleased when she found out that I spoke Greek and could become a friendly Caliban for her; myself, as I was passing through a particularly lonely period of my life, I was delighted by such a chance friendship. From then on we met once or twice a week for dinner—and when there was any need for an interpreter she had no hesitation in driving up to Bellapais and digging me out.

Our friendship prospered in the very notion that we were going to become neighbours; and that we were both going to live alone and work. I showed her a half-finished novel called *Justine*, while she, with much hesitation, entrusted me with a half-finished travel-book called provisionally *The Bamboo Flute*. It was about her first solo flight around Indonesia and Bali and it was organised in a series of cinematic rushes which at that stage had a bright but highly provisional air. But there were good things in it about colours and smells. I remember one sharp comparison of smell between a crowded country bus in Indonesia and the London Tube; the Indonesians however primitively they were forced to live, she said, smelt of nothing, were astonishingly clean; but the London Tube smelt of wet mackintosh and concrete and damp hair-do's.

Inevitably our book discussions found a place in the general context of all the others—of the readings of Indian texts, of the amateur attempts upon the world of breathing exercises, attempts at meditation. It was an idyllic time spent in blue weather on the green grass of the ancient Abbey; I had been elected what the Chinese called (so she said) "a friend of the heart". And indeed so had Piers who made frequent summer appearances in order to advise her about her house and add afterthoughts to his own beautiful house in Lapithos. It was the last summer before the Fall—before the political situation, envenomed by neglect and stupidity, burst into flame and turned into a fully fledged insurrection. For a longish while, however, the manifestations of the crisis remained quite moderate—for the Cypriot Greeks were most peaceable people and they knew that the British people in the island were not the architects of the policies which ruled it. But with the arrival of troops and the gradually mounting toll of incidents and counter-incidents tempers wore thin and at last wore out altogether. All our hopes of a peaceful and productive life in this paradisiacal place went up in smoke.

As the problems connected with the buying of her land, and permission to build upon it, proved somewhat long—for the Government, if honest, was somewhat dilatory—Piers persuaded Martine to build an encampment of mock Indonesian huts on her land where she could live during the summer and see her house emerge from the scrub and arbutus of the little promontory. The island, we discovered, produced an excellent rush-matting in several thicknesses and the heaviest proved tough and weatherproof for walls and roofing. The idea was miraculous in its simplicity—the local carpenters could run up a whole room in a day. It was like playing at dolls' houses; for a couple of hundred pounds Martine built herself a temporary matting house with room enough to invite her summer guests, with kitchens and bathrooms—everything, for there was water on the land which Piers could later draw off for the big house.

Intoxicated by this discovery she at once launched into what gradually turned into a miniature village almost, with a main square from which all the huts led off, with grouped water points and drainage and septic tanks. Piers, the born architect and planner, was lost in admiration and envy at this free-style building and often, when he ran into problems with the big house, would swear and ask her why the devil she could not live forever in a matting house, repairing it at little cost as fast as it deteriorated? There were times when she almost agreed, when the big house seemed too solid and too consciously thought out—for at heart, like all the family of Gainsboroughs, Martine was something of a gipsy. The instinct had perhaps worn itself out a little—though her father, old Sir Felix, had expressly chosen a travelling profession—diplomacy—which sent him to a new country every few years. She had been marked by this wandering life, and she spoke with eloquence and insight of what it had meant to her and to her brother, in terms of actual domicile, to inhabit buildings which were beautifully appointed but in which nothing belonged to one—everything belonged to the Office of Works, even the choice plate. One brought one's books and pictures into play to be sure, but an embassy for all its comfort could never be a home. But this was how she knew Rome, Moscow, Buenos Aires: and this was how she had become a linguist. But her childhood had been full of this strange sense of not-belonging; lying awake at night listening for the official Rolls which wheeled on to the gravel after midnight, bringing their parents back from some boring reception—so fatigued by their social duties that they could hardly exchange a word and often even dined alone in silence; simply to recover from the deep wasting fatigue of a life which was a mirror life. Only at holiday times did things seem to come alive, but then the cottage in Devon was *owned*, it was theirs like the mill in Ireland and the flat in Capri. The subtle difference cut very deep; but was it really necessary to own the house one lived in in order to feel happy? Surely there was something false about the proposition? Then perhaps it was simply the artifices and limitations of the diplomatic life? She had begun to look upon diplomats as kindly lampreys gesturing in the dark pools of the profession among the fucus and drifting weeds of protocol and preciousness. Nor was this really fair—for Sir Felix was far from being a mountebank, hence no doubt his frequent relegation to quite minor missions in the role of a lifesaver or lifegiver—to ginger them up, or to create new openings as he had in Latin America. But Martine in a dim incoherent way wanted a different life: and here it was.

These long-lost events, which my memory had so carelessly and capriciously stored away, came back to me now with full force as we munched our stale pizzas and drank heartening draughts of Chianti; it was a memory touched off by the fact that here, like in Cyprus, we were seated on the hot time-worn stones of a vanished Greek civilisation, in the drowsy heat of the Mediterranean sun. Sacked temples, quake-shattered citadels, ruined fortresses, exhausted wells . . . the old tragic pattern was the same, a long barren lesson in history which seeks always for the stable and is undermined by the shifts and betrayals of man's consciousness itself as reflected in the ebb and flow of temporal events. And yet —what was he not capable of, man? Any benevolent tyrant who could enjoy a thirty-year rule was capable of launching humanity on a new vector, on to the peaceful pursuits of husbandry and art and science. Then, abruptly, like the explosions from some Etna of the mind, the whole thing overturned and both guilty and innocent were drenched in blood. One would have to believe very deeply in Nature to expect a meaning to emerge from all this senseless carnage; if one were really truthful one could not help but see her as some frightful demented sow gobbling up her own young at every remove. But Martine, underneath the spoilt playgirl or fashion-plate, was hunting after some absolute belief in the rightness of Process—and only the philosophy of the Indians seemed to offer that.

Nearby in a mulberry tree, half dead and desiccated by the sun, there was a great concourse of ravens or rooks—I could not tell which. They were like Methodist parsons holding one of their amusing conventions in some Harrogate hotel. They submitted with modest attention to the theological addresses of two obvious elders of the church. Almost they made notes. We watched them with wonder and curiosity, trying to imagine what could be the subject of their grave colloquy. In vain. After a long moment, and in response to no immediately visible signal, the whole company wheeled suddenly up into the sky and performed several slow and rather irresolute gyrations—as if they were trying to locate a beam of light or sound, an electrical impulse which would orient them. They wheeled several times in a most indecisive manner; then suddenly a break-away group detached itself and headed northward, and the rest, their minds set at rest, wheeled into line and followed them. Direction assured, they broke into several clusters the better to talk; one could hear their grave club-chatter as they diminished in the distance, leaving the field clear for the drone of bees and the sharp stridulations of the cicada. I was dozing. I was nearly asleep in fact. It was a good way to start off, with a siesta in Sicily.

It had become very hot up there in the dusty foothills, hotter than Provence at this hour in summer. The light wind which had cooled us all morning had subsided and the whole of nature, it seemed, was itself subsiding into the death-like composure of the siesta hour. Sensible men in such places preferred to sleep in a shuttered room until almost sunset when the coolness once more started and when a walk upon the Corso and a Cinzano at a café became imperatives. I lay for a while in the shade with my eyes closed, recalling another anecdote which had emerged from the casual conversation of Martine. Once upon a time, as children in a foreign capital, she and her brother had been sent to play with the children of a fellow-diplomat whose little girl and boy were about the same age as they were. They were accordingly decanted by their nurse at the Japanese Embassy where the two Japanese children waited for them with friendly politeness. Introductions once effected, their small hosts led them to their playroom—a large studio with high bright windows. "You must not forget that we, like all English children, had a playroom stuffed with toys, from rocking-horses to bicycles and model cars—just about everything. But when we entered the Japanese playroom we were struck dumb, we were thunderstruck. There was nothing in it save for one solitary object on the window-sill against the studio window. This was a great white ship, a fully rigged Japanese galleon in full sail. Just that and nothing more in this spotless shining room. We stood still in front of our Japanese hosts feeling suddenly terribly ashamed."

Sleep had almost wrapped me up when I felt a restraining hand upon my arm, and Roberto stood smiling before me. "We are off," he said, and as if to underline the thought the far-off bus gave a little whiffle of sound. Languidly we returned to it to find Mario sitting on the step sorting out his first-aid kit with pensive attention. "Yes," said Roberto catching my eye, "we must take every precaution. You tourists are capable of anything from dysentery to sunstroke, from fever to broken bones. And it's always our fault! That is why we carry a full medical kit with us." He had hardly uttered the words when the American dentist advanced and requested a Band-Aid as he had cut his finger in some mysterious way. More classical was the wasp-sting incurred by one of the French ladies. Pleased to show his medical prowess, Roberto whipped out his tweezers and drew the sting before drenching the wound in ammonia. "He's right," said Deeds, "people are such fools anything could happen." And so we rolled down the dusty inclines towards the far-off blue promise of a first sea-bathe, though truth to tell the little beach was not the prettiest I had ever seen, and there was quite a disturbed little sea running. Beddoes would have things to say about it!

But no. He just sat and scowled upon the shingle, sucking at his pipe. The rest of us showed a commendable burst of energy, changing into our bathing costumes in a nearby thicket and advancing intrepidly towards the sea, which frolicked about in a disconcerting manner—at least for those who did not, or could not, dive through the waves which broke on the shore, in search of the relative calm beyond. The American dentist's lady friend behaved too irresolutely, too pensively, and was knocked down in a heap—or perhaps she had decided to fall in just this beautiful soft waxen way. We all rushed to help in order to get our hands on that beautiful form but her man was there ahead of us, alive to every eventuality. Deeds bumped his toe. The pebbles were blazing hot and we all scuttled about with burning soles, to cool them at last in the innocent surf. I swam a little, regretting that I was not in better shape physically; a winter of French cooking had done me in. Perhaps the modest fare of Sicily—if one could defeat its copiousness—might do the trick? But no, because when one travelled this way one was always famished, and the only choice lay between spaghetti and rice. . . .

The sea tasted of oysters and brine when I inadvertently swallowed a mouthful. Some anxiety was now caused by the German beauty who had apparently decided to swim over to Piraeus, so far out was she. (She explained later that she was simply keeping pace with the sinking sun.) But how was Roberto to know this, as he stood shouting at her on the brink and wringing his responsible hands? She was finally persuaded to come back to us, which she did at a smart crawl—to be fiercely rebuked by the guide who said he would post no more letters for her unless she showed more good sense. But she seemed unaware that she had done anything to cause alarm and annoyance. She shook out her blonde hair and of course the gallant soul of Roberto melted, his wrath cooled like lava. But the sun was already behind the hills and the night had begun to fall. We should arrive after dark in Syracuse—the town which Martine had esteemed superior to all the towns of Sicily. We dressed once more, relaxed into happy fatigue by water and sun, and recovered the saturnine Mario and our little bus—together with all the belongings we had left in it. The atmosphere of the interior was now becoming ever so faintly disorderly—the disorder of gipsies who have no time to be tidy when they are on the road. Binoculars, scarves, Thermos flasks, picnic baskets and cameras; we carried all this lumber with us like all modern pilgrims do, and Mario watched over it all while we were absent, sitting to play himself a hand of patience on a little board erected over the wheel; or else to study a Sicilian paper with great care and slowly while he sucked a match stick which he had carved into a toothpick.

Darkness fell while we were on the road; the familiar daylight forms receded and melted slowly away into the tenebrous hinterlands around us. We put on coats and scarves and settled into our seats, glad of the warmly lighted bus which we could feel burrowing its way through the darkness towards Syracuse. Mario played his chuckling horn, sometimes it seemed for pure pleasure as there was hardly any traffic on the road. It was a horn on two notes, like a magpie's rattling call. In silent villages he let out this pretty call-sign to register our presence. Answer came there none. Then as we climbed a hillock and took a smooth curve Roberto announced that we had reached Augusta, and this was well worth sitting up for.

It was of an extraordinary beauty, this little oil port. A thousand tulips of light and coloured smoke played about its derricks and towers and drums—a forest of refineries whose beauty was made quite sinister by the fact that the whole was deserted. There was not a soul in the whole place, not a dog nor a cat; there wasn't even a guard-post. Yet the light played about in it, the smoke gushed and spat, as if it were the very forge of the Titans, and a thousand invisible trolls were hard at work in it. Its beauty was quite breath-taking. I watched it in diminishing perspective, reflected in the windows of the bus, and it seemed like a thousand waxlights afloat on the waters of chaos. Two days later we were to pass it in daylight and to have our ardour quenched by its hideous ugliness, its ungainly spider-like instruments. But indeed it was an important guarantee of Sicily's economic progress. No more would she be a poor relation of the north. Roberto spared us statistics tonight out of sheer tact, and because he knew that in two days' time he could spout them all out by daylight. "Augusta," said Deeds shaking his head. "All through the damn war we tried to shell it, with never a single hit. How could it have escaped? But it did." I thought I knew the answer. "Every time the Fleet Air Arm tried to bomb Augusta or even Catania the Italians came back and knocked a piece off my balcony in Alexandria. Finally there was no balcony left." The little spots of light receded into the rolling hills, until Augusta looked like a small forest fire, or the brindles on a tiger's hide. It hung for a while like a sinking constellation and then extinguished itself while ahead of us, more warming but less spectacular, glowed the lights of Syracuse. We had begun to feel hungry and watched with a certain envy the Americans who poured out coffee from a vacuum flask and ate a sandwich in a lingering way. I thought that, after all, I would sleep like a lead soldier tonight once I had had dinner and a drink.

Syracuse

Marble Stele: Syracuse

One day she dies and there with splendour
On all sides of her, for miles and miles,
Stretches reality in all its rich ubiquity,
The whole of science, magic, total time.
The hanging gardens of folly, the aloof sublime,
Just as far as thinking reaches,
Though lost now the nightingale's corroboration
Of spring in meadows of dew uprising.
Only the avid silence preaches.

"Whence came we, blind one?" asks the nursery rhyme,
"And whither going, say?" The cherub questions us
"In the dark of his unknowing clad
He charms eternity, makes all process glad."
Time has made way at last, the dream is ended
Least said is soonest mended.

Hear old Empedocles as calmly wise
As only more than mortal man can be
Who stands no nonsense from eternity.

"The royal mind of God in all
Its imperturbable extravagance,
Admits no gossip. All is poetry.
There is no which, nor why, nor whence."

Syracuse

The town seemed quiet and with little movement despite the earliness of the hour; there was a trifling contretemps at the hotel, where we found that the porters were on strike for the day. We had to hump our suitcases for the night.

This would not have been a very serious matter had the lift not been so cramped, and had the French diplomatic couple learned the elementary art of packing. There seemed to be something absolutely necessary to their peace of mind in each of half a dozen suitcases—so the poor husband had to make several trips. Both Deeds and I could afford to be smug, having put our night clobber in one small case, which enabled us to forget the rest. But even this small suitcase became a problem when one found oneself in the lift with the Frenchman who was humping two large ones and a dozen assorted paper bags. We collided repeatedly and at several angles, bumping first our heads (in a convulsion of reciprocal politeness) and then our booming bags. It was hard to get in and hard to get out; the doors closed automatically if one did not keep them open with one's foot. Getting out we collided once more in the corridor, when in a sort of hissing anguish my companion said, "*Cher maître*, excuse me."

My heart sank, for I had been recognised; due perhaps to too many television appearances in Paris. But he went on, "Be assured. Your anonymity is safe with me and with my wife. Nobody shall ever know that Lawrence Durrell is with us." It was like Stendhal meeting Rossini in the lift. He almost genuflected; I suppose that I swelled up with pride like a toad. He walked away backwards down the corridor to his room—like one does for Royalty or the Pope. I went pensively to mine to unpack. Deeds came in with a hip flask and offered me an aperitif before we went down to the cold collation which had been prepared for us in the dining-room of the hotel. He approved of my neat packing, and showed quite a streak of psychological insight, for when I said: "I suppose you detect the signs of old maidishness in this mania for tidiness?" he replied, "On the contrary, I detect a camper and a small boat owner. You simply have to be tidy if you are either; since you weren't in the army I mean."

After dinner we smoked a cigar in the garden of the hotel and I tried to divine the nature of the town by sniffing the night air—which was pure and scentless. We were on a pleasant but suburban street, made somehow agreeable by flowering oleander which reminded me of Rhodes in a way, modern Rhodes whose towns are made beautiful by this graceful and tough bush which can feast on the bare rock or the crumbling shale of a deserted river-bed—as it does in Cyprus and Sicily alike. The night was still, and balmy. As we walked to and fro the Frenchman came out and spotting us came over with his visiting card in his hand. "As an *ancien préfet de Paris*", he said, "allow me to make myself known. Count Petremand at your service." His manners were delightful and innocent of guile. Then he added, "I had the great honour once to help your friend Henry Miller, and he was grateful enough to immortalise me in a short story under my own name—imagine how that pleased me. He had been picked up by the police for not having a residence permit—after two years, mind you. Luckily I was at the Préfecture and . . . well, fixed him up." I vaguely remembered him now. "But Miller was totally unknown then," I said, "and he had published nothing." Count Petremand held up his hand and smiled. "He was an artist," he said, "and that was enough for us." It wouldn't, I thought, be enough for the competent authorities anywhere else—except perhaps Greece. He joined us in a cigar and the three of us took a turn up and down the warm still garden. "I was touched by your mention of my incognito," I said with feeling. "I have never had any trouble with it before. Once or twice I have nearly been declared persona non grata but that is all. In fact the only cross I have to bear is that everywhere I go I am asked to sign one of my brother's books. It is invariable." I must have sounded rather vehement for Deeds looked at me in some surprise and said, "It hasn't happened yet." "It will, Deeds. It will." (Two days later it did. As usual I obliged, signing the book Marcel Proust, with the appropriate flourish.)

Our acquaintance was pushed no further that evening for the Count's wife appeared with a sheaf of letters for him to address and stamp; and he took his leave, once more with the same exquisite courtesy.

I spent a while longer in the garden, taking the temperature of Syracuse, so to speak; sniffing the warm night like a hound, to divine (or imagine) the faint smell of brine from the invisible sea. The place gave off a feeling of peace and plenitude, and the late moon would rise long after I had drifted into sleep to touch the graceful flowering bushes of hibiscus and oleander which lined the streets. It was in a sense the real beginning of our trip, the first great city whose antiquities we were to visit in any detail; up to now we had been mobilising ourselves, getting to know one another, improvising. But now the ice had been broken and we were a distinct party. As I came back into the hotel to go to bed I saw the Microscopes sitting in the lounge, the man with his head buried in *L'Equipe* (The Team)—a weekly sports paper which he had hardly left out of his sight throughout the trip. Either he had a number of copies or he was reading one special issue over and over again. But his concentration was quite ferocious and proof against any other pleasure one might offer him in the way of ruins or landscapes, even food and drink—for at meals he read at table. Well, as I passed them I saw his wife put her hand on his arm and say with real feeling, "*Eric, si tu continue comme ça je sens que je perderai l'oriflamme.*" It was so ridiculous as a remark that it took my breath away.

"I remember you saying once that there was something very slightly suspect about our Mediterranean raptures—I mean the islomania we invented in Cyprus and which characterised all your previous poetic transactions with Rhodes and Corfu. I suddenly recalled this remark on a sunny afternoon when I was sitting in the Greek theatre of Syracuse, knitting and reading while the children foraged for stalks of grass to chew."

She had forgotten the provenance of the remark, but I recalled it quite distinctly. It had suddenly occurred to me that we had given very little thought to what these islands, Cyprus or Sicily, must have been like before the extraordinary efflorescence of temples and statues had taken place—all the paraphernalia of a fully-fashioned and self-confident culture which had created plenty out of barrenness, beauty out of the incoherence of a nature run wild; piety, literacy, art. It is sufficient to cast an eye over the leavings of earlier cultures to be aware of the sweeping definitiveness of the Greek thrust—its glorious freedom from self-doubt, hesitation. But it was as much due to what they planted in the ground as to what they erected upon it in the way of cities, temples and harbours. In a sense all our thinking about the Mediterranean crystallised around the images planted here by the Greeks—in this Greater Greece, so aptly named. In Sicily one sees that the Mediterranean evolved at the same rhythm as man, they both evolved together. One interpreted itself to the other, and out of the interaction Greek culture was first born. If it becomes clearer in Sicily than elsewhere it is because when the Greeks arrived their homegrown culture was at meridian, and the similarity of landscape and climate did not impose upon them any modifications, either of worship or of jurisprudence or of politics. Athens evolved as piously and rigorously here as it did in Greece proper. I use the name loosely for the first settlers came from various places; but the cultural problems, even to their bitter differences and disputes, were first broached in Athens and by Athens. In a sense the word Greek and the word Athens are interchangeable except for purists and historians.

Comparing site for site—Neolithic and Greek in Sicily—one stumbles upon the fact that before the Greeks came men were terrified of rapacious nature, its excesses and its unpredictability. No evolution was possible—man stayed crouched in fear under the threat of extinction. Then something happens. Hope is born. But how? And for what reason? Nobody can tell us, but with the Greeks men began to see Nature not as hostile and dangerous, but as a wife and even Muse—for her cultivation made leisure (with all its arts) possible. What we mean when we use the word Mediterranean starts there, starts at that first vital point when Athens enthrones the olive as its reigning queen and Greek husbandry draws its first breath. . . .

Scholars will rush in at this point with their warnings against too simplified a picture—and indeed my choice of turning point in the consciousness of man is rather arbitrary; it is more probable than certain. But there certainly was such a point and the election of the olive in Attica will do as well as any other. Of course there were Gods and beliefs of all sorts circulating at the same time—local as well as imported ones; this is what makes the case of the scholar unenviably full of contradictions and suppositions. Yet there is a case to be made for the election of the olive for it was mysteriously bound up with the fate of the whole Greek people. The sacred olive tree in the Academy was an offshoot of the original tree in the Acropolis; and throughout Attica all olive trees reported to be of the same provenance were called *moriai* or seeded trees. They were state property and their religious sanctity helped to conserve a great national source of wealth. They were under the immediate care of the Areopagus and were inspected once a month. To uproot such a tree made the offender liable to banishment and the total confiscation of his worldly goods. They were under the special protection of Zeus Morios, whose shrine was near that of Athens. One of his attributes was the launching of thunderbolts upon the heads of such offenders.

But even the provenance of the olive is something of an open question. Where did it come from—Egypt? We cannot be sure. Yet of the qualities which made it valuable enough to become the Muse and Goddess of the Athenian we can speak with the authority of someone who has spent more than one winter in Greece, even modern Greece. The hardiness of the tree is proverbial, it seems to live without water, though it responds readily to moisture and to fertiliser when available. But it will stand heat to an astonishing degree and keep the beauty of its grey-silver leaf. The root of the tree is a huge grenade—its proportions astonish those who see dead trees being extracted like huge molars. Quite small specimens have roots the size of pianos. Then the trimmings make excellent kindling and the wood burns so swiftly and so ardently that bakers like to start up their ovens with it. It has other virtues also; it can be worked and has a beautiful grain when carved and oiled. Of the fruit it is useless to speak unless it be to extol its properties, and the Greek poets have not faulted on the job. It's a thrifty tree and a hardy one. It has a delicate moment during the brief flowering period when a sudden turn of wind or snow can prejudice the blossom and thus the fruit. But it is a tree which grows on you when you live with it, and when the north wind turns it inside out—from grey green to silver—one can imagine with accuracy the exact shade of Athena's smiling eyes.

All this, and the human attitude which flowered from it, was brought to Sicily in the long boats and planted here in the thoroughly Greek cities of Syracuse, Agrigento and Gela. To be sure, thinking of Zeus as a watcher over the olive one feels that he belonged to an older religious culture of which the oak and the other mountain trees were perhaps fitter symbols. As for the olive, it was left as a simple phenomenon, accepted as a free gift from Athena after she won the contest with Poseidon for the patronage of Attica. To the old sea god belonged perhaps the salt-water well on the Acropolis, a mysterious feature recorded in Pausanias' account of the Acropolis. This does not help us much . . . though we are told that Athena herself was born from the ear of Zeus (like Gargarmelle?). As Deeds once remarked: "The maddening thing about the ancient Greeks, and one would like to kick them for it, is the capacity for believing two mutually contradictory things at one and the same time." It comes of being as curious as one is hospitable—all foreign Gods are made welcome, whatever their origins; hence the mix-up when one tries to establish something concrete about the home-grown deities.

At any rate the olive branch with the little owl (the *skops*, whose pretty descendants still occupy the holes and fents of the Acropolis and utter their strange melancholy call at dusk and dawn) feature upon the coinage of ancient Athens. In modern Athens, too, the children of the Gymnasium sport a distinctive button which pictures Athena's owlet, which has come to stand for wisdom: not esoteric wisdom necessarily but horse-sense of the worldly kind. And while we are on the topic of the olive I must not forget to add that the cultivated tree, which is harvested in November and December, is grafted on to wild stock—so perhaps we should look for its origins in the historical side of grafting as a technique; it argues a highly sophisticated knowledge of agriculture in the country which first adopted the practice. Was it India? If so how did it come into the orbit of the ancient Greeks? I am not competent to answer all these questions, though my mind occupies itself with these and other questions as I travel. Indeed I hold long conversations with the vanished ghost of Martine who was always hunting for answers, and was not slow to disagree with the propositions I enunciated. I could see that she would have a hole or two to pick in my olive theories; but in fact if one were to ask how the word Mediterranean should be defined I should be tempted to answer: "As the country where the olive-tree is distributed and where the basic agricultural predispositions such as the cuisine depend upon its fruit either in the form of oil for cooking, oil for lighting, or fruit to eat with bread. It has fulfilled all these functions from time immemorial and in the countries bordering the inland sea it still does."

But I had strayed a little in my thoughts; I had not touched upon the central question raised by her remark. What happened before *this*—what was the island like?

Long before the owl-eyed Athene came into her own the island was settled by men whose history has been obscured by the fact that they left nothing behind for us to admire. Many strains, many invasions of tribes from different quarters must be envisaged, but the historically predominant inhabitants were the Sikels whose alphabet, if I am not mistaken, has not been deciphered as yet; nor are their inscriptions very numerous. It is a dead end where the prehistorian ekes out his scanty certainties with large conjectures; a few tombs, a few clearings and stone houses worthy of the jungle cannot go far to excite our minds or our aesthetic sense. It is really idle to dwell upon them. (I am talking in my sleep to Martine with one half of my mind; with the other I am trying to rough in the outlines of the pocket history which she had once demanded for her children.) One should concentrate in such cases on what is striking, and leave out the rest. Good histories of the place in yawn-making detail—there are a number; but in shortening sail I would build something more like a companion to landscape than a real history.

It is not the Sikels as such, then, who are interesting; what is interesting is trying to visualise the state of the island which they inherited—a pre-Mediterranean Sicily, if I could dare to call it that. In its Pleistocene period, for example, it must have been a desolate and forbidding place with nature far outstripping man in the luxuriant prolixity of its inventions. All that man could do was to cower superstitiously under it in fear—without the tools and intelligence to shape or combat it, or even to defend himself against the wild animals which abounded in these fastnesses of oak and beech, the boars, the leopards and the stags of great tine; not to mention the snakes and wolves and insects which harried these forlorn little settlements of volcanic limestone where the only household tool was obsidian—a volcanic glass—which offered a limited scope in cutting up meat or vegetables for food. One must presume that man at this time was a debased sort of creature from the cultural point of view—unhappy on land as on the sea because he was the master of neither. I picture a sort of Caliban of the woods, living on grubs and worms when he could not find animal carcases to nourish him. In Africa and in Australia there are such cultures existing to this day. Perhaps the Sikels were not quite as primitive, but in the absence of any firm facts about them one is at liberty to imagine; nothing they did seems to indicate that one day Syracuse would arise, white and glittering on its green and blue spur between the two perfect harbours—a home from home for Corinth, for Rhodes, for Athens. . . .

The imaginative jump is a big one; but it is not less of a jump to try and imagine what the landscape must have been like without most of the fruit and flowers that we see today and which characterise our notions of the Mediterranean scene. So much of what surrounds us today came to the island very late in its history, sometimes as late as the sixteenth century. The long straggly hedges of prickly pear came from the Americas, as did the agave and the tomato. The Arabs imported lemon, orange, mulberry and sumach. Papyrus from Egypt still flourishes in some corners. The land is bounteous, and it varies in exposure and elevation to a considerable degree. But then, if one reflects, even the olive and the vine were originally not native to Athens, though where they came from we can only conjecture. But as for Sicily, everything "takes" and there is a suitable corner where soil and temperature combine to welcome almost everything. Deeds had seen tobacco as well as avocado doing well here.

Indeed a stable sub-tropical climate is ideal for all crops—if one wishes to enjoy the best of all worlds. Here for example one can see stands of banana, grape-fruit and sugar-cane in the hot lowlands. Even carob-trees must have come from somewhere like the Lebanon. . . .

But how hard it is to imagine this "granary of Rome" without lemons, oranges or grapes, without the cactus and the sentinel aloe. While in the cool misty uplands the conifers and berries remind one of Austria or England. Even the sweet orange was brought here from China by the Portuguese in the sixteenth century.

Is it any wonder that the Sikels, eking out a fearful life without all these glorious fruits in which to exult, left us nothing to admire? Not for them the final conquest of the land which brings wheat and barley, nor the control of the sea which brings the produce of other lands, other cultures to one's door. They were locked up in their loneliness like the inhabitants of another planet and it is impossible to feel much sympathy with them, or gain any insight into their characters.

But if the arrival of the Greeks so much marked agriculture and city growth it was, so to speak, only the historical topsoil which was changed; underneath it all the island climate was that of Attica or perhaps the Argolid. The limestone valleys were quick with fresh-water springs; the land was as beautiful as Greece and quite as rich. And in the first spring showers Sicily must have put forth as rich a crop of wild flowers as Attica itself for it still does to this day. The Greek garden described by Homer in the *Odyssey*—it could and perhaps did flourish also here in Sicily: "In this garden flourish tall trees like pears, pomegranates and apples thick with fruit, also sweet figs and bounteous olives. Moreover a rich vineyard has been planted hard by, beyond the last row of trees; there are garden plots also blooming all year round with flowers. . . ."

These new and picturesque additions to the domestic scene spelt leisure and plenty, and with them came the first thrust of the vase paintings and the first verses of the poets who peopled the streams with nymphs, the oak groves with dryads, the caves with Pans and centaurs and the forests with satyrs and silens. In the culture which followed each plant and flower had its story, its link with the mythopœic inner nature of man—which he can only realise when he has a chance to dream. Yes, Martine, that was it! A chance to dream! So Daphne turned to laurel, so Persephone broke her fast in nibbling pomegranate seeds—and poetry itself became domesticated.

But the fruits of all this were not necessarily the sophisticated blooms of enclosure, they were simply the fruits and flowers of the earth. It is significant perhaps that there were no treatises written upon gardening until the late Hellenistic era. Temple groves and gardens followed—I am thinking that Plato (who was nearly murdered in Sicily by the tyrant of the day) rejoiced when his academy in the valley of Kephissos was transformed into a "well-watered grove with trim avenues and shady walks"; nearby too was the academy of his rival Epicurus, laid out, they say, at the cost of seven thousand drachmae. (One drachma was a day's wages.) Here he lived and taught in his three-wheeled chair, and when he died he willed the garden and the little house to his fellow philosophers. It has vanished. Everything has vanished. Fussy old Cicero was the last to set eyes on the place when, some two hundred years later, he passed it by accident while walking in Athens with friends. But the effect of shade and water and time upon philosophy—there is a whole treatise in it. Outside the city to the north-east in a large green park lay the Lyceum where Socrates taught and where Aristotle and his followers paced the walks in deep discussion, becoming nicknamed The Peripatetics. They were specialists in the qualities of shade as well as water—just like the modern Athenians and the Sicilians are. Indeed one can test the contentions of modern folklore by comparing the shade of a pine with a plane, the shade of a fig-tree with that of a cypress. Try them, and see which brings the deepest siesta sleep and which troubles you with dreams and visions. . . .

The Hephaisteion Garden had its echo in Sicily where history recorded a sacred grove to the god on Etna. It was guarded by savage dogs which were, however, trained to welcome decent folk and only attack visitors who were either temple-polluted or living under a curse for some act of sacrilege. Hephaistos (as brother?) shared the responsibility for the Acropolis with Athena and his shrine was hard by her own.

But this was public forestry, so to speak, and meant to echo public (or religious) statuary, like the grove of laurel and olive which surrounded the Altar of Pity where malefactors and run-away slaves often sought refuge; or the white poplar where thieves and other swindlers of a philosophic persuasion held their informal get-togethers. But what of the wild flowers?

In early spring, and again in the autumn with the first rains which herald the winter, Sicily like the whole of Greece is carpeted in wild flowers—some six thousand varieties have been listed of which some few flourish only in the Arcadian valley of the Styx. They are still familiar to us, the flowers which filled Greek gardens of old—crocus, violet, hyacinth; but northerners will be fondest of the more fragile anemone and cyclamen. Sometimes one has seen the little white cusps of the cyclamen pushing up through young snow like the ears of some fabulous but delicate creature from a storybook. Then there is Star of Bethlehem, as we call it, tulip, prodigal narcissus, humble daisy, lofty lily. . . . But for Martine there was nothing like the rose; she loved its variety and hardiness, for she had seen it bravely flowering out of dry and bony ground, almost calcarious rockface. And she had promised herself a rose garden wherever she went. Its history is as beautiful as its flower for it goes right back into the Age of Bronze as far as fresco paintings in Crete are concerned.

It appears in the *Iliad* as the flower of Aphrodite who cured the wounds of Hector with oil of roses. Thus having become sacred it descended from Aphrodite to Eros and Isis, ultimately to emerge once more as the *rosa mystica* of the Virgin.

It was perhaps the only flower to be intensely cultivated and marketed. For the Romans the rose became a rage and a fad and fresh blooms were rushed to Italy in winter by fast ships fresh from nurseries in Egypt. Rhodes took its name from the rose's and showed the flower on its coins; its abundance was so famous that a legend grew up that sailors approaching the coast would smell the flowers before they sighted the land. Athens—no don't tell me, I know—was always for Pindar "the violet crowned city", though he may have meant the violet-magnesium light which plays about Hymettus at sundown, and not the flower at all. . . .

But here my memory recalled a warning she uttered in a later letter—the one about Agrigento where I had not yet been. "The yardstick is Athens if you like, but we always forget that almost *all* we know about Athens as a town comes from a very late witness, Pausanias, writing in the second century. I imagine him as portly and meticulous, a Roman Gibbon, working up his travel notes in his depressing office in Asia Minor. Thank God for him—but of course he was the first tourist and perhaps the greatest."

Yes, the caution is worth heeding, and luckily I was able to turn to the admirably phrased introduction of Jane Harrison on the subject—for she had chosen him as the only real guide to Athens. The Emperor Hadrian (who by the way was much beloved by the Sicilians because of all he did for the island) made a valiant attempt to make-over Athens anew, to restore its former glories by the addition of new temples and restored monuments. His passion was an antiquarian one which reminds us very much of the contemporary British or German attitudes. But work as he might the soul of the city had fled, and all he ever achieved was the snobbish embalming of a once magnificent corpse. "He supplied anew all the outside apparatus of a vigorous city life but he could not stay the progress of the death that is from within. Accordingly this prosperous period of Hadrian's reign has the irony of a magnificence purely external. Pausanias, of course, did not feel the pathos of the situation; perhaps no contemporary thinker could have stood sufficiently aloof to see how hollow was this Neo-Attic revival. Greece endured to the full the last ignominy of greatness, *she became the fashion of the vulgar.*"

I fear these last fine phrases could be aimed a little bit in our direction—in the direction of the little red bus with Mario at the wheel, and the twenty or so captives of tourism tip-toeing around monuments they do not comprehend with a grave piety they do not feel. Pausanias himself complains petulantly against the tourism of his day, for the Romans could not help but feel that Greece had the edge on them, that in some undefined way they remained forever provincial, out of the mainswim of culture despite all their own real greatness and their own mighty and original culture. Somehow there was a tug towards Greece, and the young Romans must have made a sort of Grand Tour of the now ruined and blasted land, still eager to be accredited to the mysteries (which had lost all their *numen*, all their spiritual sap) or to win a prize for a chariot-race at Olympia, or a derivative play in a Greek theatre. They were marked by the thumbprint of an unnatural vulgarity, which they never succeeded in surmounting.

But as for Pausanias, thank goodness for his passionate antiquarianism; at least he has managed to leave us an extensive notebook of all that we have lost. It is something. For most of us tend to think of the Acropolis, for example, as a stately marble hill approached by the Propylaea and crowned by the austere, almost abstract beauty of the Parthenon's white catafalque. But it is from the jottings of this little Roman antiquarian that we see something much closer to the original during the days when it still "worked", still performed its vatic duties for the whole Greek race. How different a picture! In its clutter and jumble one cannot help thinking of the equivalent jumble of modern Lourdes or Byzantine Tinos today.

"Only Pausanias tells of the colour and life, the realism, the quaintness, the forest of votive statues, the gold, the ivory, the bronze, the paintings on the walls, the golden lamps, the brazen palm-tree, the strange old Hermes hidden in myrtle leaves, the ancient stone upon which Silenus sat, the smoke-grimed images of Athene, Diitrephes all pierced with arrows, Kleoitas with his silver nails, the heroes peeping from the Trojan Horse, Anacreon singing in his cups; all these, if we would picture the truth and not our own imagination we must learn of from Pausanias."

Those who tiptoe round the Acropolis today in their thousands hardly realise that they are looking at something like an empty barn. . . . "And by the same token," I told Deeds, who was standing on his head on the sunny balcony next to mine, for he did yoga like most Indian Army officers, "by the same token it is the merest vainglory to tell ourselves that we are going to see anything in Syracuse as the Greeks left it—it's simply a hollow shell from which the spirit has fled. Even the temples are for the most part wiped out, gnawed down to their foundations like the molars of some old dog." I was repeating and improvising upon the caveat of Martine who had once written to me about Pausanias apropos of the Minoan reconstructions in Crete, saying how tasteless they seemed to her. "They robbed my imagination of its due, and vulgarised something I expected to find elegant and spare and cruel—a fit sea-nurse for the mainland cultures which Minoa influenced, perhaps even founded."

"If you tell Beddoes that," said Deeds, "he will at once ask for his money back." I could see that he was not going to let these grave considerations disturb his mature pleasure at sight-seeing in an island which had become as precious to him as it had once been for Martine. In a sense he was right. If the Greeks were gone and their monuments were dust there were still vestiges of their way of life to be found in the food, the wine and the wild flowers of the land they had inhabited and treasured.

Today, then, Syracuse waited for us to disinter its ancient glories by an act of the imagination, aided by whatever Roberto could tell us, which was not much. Oleanders, however, and sunny white streets leading down to a bright dancing sea! There was pleasure in the air, and I did not need to sniff the horizon to determine that we were in one of those benign spots which favour happiness, encourage "all the arts—even love and introspection" as Martine used to say when she awoke from a spell of sleep on the green grass of the Abbey. Today the Carousel tackled its breakfast with despatch and good humour; the Bishop forgot to tell the world how much he preferred bacon and tomatoes in the morning, a very good sign indeed for the rolls were not very fresh and the coffee insipid.

Even Beddoes—Beddoes had *washed.* He had parted his hair in the middle and combed down his thatch of wet ringlets with energy and science. He came up to me as I stood on the terrace with my coffee, watching Mario growling at the porters and feeling the fine morning sun on my fingers and forehead—omens of a good day to come. Miss Lobb was already aboard the bus, and remarking this Beddoes said: "If you asked me why one felt compelled to like Miss Lobb I should reply that it was because she was so completely herself. She has grown on me. Or perhaps it is the heat." It was not the heat, for Miss Lobb had grown on us all. Gradually the outlines of her splendid personality had flowered in the Sicilian summer, her robust but handsome figure had emerged now clad in those rather expensive summer prints from Liberty's or Horrocks with becoming style. There was a touch of cretonne-covered sofa about her which was somehow suitable to her general style of mind. She introduced herself with simplicity as Miss Lobb but always added the phrase "Of London" as if it were a lucky charm. She was indeed the spirit of London—the "best-foot-forward" of that rainy but warm-hearted town.

Miss Lobb was a barmaid and she worked in the Strand in what she described as a "good house"; once again adding an explanatory phrase in the words "a tied house", whatever that was. Her warmth and good humour were infectious, and she talked English loudly but with grace to everyone, even when she fully realised that they did not understand what she was saying. "I think what I like about her," said Beddoes, "is her way of saying 'OOPS!' when she trips over a bush, and then flicking up her skirts in a skittish manner." Yes, but that was not all. She also had a way of crying "Righty ho!" which brought all hands running on deck to reef sail. Beddoes watched her fondly as she sat, reading a novel by Marie Corelli which she had stolen from the last hotel. Perhaps it was the association with bars? Though Miss Lobb did not herself drink, or so she said. Yet her frame was broad and buxom and her face large and red with a strongly arched nose and large sound white teeth. Later she was to explain to Deeds that even if one did not drink the mere fact of working near the stuff made one breathe it in through the pores—the reason why barmaids were always on the stout side. I forgot what he answered to this; but he too like the rest of us was a willing captive of her charms. And when she began a sentence with the phrase "Lord love yer now" he winced with pleasure; it was the very soul of London speaking. "I think I am deeply in love with little Lobbie; in love for the first time in my life," said Beddoes and I gazed at him anxiously, wondering if perhaps he had been drinking before breakfast. Little Lobbie!

Such was the prevailing good humour—and I am disposed to attribute this to Syracuse itself, for the whole place radiated good humour and mildness—that even the Bishop unbent and became almost expansive; he strolled over to us and asked Beddoes what he did for a living. "At the moment I am on the run from the police," said Beddoes unexpectedly, and after a moment's pained surprise we all laughed heartily at the supposed witticism. "I got flung out of Dungeness Junior for setting an exam paper which they said was far above the heads of the children." The Bishop looked perplexed and concerned. "But there were other reasons too," said Beddoes and gave his yellow smile. "For instance, my paper said 'Enumerate all the uses of adversity and explain why the hell they are sweet'." The Bishop's wife beckoned him, and he left us with obvious relief. It was time to crawl aboard the little bus. Today there was no problem with our gear as we were staying in Syracuse for a couple of nights or so. There was simply the organisation of the medical supplies and the lunch-boxes of Mario and Roberto.

So we began to sidle down the inclined planes towards the little island of Ortygia, the original site from which the ancient Syracuse had grown up into a capital of 500,000 souls—a giant among ancient cities. There was not much traffic along the broad avenues but I was glad that Mario was taking things softly—I felt that there was something precious about the place and that one should not damage its atmosphere by rushing greedily about. The modern town has spread in a smeary way towards the landward side and the little island of Ortygia is slowly becoming depopulated, though for the moment it is full of tumbledown houses of great charm—like a little Italian hill-village sited upon an ancient fortress. But the presence of water, of the blue sea, gave it radiance and poise. Like so many choice Greek harbours (Lindos, Corfu, Samos, etc.) it had been sited on a spit between two perfect anchorages; owing to the stability of the Mediterranean weather, and its predictability, one could always live upon a double harbour like this, confident that when the south wind blew the north wind packed up; there was always a good lee. So with Ortygia. It must have made an instant appeal to Greeks who had known the beauty and security of Lindos in Rhodes or Paleocastrizza in Corfu. The actual soil erosion in limestone lands must always produce this sort of configuration under the rubbing of the sea; I can think of dozens of such harbours and have often wondered whether the Cretan or Minoan symbol of the double axe was not a reproduction of this sort of ideal harbour. . . . Alexandria too had this to offer the sailor, the safe anchorage during the winter storms, and the safe lay-by for the spring and autumn squalls brought by the changing equinoxes. I made a mental note to try this theory out on Roberto when next I got the chance; at the moment he was vaguely describing the streets through which we were passing as we moved towards the narrow causeway which led to the island.

"I have a nagging memory about the word Ortygia," I told Deeds; "I think that somewhere I saw that it really meant 'Quail Island', and that it was one of the possible sites where Ulysses (always accident-prone when it came to females) ran into a lot of trouble with Circe." It would need the Lexicon to check this vague and irritating notion. Deeds said that in the islands off the coast of Turkey there were some small and remote ones famous for their quails; and that the women hunted them with a curious kind of little net like a lacrosse-stick which had two large eyes painted on it. It resembled a strange savage totem. When the quails saw the eyes they crouched down and seemed hypnotised, and they were easily netted. He had often wondered whether this was an ancient survival, this curious hunting art.

Today, however, Quail Island was agreeably crowded with loafers drinking lemonade and waving to us as we passed over the narrow causeway and slowed almost to a halt in front of the Temple of Apollo—disappointingly battered and placed all askew with reference to the modern town in which it had got itself stuck—it seemed almost by accident. It had a forlorn benignity in the sunlight but it would need a very advanced state of rapturous romanticism to feel deeply moved by it. Mario drew rein for the statutory pause and himself rested with his forehead on his arms; he did not give poor Apollo as much as a glance. I think that he never had given it a glance or a thought. Was he right or wrong, I wondered? Here we were all politely craning our necks, while the more industrious had their noses buried in their guides. The bus had attracted a crowd of children who were equally indifferent to Apollo and found us much more interesting; they proposed to try and stick us up for the price of a drink. Negotiations were opened in a strange lingua franca which seemed part Swedish and part English. They did not get very far, for suddenly, like a lion waking and bounding from his lair Mario rushed out of the bus and after them with a deep and frightful growling which sent them rushing widdershins. It was as decisive as the Battle of Himera, the enemy forces were scattered and ran screaming down the side streets while Mario with a grin like a harvest moon, regained the bus and started up the motor again.

Deeds' *Guide* was all carefully marked up with symbols which strongly suggested the Sikel alphabet or Linear B. Intrigued, I asked him what they represented. "I am evaluating my own Sicily," he said. "There are four terms, four values for the monuments. Together they form the word Moss. M is for must, O is for ought really, SH is for should really, and SK is for skip. Over the years my taste has varied a little but not so much. I see for example that for old Apollo I have given him an 'ought really'. . . . We can't afford to skip him outright on historical grounds, but he doesn't invigorate one. But just you wait a moment." I waited and it was not for long, for Mario crawled down a couple of streets so narrow that we could have touched the walls without leaning forward—and at last into the fine airy cathedral square. It was not only spacious but it was smothered in oleander blossom—full-grown trees this time and in full flower. It was no surprise in this halcyon air to hear a girl singing, the cooing of doves, and the brisk clip-clop of the little coloured *fiacres* which plied for hire in this enchanted corner of Quail Island, as I dared to call it in my own mind—until either Liddell or Scott or both told me I was all wrong. We drew up outside the cathedral and Roberto had a sudden access of hopelessness. "There is so *much* to tell," he said wringing his hands at the immensity of the task, "we should really stay a week or a month. . . . But the important thing is to *look first*!"

It was a happy injunction, and we clambered down from the bus in a sunshine fragrant with flower smells to follow him into the deep booming warmth of the old church which was surprising and unreal—and above all sublimely beautiful. One felt that little knock at the heart which told one that we were really visiting the heart of the island—the quick or quiddity of Sicily. Why is it so astonishing a place? It takes a moment's thought and a hundred paces down the side street to analyse its singularity. For the ancient Greek temple, or what remains of it (the remains are really considerable), has been comfortably and capaciously cocooned in the Christian edifice without attempting to disguise the modernity of the successor to Gelon's noble construction.

You would think that this simple but daring idea would result in a dreadful fiasco. But you are astonished to find the result deeply harmonious and congruent; it has a peaceful feeling of inevitability, as if it had been achieved during sleep, unerringly. I think everyone in the party felt a strong tug of admiration at these fine proportions, and the simple dignity of the whole conception. It was also a sort of living X-ray of our whole culture, or let us say, the history of the religious impulse in one vivid cross-section. Usually the age that succeeds manages to smash everything and sweep it, if not under the carpet, at least into the new construction. Here we were standing on a spot which had been consecrated ground before the Greeks, then during the Greek reign, and finally for the Christians. . . . The past had been not razed but accepted and accommodated with reassuring tact and ampleness. I felt suddenly like chuckling as I walked about inside this honeycomb—so full of treasures, a real Ark of the human covenant. For the first time in my life I didn't feel anti-Christian. Roberto must have been used to seeing the impact of this lovely spot upon his tourists for he did nothing, said nothing, just stood by with his hands in his pockets, waiting to brief us when we so desired.

In one side-chapel there was some sort of office being read aloud by a young sleek priest. His only congregation consisted of two old washerwomen who seemed to be half asleep. But in the duskier hinterland of the church there were children skirmishing and their sharp little voices made the priest half cock a reproachful eye in their direction. But the reading went on with a suavity which suggested not only his pleasure in language but also the knowledge that he had a fine voice for poetry. He was clad all in green, a colour which I usually associated with Byzantine robes. He looked like a slim and self-possessed green lizard standing at the elaborately carved lectern.

But while we were all marching about the great cathedral, full of the pleasant inner disturbance which comes from a shock of aesthetic pleasure, it was Miss Lobb who hit upon the most appropriate gesture with which to acknowledge it. She walked quietly away into the body of the church and, kneeling down in a pew, covered her face to pray. It was rather moving, the simple inevitability of the act. After a moment of hesitation the dentist and his lady followed suit. It was then that I saw the Bishop's throat contract with sympathetic emotion, and he gave a distinct sob on a funny juvenile note—like a boy of fourteen. It was another revelatory moment of insight, the little gesture of concern and affection sketched by his wife in taking his arm. That sob of a choirboy with an unbroken voice somehow made me see in a flash that he had been wrestling with weighty inner stresses, problems, in a word, Doubts. Later when Roberto told me about his nervous breakdown—his losses of memory, nagging insomnia, bursting into tears in the pulpit . . . it all related itself back to that moment of stress and the little sob. Yet—am I wrong?—I felt that he had an overwhelming desire to imitate Miss Lobb and kneel down in prayer but was held back by some unconscious and unformulated scruples against the heathen relics embedded in the church walls; the presence of Athena, in fact. But perhaps not, perhaps I am just romancing. At any rate the fact remains that he watched Miss Lobb with a kind of hungry envy, but just stood there, with his wife's sympathetic and restraining and comforting hand on his arm.

I was not too sophisticated to follow suit though what prayers I had to offer up were addressed rather in the direction of Athena than in that of the Virgin. But the pleasure in the graciousness of the building persisted. And it was here that Martine had tried to interest her children in the history of Greek Sicily—which is really to say Syracuse, for everything started here on this queer little island. At first she was exasperated by the flatness of the guide-book accounts, but gradually as she went on trying to make the history come alive to the children she began to "see" it herself as something real and full of colour. It is not the fault of the guides for they are forced to be dryly accurate; they cannot afford the colouring matter which gives such pith and vision to master journalists like Suetonius, who knows exactly when to add that small distinguishing visual touch which brings the subject alive. With a hare-lip, a mole, a squint, a tonsure . . . with one little attribute the whole portrait breathes. But now, in Syracuse, reading about the great Gelon of Gela all the guide book is allowed to do is to repeat the name of this remarkable but unknown man—the man who began everything here that gathered weight and shaped itself into the great efflorescence of Greek culture which even today as a relic quickens and moves us. Who the devil was Gelon when all is said and done?

The ambitious and energetic tyrant of Gela had already shown his restlessness and administrative skill by making a diplomatic marriage to Damarete, the beautiful daughter of a neighbouring tyrant at Akragas, Theron by name. But his real chance came when he received an invitation from the aristocratic party in Syracuse to come and govern the city. He seized it with both hands, happy to see his powers extended further still in a three-cornered diplomatic federation which was to stand the acid test of the Carthaginian assault at Himera.

The numerologists insist that both in individual lives and in the lives of nations there are fateful days and fateful years; for England 1066, 1588, 1814, 1940. . . . For ancient Greek culture there came such a day in 480 B.C. when the Greek spirit asserted once and for all its powers of light and its resolve to flower into its prime. On this same day while Gelon and his confederation were securing for Sicily almost a century of peace and security, the Athenian forces were defeating the Persian armies and clearing themselves a same sort of space in which to grow and flower and assume their birthright as a mature nation. It is not recorded whether the astrologers played any part in predicting these two immortal victories. Even at this remove in time they seem by no means a predictable thing—when one considers the massive forces ranged against the Greeks, both Sicilian and metropolitan. Yet the historians do not seem to be unduly surprised, or perhaps we do not catch their tone correctly. But nothing more decisive could be imagined, and in the aftermath of victory there came a flush of triumphant and triumphal building, of which this fine cathedral is one of the late results. Thousands of slaves were taken prisoner after Himera and set to work on these projects. The new temple of Athena was especially designed to reflect and celebrate the decisive battle. Gelon's reign was astonishingly short—as short as it was decisive. Yet he had burst open the doors of Greek history.

As for the famous temple, he did not live to see it completed as he died in 478, but he bequeathed all he had to his brother Hieron I who had been his deputy at Gela. His was not a long rule either but such had been the decisiveness of the victory over the Carthaginians at Himera that he could afford to draw breath. A period of peaceful prosperity and culture dawned in Syracuse; Hieron showed himself a discriminating patron of the arts and the list of visiting luminaries is impressive; it allows one to have some reservations as to the appalling portrait of Hieron painted by worthy Diodorus, who says he was as avaricious as he was violent, and an utter stranger to sincerity and nobility of character. We must weigh this bit of character-assassination against the fact that Pindar, Aeschylus and Simonides all found a generous welcome at his court. Pindar (am I wrong to think of him as a somewhat laborious poet?) stayed a whole year and extolled his host's skills in several unusual domains like chariot-racing. Aeschylus seems to have had quite a love-affair with Sicily; it is believed that he had the luck to get his *Prometheus Bound* and *Prometheus Freed* produced in the theatre here, presumably at a time when his work was still felt to be modern and rather revolutionary in style. But then there is so much that we don't know, presumably may never know. Eighty of his plays are known only by title, and a mere seven survive. In the puzzling epitaph he wrote upon himself he seems to extol his military service at the expense of his art—which makes Deeds rather distrustful of his sincerity. The soldier has an absurdly high opinion of men who can write, and not much use for the "service mentality" as he calls it. But then civilians are always prouder of having borne arms than regulars are. At any rate the dramatist actually retired to Gela to live out his declining days; perhaps the very things which made old Gelon fume with impatience—the absence of a harbour, the seclusion of the quiet little town on its promontory high over the sea, its remoteness from the bustle of everyday politics . . . were the very things which made it precious in the eyes of Aeschylus. Or was it perhaps something else of which the tyrant himself may never have been aware? I mean the existence of the secret religious sect professing a Pythagorean life and principle? We know that there was such a sect of philosophers in Gela.

But enough of these idle imaginings; one day (I made a mental note) I would ask Martine's daughter just how much she remembered of the history of Sicily—the potted history her mother had once given her as they sat in the cool darkness of the great church listening to the cooing of doves in the brilliant sunshine outside.

So bright indeed was it that those of us who had dark glasses must have been glad of them. Mario had gone off with the bus telling us that he would pick us up by the Fountain of Arethusa in an hour or so—leaving us time to loiter away a moment in the museum which stood just opposite the cathedral—or in any other place of our choosing. The Microscopes, for example, recoiled at the very word Museum and retired to a pleasant bar, and I may have well done the same, but as Deeds had marked the place with an "Ought" I thought I would please him by giving it a look over. To be truthful, despite its handsome rooms with their fresh and open views over the harbour it is rather disappointing—a prodigious jumble of bits and pieces of pottery and stone, for the most part without any kind of aesthetic importance but simply preserved as a historical illustration of an epoch or a trend. Yes, there is an elephant's graveyard of such vestiges and one cannot help feeling a certain sympathy with Martine's contention that "we are in danger of preserving too much worthless stuff." However, it gave me pleasure to watch Beddoes staring vacantly at the Paleolithic fossil of a dwarf elephant and then turning to Deeds with a "I can't see any point, can you?" It was all right, I suppose.

I even did my duty by the famous Venus Anadyomene in Room Nine, which the guide assured me was remarkable for "its anatomical realism" which is a polite way of dealing with the more vulgar aspects of its style. Haunchwise, as they would say in New York, she is anything but kallipygous. She is softer than cellulitis and her languorous pose feels debased in a fruity sort of way. She could have gone back into stock without the world needing to feel too deprived. The fame of this insipid lady is due not to the poets but to the historians.

There were indeed one or two fine smaller pieces but truth to tell it was the cathedral which was nagging at me and I could not resist slipping away for another quick look round in it. The service was over but there were still candles burning in the side-chapels with their characteristic odour of waxen soot. A fly flew into the flame of one and was burnt up—it expired with the noise of a match being struck. What was it that was really intriguing me? It was the successful harmonisation of so many dissimilar elements into a perfected work of art. It didn't ought to be a work of art but it was. It is true that the builders of the great cathedrals did not live to see their work completed but they were operating to an agreed ground-plan; here the miracle had been achieved by several sheer accidents. And with such unlikely ingredients, too. Start with a Greek temple, embed the whole in a Christian edifice to which you later add a Norman façade which gets knocked down by the great earthquake of 1693. Undaunted by this, you get busy once more and, completely changing direction, replace the old façade with a devilish graceful Baroque composition dated around 1728–54. And the whole thing, battered as it is, still smiles and breathes and manifests its virtue for all the world as if it had been thought out by a Leonardo or a Michelangelo. I caught them up in a side street wending their desultory way to the point of rendezvous with Mario.

Not many had taken advantage of the pause which we had devoted to culture; the French ladies had bought thousands of postcards, and were clucking with pleasure like hens because they were so cheap. The Bishop—where was the Bishop? I had not noticed him in the museum, and I wondered if he had really stroked the haunches of Venus in passing. Beddoes swore that he had seen him do it, but then he was not really to be trusted. But when we got down to the little square where the fountain stands we found that they were all already there, hanging over the railings. It was here that tragedy was to overtake them. The Bishop, like a sensible man, had brought along a tiny pair of opera glasses with which he examined architectural details with scrupulous attention—"standing off", as he would put it, from them, and taking up a special stance, as he gazed up at the gargoyles and saints in remote corners of the edifices we visited. It was really sensible; how else, for example, can one really take in places like Chartres? I regretted my own heavy binoculars as being too big and clumsy for this function; they were good on landscape, yes, but too unwieldy for niceties.

His meek wife had already been down to touch the waters of the fountain and proclaim them rather cold; for my part I had lively regrets that the Italians were in danger of turning the place into a rubbish tip—I exaggerate, but there was a Coke bottle and a newspaper floating about in the swirl of the fountain, which had quite a strong central jet and must obviously have been rather pretty when kept in better trim. I leave aside all the nympholeptic legends concerning it for they can be found in all the guide books. But there were some large darkish fish with speckles—they looked rather like trout—which sported with the brisk current, turning and twisting and taking it on their flanks with obvious pleasure. There were also clumps of healthy papyrus growing in the fountain. The site was also charming, being as low as a reef at the sea level, which suggested that the slightest wave would bounce into the fountain and disturb the peace of Arethusa, if indeed she still lived there. But leaning over the parapet in a trance of pleasant sunlight the poor wife of the Bishop suddenly let slip the little opera glasses and, stiff with horror, saw them roll down the stairs and tumble into the fountain. No one spoke. She turned pale and the Bishop had a look of uncomprehending rage—as if this injustice had been wished upon him by the Gods, perhaps by Arethusa herself. His wife had simply been a passive instrument of the Nymphs. (Perhaps it was a punishment for stroking the amenities of Anadyomene?)

The silence of doom fell over us. It was clear that here was a matter for at least a divorce. The poor lady, her face worked, as they say in the popular press; she opened her mouth to speak but nothing came save a terrified smile of pure fright and idiocy.

Our hearts went out to her as we turned our gaze upon the Bishop and saw his own grim expression. All this, which takes so long to describe, passed in a second. Then came Mario to the rescue with a whoop of joy—as if he had waited for a half-century for the event. He clattered down the steps and, tucking up his trousers, shed shoes and socks and waded into the place, wincing with cold but grinning with pleasure. He restored the glasses to the Bishop who thanked him warmly and declared that they would have to be dried out, and even *then* one could not be sure (a glare at his wife) whether they would ever work again without being completely taken down and cleaned. It remained to be seen.

And on that note Mario whiffled and we straggled back to the bus which was drawn up in a shady corner—the heat had really begun. We made a slow circuit of the little island, which reminded me a little of the circuit one can make round the town and battlements of Corfu. The sea glittered and winked and here and there in a shady nook there was a sudden blaze of bougainvilia or oleander to temper the stone. But everything seemed deserted—all the raffish lower life of the town centred upon the Apollo square; up here the buildings opened inwards; they were full of the inner reserve which is expressed in courtyards and patios. The answer of course is the sea with its salt which rots everything. I am thinking among other things of the huge Castello Maniace which offered a total contrast in epoch and style to all the Greek remains we had been concentrating upon. It was, according to Roberto, only one of many such features on the island, and if people were not so damned obstinate about Greek remains they would really profit by having a good look at the palazzi of Ortygia. We only got a glimpse of two of them but they certainly bore out his contention by their reserved nobility. And so through a network of narrow streets which Mario navigated with an effortless skill which was quite astonishing; in places his outside mirror passed within a couple of centimetres of the street wall without ever grazing it. Presumably long practice was responsible for this. I wondered how many carousels a season fell to his lot.

We rolled back across the causeway into fairly dense traffic and bore steadily right, gradually emerging from the press of buildings until we reached the sea, and a pleasant-looking fish restaurant placed right on the beach; with its own little jetty too, and wooden diving pontoons floating off shore. A swim in that blueness would cure all rumples, I felt, and indeed most of the party must have felt the same to judge by the alacrity with which they alighted and sought the terrace where, while sorting out where to change, we all profited by a shrewdly aimed *apéritif* which the good Roberto paid for out of his own pocket, though he swore, without much conviction, that he would get it back from the Company. He was so happy; our behaviour had been decorous; there had been no scenes and no bad blood. Lunch stretched before us, and it was one of the better and more characteristic Italian meals—mixed grilled fish of every variety with fresh lemon followed by an eggplant pie which reminded me more of Greece and Anatolia than Italy. And then the wine was potable red with a slight "nose"—it avoided fruitiness, that besetting sin in lands where people seem to adore drinking pure diluted sugar with just a sniff of alcohol in it. We hailed the wine and behaved like masterful Sileni, smacking lips, holding it up to the light. Vino! Not all of us bathed, so that we had to wait for the general assembly of all before the hot food could be served; *amuse-gueules* of cucumber and radish staved off that caving-in feeling. The light was prodigious, the light wind off the lustrous sea made everything throb with importance. Whatever we might forget about Sicily we would remember this newly minted day.

The caverns and the quarries called the Latomie are nowadays one of the sights of the city; once they quarried stone from them for their temples and palaces. But since they were abandoned for this use they metamorphosed to underground grottoes thick with a luxuriant vegetation so dense that it needed the skilled services of landscape gardeners to control—and indeed the work of engineers to cut paths and asphalt them securely down so that the public could take extensive strolls through this underground jungle. But this excursion was planned for the cool of the evening, and the general idea was that we should have a siesta after lunch back at the hotel. Nothing more pleasant to think of—that seemed to be the generally accredited view. The French Count was pleased when I said how much I regretted that we did not have a quirky guide of Sicily by Stendhal to match his *Walks in Rome*. Indeed he would have been the ideal companion for the trip—perhaps with Goethe as well.

There would probably have been a good Sicilian candidate also, but our ignorance of the island's letters was abysmal. Yes, Pirandello and Lampedusa, and someone that Lawrence translated successfully; I had heard of others whose renown was also widespread but could not recall their names. Roberto was impatient too and ate in a boneless exhausted sort of way. He had had a long morning march and was not disposed for any more casual gossip before his nap.

So we returned, well fed and rested by a bracing cold swim in the sea. By contrast with the sea-coast the hotel which was a little way inland was somewhat hot. I opened my shutters and stepped out on to my balcony to judge what siesta-conditions were to be like. To my left a thoughtful Deeds was hanging up a bathing-costume; to my immediate right the Bishop's opera glasses had been placed on the balustrade to dry out; they indicated his presence next door. Beyond the Bishop stood the figure of Beddoes engaged in some domestic pursuit—he seemed to be darning a sock. I set out these dispositions in some detail because a small incident took place which lent depth and perspective to the portraits of the ecclesiastical pair—putting them in a somewhat intriguing light. Neither was on the balcony but their shutters stood open. Beddoes was about to address some cheerful remark to me across the gap when I shut him up by pointing to the Bishop's balcony and miming people asleep. He duly broke off and it was at that minute that we heard the voice of the lady lifted in plangent rebuke. She said: "O yes, you *are* and you know it, *you are against the whole universe*!" This sublime accusation, searing enough to become the foundation of a new Council of Nicea, reverberated on the silence and hung there, so to speak, unqualified by further noise or gesture. Beddoes and I gazed at one another. Deeds discreetly withdrew. I was about to do the same when a slap rang out, a distinct and unmistakable slap, followed once more by a wave of silence. We hovered there for a moment, Beddoes and I, like figures hastily improvised with the airbrush, or graven images reflected shimmering in a sunbeam. Nothing further happened after this and we both beat a tactful retreat into our rooms where in a matter of moments I was asleep, having set my little alarm for four. I wondered for a moment which of the two had slapped the other—had she swiped him? It was hardly conceivable that he had landed her one for such an impudent remark. And anyway what did it *mean*? Have women no innate respect for the Cloth? But sleep came to dispel these useless questions, and it came on bare feet, noiseless on the tiled floors. The alarm set me by the ears with a shock of surprise—it was like being hit by a thunderbolt.

When I got down to the terrace we were nearly all present tucking into an excellent tea with several kinds of cake. The transformation in the Bishop was marvellous to behold; he was expansive and smiling and relaxed. He caressed his wife's arm like a clumsy but affectionate gundog. She too had a touch of red in her pale cheeks—had she made up? At any rate she was less pale than usual. Beddoes caught my eye from a neighbouring table and gave us a wink of complicity which Deeds did not acknowledge; but undaunted he came over to us and whispered hoarsely: "After the slap they made love all afternoon in a disembodied way—perhaps for the first time since their marriage fifty years before; but I couldn't make out who hit who, could you? At any rate that humble slap uncorked an unearthly lust. . . ." Deeds got angry and said, "I wish you would go away and take your rumours with you." Beddoes looked hurt. "It's not rumours," he said, "I watched them through the keyhole."

The man was incorrigible and Deeds told him as much with a vehemence controlled only by good breeding; but undaunted by this the fellow followed us still and took a seat near us in the bus. The ride was not a long one, though my sense of direction was fazed and I could not tell if we went east or west. But today was to be a great treat for we were decanted upon a shady walk where another guide awaited us—to the relief of Roberto. This was an elderly man in dark glasses who looked like a policeman or a spy in a story of detection or espionage. Dark glasses—but so dark you could not see his eyes. He wore a bow tie and a Homburg hat with his well-cut but rather weary suit. Cuff links, also. He was rather hard to place at first for his manners were somewhat seigneurial; was he an aristocrat down on his luck, and doing this job for the tips? But I think that Deeds had the right idea when he insisted that he was a university professor in classics who had become bored with retirement and was glad to use his knowledge in this way. He was certainly a most instructed and knowledgeable man, and his English and French were extremely good despite a bit of an accent. Moreover, he was mad about his subject and knew how to convey his enthusiasm. We were in good hands for a visit to the Roman and Greek treasures—the Roman amphitheatre and the Greek theatre which lay there, so fortunately rump to rump although belonging to different epochs of time. To have them both under our noses for comparison was a bit of luck—and the old guide told us as much. . . .

But I am going too fast, for our attention was first directed to the huge altar to Zeus built by Hieron of which nothing remains save the stone emplacement with a few shattered stone suggestions as to its erstwhile function when it was used for the giant sacrifices to the god. There was still the ramp up which the animals were driven to the place where the priests waited to despatch them. This gave our guide the chance of a little disquisition upon the nature and function of the Greek sacrifice—and of course here one could see all the difference between him and Roberto. He knew his Ancient Greece and had extensively visited the modern one—so he had a yardstick with which to compare Sicily. (Diodorus records a sample sacrifice here as counting 450 oxen, a prodigious number.) But our guide made haste to point out that there was nothing gloomy, or cruel or depressing about such a custom—for the whole town ate the sacrifice after it had been consecrated by the priests. It was a Bank Holiday celebration with everything on the house. "Greek writers of the fifth century have a way of speaking of, an attitude towards, religion which is wholly a thing of joyful confidence, a friendly fellowship with the Gods whose service is but a high festival for man." He was quoting, of course, and Deeds, who had already been on this tour once before whispered to me that it was from Jane Harrison (peace be to her shade!). But the guide was in full spate now and we got a chunk of Xenophon thrown at us which later I noted down from his little black notebook. It was very much to the point, running: "As to sacrifices and sanctuaries and festivals and precincts, the People, knowing that it is impossible for each poor man individually to sacrifice and feast and have sanctuaries in a beautiful and ample city, has discovered by what means he may enjoy these privileges. The whole state accordingly, at the common cost, sacrifices many victims, while it is the People who feast on them and divide them among themselves by lot." The old guide made no bones about the fact that he was reciting, for he beat time with his fingers to the English text; and added in English and French: "It was a great fiesta, religion, then. Nowadays, we Sicilians still keep quite a shadow of the sentiment—unlike the Italians." O dear, another fanatic nationalist!

But he was the complete master of his subject and in that hot afternoon light, westering now, he gave an expressive account of these once beautiful monuments which now lie, shorn of all decoration, unprotected by shade and stripped of all statuary. It is hard work, too, to try and visualise the great altar as it once must have been. All the statues have vanished and also the pillars. But even if they had survived they would presumably have been like those in the existing Sicilian temples—stripped of their false marble surfaces and now the colour of dry tobacco. "I suppose it is silly to regret the wholesale destruction of fine objects as one culture succeeds another; after all, if nothing ever got destroyed where the devil would we put everything?" The musings of Deeds as we sat in the hot Roman amphitheatre, chewing blades of grass and smelling the rich resinous smell of the hot pines which instantly brought to my memory the slopes of Acropolis or Lycabettos where as a young man I so often slept out on warm windless summer nights, brilliant with starfall. It must be the same here.

But the guide was harping on our good luck to have the Roman and Greek cultural world set side by side in Sicily as nowhere else. "The very architectural shape will tell you of two different predispositions. In this great amphitheatre the Romans were organising for the eye, for a *show*, a public show. Now just a few yards away you have the Greek hemicircle, organised in a different age for the *ear*. The difference between art as a quasi-religious intellectual event and a popular spectacle. Aeschylus and his Gods against bread and circuses. Here you can study both predispositions as if they were historically co-existent while in fact they are separated by centuries." It was astute and highly suggestive as a way of looking at these now shadowy monuments of a lost world. The heat of the declining sun still throbbed, the rocks were dazing. Capers grew in the white rock as they did in Athens. There was even a little owl which flew into a cypress tree with the unmistakable melancholy little whoop of the *skops.* But what is astonishing is the speed with which the exact nature and function of things becomes forgotten; the archaeologist tries to read a sort of palimpsest of superimposed cultures, one displacing or deforming the other—and then tries to ascribe a *raison d'être,* function, to what he sees. In vain. Or at any rate in Sicily, and more specially here in Syracuse. The ruins keep their secret. The monuments have been worn down like the teeth of an ancient jawbone; what was exportable was expendable, what was beautiful had a value worth despoiling. Only the hot bare rock still contains the imprint of a half-obliterated inscription here or there, or the pedestal of a vanished statue, or a carved hole to admit the locking elbow of a stone mortice. It had all been eaten up as flesh is eaten up by the ground. Yet sitting in this old Roman theatre it takes no great act of the imagination to reconstruct the crowds, themselves now swallowed up by the centuries, as they watched the sports offered to them by the state—sports of blood.

All round the arena were the gloomy and secretive cages where the lions and tigers for the combats were lodged; the gladiator or the slave had to open the door of his choice—and here luck took a hand, for not all had animals in them. I did not know this. According to the old guide the crowds respected a lucky choice and set the slave free if he did not wish to exhibit his skill. Nor, he went on, need one imagine that in terms of danger this sort of combat represented anything peculiarly terrible for the experienced gladiator—usually an ex-soldier in retirement. It was not more dangerous to take on and despatch a lion than it would be today for a boxer to undertake to win a match against a heavyweight champion. I wondered. The German girl appeared to disagree with this; she had become quite perked up by the discovery that one of the rather duller looking sandy men of the party (I took him to be Dutch) was actually a compatriot of hers, and an architectural student who had done a sketch of her on a paper napkin during the seaside lunch. This sudden *rapprochement* had thrown a spanner into the works of Roberto who had been gradually cementing his acquaintance with the blonde beauty by judicious gifts of sweets and bulletins of special information intended for her alone. All this quite decorously—a mere sympathy had flowered between them. They bent their heads over a map or a plan until they just touched . . . by accident it would seem. And now this damned German student with freckles and knock knees. . . .

"We do not know enough about the matter but there is no reason why the gladiators should always die—some more lucky or more skilful must even have made a living with the sword. Why not?"

My mind went back to those modern versions of the Roman gladiator—the *razateurs* of Provence who make a good living in prize money from the dangerous game of cocarde-snatching, the bull-dusting form of bullfight which does not kill the bull and which is widespread in the Midi.

"Even the slave or the Christian lucky enough, say, to open two successive cages with no animal in them—almost certainly he benefited with a thumbs-up, was released. Underneath it all must have been a respect for destiny or luck—there was a certain magnetism in chance—*rouge ou noir*, life or death. . . ."

The German girl had descended now and stood in the centre of the amphitheatre to test the acoustics. She sang a little bit of a folk-song in a beautifully modulated contralto which made Roberto's blood fairly whistle in his veins. Then she turned smiling to the awful compatriot and patted his arm. *She patted his arm!* Miss Lobb got a stone in her shoe.

"Before we leave the Romans—this is one of the largest amphitheatres in existence—I have to confess that we still cannot deduce everything we would like from it. For example, that little water-tank in the middle of the arena—too small to be of any aquatic significance. A holy water stoup? We don't know."

Here I had a brainwave, for back in the Midi, apart from the professional Spanish-style bullfights they also have the odd evening of bull-dusting where they try out the baby bulls and cows and then young people are invited to leap into the ring and have a go. The horns of the young bulls are padded so they can do no harm. These evenings of absurdity and fun are called *Les*

Charlotades in memory of Chaplin, and indeed a couple of village boys often dress up as Charlie and enter the ring with umbrellas in order to do battle with the bulls. The antics of both bulls and Charlies provide great fun and an occasional brisk knock in the behind from a frisky young cowlet. Now one of the special features of these evenings is the *piscine*, a water tank in the middle of the arena over which and into which the young amateur bull-fighters jump. The antics of the bull, puzzled by the water and with its attention scattered by all the yelling children, are amusing to behold. But the *piscine* is a regular feature of an evening of *charlotade* and all the posters announce the fact—*course libre avec piscine*—which makes one wonder whether the Romans themselves were not given to bull-dusting and whether the faint echo of their passage in Provence (a country still sown with their grandiose monuments) has not remained in this puzzling feature of the ancient bull-fight. But it was not the moment to try out my knowledgeable theories on the old guide who was now showing a little bit of well-earned fatigue, and so I let the matter pass, promising myself to investigate it in detail when I got back to Provence.

At last, when the cameras had stopped clicking, we straggled back the hundred yards or so into another world—so different in its white presence that the whole Roman venture in its vastness and impersonality seemed hopelessly debased in comparison with this white almost prim little theatre which expressed a world of congruence and vital intelligence where the poets were also mathematicians—the imaginative link had been made which we are only just beginning to try and recover. The blue infinity of sky and the white marble were the keynotes to the Greek imagination; somehow one associates the Roman with the honey-coloured or the dun. A massive eloquence which was intended to outlast eternity. The Greeks felt time slipping through their fingers—one had quickly to seize the adventive minute before it trickled away like quicksilver and was lost. Yet there was strictness in this urgency—the singing for all its purity (perhaps because of it?) was based on an equation which linked it with its celestial parentage, the harmony of the all.

Martine: "I don't know what you will make of the quarries. Holes in the ground have always had a depressing effect upon me, and the Latomie proved no exception, specially as I wandered about them in the afternoon with a westering sun and lots of dense shadow which gives off waves of humidity. Beautiful yes, the gardens and their luxuriance. But once or twice when I found myself alone on the asphalt paths among the dense lemon groves with their great clutches of fruit . . . I felt a kind of panic, a sense of urgency, a premonition of doom. Almost the desire to cut and run back, back into the warm sunlight of the open earth above. It was the original 'panic' sense about which you talked—but in Greece proper it is that moment of noonday when suddenly silence falls, the cicadas stop, the sea subsides, the whole of nature holds its breath. And you hear the breathing of Pan himself as he sleeps under an olive tree. We have all experienced it. It is a terrifying experience. Well, down here in the Latomie I experienced it all over again, and cried out to call the children who were clambering about in the Ear of Dionysos testing the echo. Whew! I was glad when they came running." So Martine on the subject of these singular caves—the one we visited was precisely the Paradiso which contained the strange feature which Caravaggio is supposed to have christened The Ear of Dionysos.

Our guide, now somewhat exhausted by his long and admirable disquisition of the monuments above ground, led our loitering crocodile down the sloping ramps and paths into the Paradise Quarry where I looked forward eagerly to encountering Martine's version of the Great God Pan. Certainly it was a little heavy and tideless as a place but there was no doubt about its singularity—one almost felt that it had been designed this way, and not just carved out in haphazard fashion by the architects who had other things in mind. It was not simply the layout of the gardens—which had an almost Turkish prolixity and richness. There was water here and shade and humidity below ground where every sort of fruit and flower flourished in a luxuriance which was really paradisical. But the actual cuttings themselves seemed somewhat artificial, in the sense that everywhere there were grottoes and caverns, pediments and columns holding up large sections of undercut ground in the most precarious fashion. It was very much after a sketch by Doré or Hugo.

But of Pan himself honestly no trace, alas; I thought it might perhaps have been the time of day—perhaps she had been down here at high noon? But no, for she had spoken of a westering sun. For my own part, apart from the luxuriance—you could see vines literally leaping up into tall green trees to dress themselves on their outspread branches—I felt most the heavy melancholy of the passages in Thucydides describing the fate of the prisoners who were once herded here. There was even a passion-flower which had wound itself about a young cypress—its flowers giving the tall tree the strangest appearance. As to the prisoners, in their time these quarries must have been bare; all this luxuriance is relatively modern. In the great battle against Athens some seven thousand prisoners fell into the hands of the Syracusans; there was nowhere to put them, so they were shoved down in these ready-made cages, easy to guard. One thinks of the Mappin Terraces in the London Zoo with their puzzled-looking inhabitants. But here life was no joke for the prisoners. The historian who records the Athenian defeat in great detail—Deeds had the advantage of reading Thucydides during the Eighth Army's advance through Sicily—made no bones about the great heat during the day, and the great evening damps which followed, particularly in the autumn with the turn of the equinox. Illness ravaged them. "During eight months the daily allowance per man per day was half a pint of water and a pint of corn," he adds.

Later, one supposes, when the war had been won, these prisoners were either sold as slaves or used as directed labour on the new monuments which celebrated another era of peace and plenty.

The so-called Ear of Dionysos is hardly less of an enigma than so many other features among the monuments of Sicily. The echo is prodigious. And it suggested immediately the cave of the Cumaean sibyl (my guide book told me it would). But our guide had other notions, based on the fact that the issue of the cave comes out just above the prompter's place in the Greek theatre and he seems convinced that the two things are somehow connected. The cave for him was a sort of sound-box—his image is the case of a violin or the body of the cicada. As far as I could understand his notion the echo of the cave lent strength to the acoustics of the theatre—but somehow this pretty theory seemed to me a little doubtful. I preferred the sibyl as a notion. But of course unless some literary reference is unearthed we shall never really be sure. For my own private satisfaction I did what one should do in sibyls' caves—I addressed a direct question to the nymph which concerned Martine. It was to be answered if she so pleased with a yes or no, and I would count ten words along in the leading article of the daily paper on the morrow in the hope of an answer. In part it was silly, I knew that; but I am superstitious. So had she been.

Moreover, on reflection I had come to the conclusion that the panic which Martine had felt was not that of Pan but that of Persephone—the horror of the deep ground in contrast to the pure open air, the flowers and trees of our mother, the earth. All grottoes and caverns and labyrinths have this enormous brooding melancholy about them, and this huge prison with its grotesque name is no exception.

Yes, we were all glad to regain the outer air, to be liberated from that hangover-like presence of darkness and shadow which reigned below ground. When the wind swept through it the foliage shuddered and twittered—it sounded like the souls of all the prisoners who had died here, so far from baking Athens. Whatever one may say to oneself it is hard to swallow the fact of death—the blank white space that follows a name about for months and years after its owner's disappearance. I saw the German girl Renata with her burnt-sugar tan and blonde bell of thick hair walking lightly down the paths ahead of me with her little finger linked to the little finger of her compatriot as they talked about Greek tragedy; I wished my German were better for he spoke with great animation and eloquent gestures. For my part, in searching for a definition of what constitutes the tragic element in people and situations, I had evolved an explanation which seemed to me to meet the theatrical case as well. It is not the simple fact of great beauty being wantonly, mindlessly destroyed by a cruel force called Nature. We would by now have become blunted in our feelings about the matter—the poignance of this inevitable destruction. No. The Greeks had from early on transplanted the Indian notion of karma to Greece, and in Greek tragedy what assails us is the spectacle of a human being trapped and overthrown by the huge mass of a past karma over which he has no control. Beauty is born of the spectacle of a perfect life or a perfected action in *this* life doomed by something emanating from an unknown past. The accumulated weight of—no, evil is not the word—of misconduct in the pure sense which occurred far beyond the range of his present awareness. In the shadows of a past which he has forgotten and which he once inhabited under another name. The Hero's fate is the past, the unknown past; and in watching him sink and fall under the blows of destiny we feel how inexorable is the nature of process. The satisfaction, the Aristotelean catharsis is contained in the fact that in its realisation we feel we know the worst about life and death—and once you know the very worst about anything you are automatically comforted, delivered.

I did not think this a suitable line of talk to embark upon with my companion, for he was full of funny little inferiorities, and tended to panic in the face of an abstract idea. No, I held my peace as we returned to recover our coach in which Mario and Roberto were playing cards.

We had made good time apparently and our next port of call was to be the network of Christian catacombs which honeycombed a whole sector of the town not far distant from these broad and smiling slopes. It was so well grouped—the cluster of monuments—that there was time for one swift parting glimpse of the theatre which was now cooling rapidly in the westering light. In ancient times the whole auditorium, which could seat up to fifteen thousand people, opened upon the slopes leading to the harbour of Plymerion—a wonderful backcloth as in almost every ancient Greek theatre in Greece as well. It is always a little pang, and indeed a sense of puzzlement, to realise that there was always a backcloth to the stage, shutting in the action, condensing and concentrating it, I suppose. One wishes one could read a little more accurately into the monuments and their ancient functions. Who produced, who stage-mounted these strange hieratic pieces of theatre? It could not have been a committee. Perhaps a small group of select priests? There is something we have not yet grasped, and it has to do with a different notion of the sacred and the profane from our own.

Deeds went to some trouble to explain the intricacies of the Athenian war and the resounding defeat of Athens by the Syracusans; it was a homely way to do history, describing how Alcibiades, that "disreputable feller got a bowler hat and was sent back under arrest, only to escape to Sparta." This exposition only elicited a grave and sympathetic clicking of the tongue from Beddoes, who added under his breath something about not being able to trust a queer. But all these speculations were pushed awry by the Bishop who suddenly announced that there never had been any prisoners in the Latomia del Paradiso—they had all been herded into another and more sinister cutting not far from Santa Lucia—the church of which, with its famous Caravaggio, we had been hoping to catch a glimpse. Here indeed some asperity had developed as it was not on our official itinerary and the lapse seemed inexcusable. Was it not a renowned setpiece for the curious tourist? Roberto was plaintive at first—the tour had not been arranged by him personally. But after more argument in which almost everyone seemed to have something to say, he agreed to foreshorten the catacombs and try to cram in a brief visit to the Saint before we were expected back at the hotel for dinner. This little argument occupied us while Mario grimly circled the town and finally drew rein before the catacombs. There was an unhealthy-looking monk on duty at the picture-postcard stall. He looked as if he had just been disinterred himself. The catacombs were not unimposing, but to tell the truth it took a good deal of imagination to repeople them with the stiffening dead in their winding-sheets—a coal-mine would have offered the same spectacle, really.

Moreover, if we had found the gloom and shade of the Latomie disagreeable how could we be disposed to relish the even more absolute gloom of these long sinister catacombs with their marker-points of light and their dank pesty atmosphere. Nor was the wretched church where St. Paul is supposed to have preached of any great aesthetic interest. This is the whole trouble with guides and guide books—the difficulty of disentangling what is historically important from what is artistically essential. So far the annotations of Deeds seemed the best way of dealing with the problem; though it must be admitted that the great Baedeker did his best in this field of appreciation with astonishingly good insight and great care. But ages change, and taste which is so unstable an element changes with them. There is no certainty to be found in judgement. We were glad when at last we assembled at the little postcard kiosk with its hangdog monk, where the French ladies once more slaked their unquenchable thirst for picture postcards.

And so downwards, seawards, to keep our tryst with Santa Lucia, the patron saint of the town who was done to death among these peaceable streets and squares in 304. The church is supposed to mark the site but . . . there was a surprise in store for us. It explained why the tourist itinerary had left out this object of veneration; everything was all closed up for repairs. The two ancient and queer crucifixes which one has seen on film and read about so often had both been carted off for cleaning; worst of all, so had the Caravaggio. We hung about in the neighbourhood of San Sepulcro (also closed) and felt rather sheepish about having complained so bitterly to Roberto about the shortcomings of the trip. Nor did he himself crow—he was too nice for that; he looked as chagrined as the rest of us by this unexpected vexation. There was nothing to be done. But at least he had kept his word and tried to show us the great painting.

Dinner was some way off as yet so we took a brief stroll among the network of pleasant streets leading down to the waterfront and it was on our return to regain the little red bus that a new diversion was presented to us by the female Microscope who was taken suddenly ill. She had been eating sweets or cough-drops all day, and also drinking iced almond-milk. Suddenly she turned an anguished, pewter-coloured visage towards us and took a few lurching steps forward to fall flat on her face at our feet, shuddering slightly as if with an attack of epilepsy. Roberto showed great consternation, and Mario positively bounded from his perch in the bus to help lift her. She was trying to be sick it appeared but without result. Everyone fussed. Her pulse was faint and her gunmetal colour was far from reassuring. Roberto decreed that we must get back to the hotel with all despatch and ask a doctor to come at once and examine her. Her husband who showed little alarm put his arm round her and said: "It is nothing. It will soon pass. It is just a little *aérophagie* to which she has often been subject." This is an extraordinary French disease which is quite common in the Midi and is based on the notion that there are some people so singularly constituted that they involuntarily keep on swallowing air until it gets to such a point that they either go off with a bang or develop a tremendously painful series of symptoms like colic and gastritis. I have known a number of cases of this scourge; and here was another virulent example of air-swallowing which had turned this harmless lady into a gulping, pewter-coloured wreck with heaving stomach and rolling eyes. She really did look awful and I wondered what sort of remedy might be proposed by an Italian medical man—perhaps to give her a potion of castor oil and then stand back with his fingers in his ears? But it was all very well to joke—poor Roberto was in a fearful state and with reason. He was more or less in charge of us and naturally dreaded anything going wrong which might hamper the smooth working of the tour. We had, after all, embarked so lightly on the Sicilian Carousel, giving hardly a thought to doctors or undertakers or insurance lawyers. And here we were with this cautionary attack of airtightness.

The lady was now moaning slightly and rocking and had folded her hands across her middle in a childish (and curiously reassuring) gesture like a small girl who had eaten too many green apples. But Mario got us back to the hotel in record time and here everyone showed anxiety and concern for the patient as we helped her out of the bus and up the steps into the hotel. The infant was there, all eyes, but playing no part. It was one huge gape—if a microscope can be said to be a gape. Our faces would have made an interesting study in concern—selfish concern, for we did not know whether this attack of illness might not prejudice the tour. Also, as almost nobody in the group liked the Microscopes there was a good deal of hypocrisy mixed into our concern and perhaps clearly decipherable in our expressions. There was general movement to get the lady up to her room where she could be undressed, but perhaps this is what she feared for she refused to move off the sofa in the lounge and elected to treat with the doctor there, upright and in full public view. It was not satisfactory from a medical point of view but as she was French and extremely obstinate there was little to be done about it. Here she waited then, gulping and closing her lidless eyes like a sick lizard, and here we hovered around the outskirts with well-meaning solicitude, waiting for the doc who would certainly be called El Dottore and would flourish one of those continental-type thermometers which are large and impressive and have to be operated in an embarrassing posture.

He was some time coming, but come he did at last and it was clear that he had dressed for the event for he wore an elaborate outfit topped off by a sort of white silk stock. The material of his dark suit was of obvious weight and quality—it made one perspire just to look at it; but the whole ensemble was beautifully tailored, while his small feet were encased in elastic-sided boots. He was youngish, a man in his forties, with a large dark head, furry as a mole, and skin the colour of plum cake. He had a singular sort of expression, a sort of holy expression which one suddenly realised came from the fact that he was scared stiff in case someone asked him a question in a foreign language. His cuff-links gleamed, so did his teeth. He carried pigskin gloves. But he was scared. He looked in fact as if he had just emerged after partaking of the Eucharist with Frank Sinatra. He sat down uncomfortably facing his patient and put a bag containing his instruments on the floor. Roberto now intervened with a spirited outline of the case and everybody's hands began to move in rhythm with their inner rhetoric—Roberto staggering, falling, holding his stomach.

The lady was looking less alarmed and seemed rather pleased to have merited such a lot of attention. El Dottore listened with a dark and disabused air, nodding from time to time as if he knew only too well what made people fall about and hold their stomachs. From time to time he allowed one hand off the leash, so to speak, and allowed it to describe a few eloquent gestures to illustrate his discourse—he had a rich and agreeable voice as well. The hand evolved in the air in a quite autonomous sort of way and if one had not been able to understand what its owner said one might have imagined it to be picking a grape or milking a goat or waving goodbye to a dying patient. It was expressive and strangely encouraging, for he did have a definite presence. He produced a stethoscope and after waving it about as he was talking made a sudden dart for his patient's wrist. This she did not mind. He planted it on her pulse and listened gravely and for a long time to her cardiac performance. He nodded slightly. They had now got on to trying to explain to him what her illness was and how she had come to catch it. He did not understand. So everyone, led by Roberto and the woman's husband, began to make as if to swallow air like the French do. The doctor swallowed with concern as he watched them; he did not seem to have heard of this disease—are Italians immune to it because they talk too much: the air can't get in? At any rate he did not get it. He raised a carefully manicured finger and scratched his temple as he thought. Then he bowed once more to his pulse, hearkening with great concentration. Ah! After a long and pregnant pause the truth dawned. He put away his little stethoscope with a snap and locked his bag. Sitting well back and with an aggressive tilt to his chin he came up with a remedy which certainly matched the singularity of the disease. "In my opinion the spleen must come out at once," he said. The translation was handed about to the party in several tongues. The spleen! So that was it!

The only person who refused to register surprise whatever happened—nothing could surprise him, it seemed—was the male Microscope. The spleen, pouf, of course he had heard all about it before. She had always been splenetic—if that is the *mot juste*—and had had numberless attacks which always wore off after she had been treated in the ordinary way for wind in the rigging. One gathered that there was some immense mauve suppository manufactured in Geneva which would meet the case. Nor were we wrong for the doctor produced a gorgeous fountain pen and wrote out a prescription with untrembling hand which he handed over to Roberto who glanced at it and offered to send someone out to the chemist at once. And the spleen? One could hardly launch her into an operation of that order while we were on the move. She would have to go into hospital. Roberto's perplexities were grievous to behold. Would her damned spleen hold up until he could get shot of her, could push her over the border? That is what he wanted to know. The doctor shook his head, smiled persuasively and said that it was up to God. Strangely enough the woman's husband took the whole matter with a philosophic optimism which seemed rather noble. Or perhaps he had been through these storms often enough to know that they subsided as quickly as they arose? But nobody thought of invoking Santa Lucia—had we been in Greece it would have been the first, the most urgent thing to do, for were we not in her domain? It was just a small indication of the degree to which we, so-called "evolved" Europeans, had become demagnetised to the sense of pagan realities. Spleen!

Well, the doctor, having pronounced upon his client, rose to take his leave; he did not elaborate about taking out the spleen—one could hardly do this in the lounge. He simply shook hands all round, discussed his fee in a gruff tone with Roberto, and slid through the tall doors of the hotel into the sunlight. Much reassured by such a matter-of-fact approach, the female Microscope rose to her feet looking very much better. Her husband, in a surprising gesture of sympathy, put his arm round her and led her up to her room to lie down. Yet all had ended on a note of interrogation, nothing finally had been decided. But Roberto sent a hotel messenger out for the medicine and we all hoped for the best. "In my experience," said Deeds, "the French have only one national disease and it is not the spleen—it's the liver. And a more honourable thing than a French liver you could not have. It comes from them being the most discriminating people on earth when it comes to food and drink." He did not want to labour the point for he saw Beddoes hovering around with the intention of making some dastardly remark, probably about morning sickness. It was time for an early dinner and bed, for we planned an early start on the morrow—unless hampered by the spleen of the French lady.

Agrigento

Agrigento

Martine: "But Agrigento for me is the acid test and I am sure you will feel it as I have; it reminded me of all our passionate arguments about the Greekness of a Cyprus which had never been either geographically or demographically part of Greece. What constituted its special claim to be so? Language of course—the eternal perennity of the obdurate Greek tongue which has changed so little for thousands of years. Language is the key, the passport, and unless we look at the Greek phenomenon from this point of view we will never understand the sort of colonisers they were. It was not blood but language which gave one membership of the Greek intellectual commonwealth—barbarians were not simply people who lived otherwhere but people who did not speak Greek. It is hard for us to understand for we, like the Romans, have a juristic view of citizenship—in the case of the British our innate puritanism makes it a question of blood, of keeping the blood untainted by foreign admixtures. The horror for us is the half-caste, the touch of the tar-brush. It is a complete contrast to the French attitude which resembles in a way the ancient Greek notion in its idea of Francophone nations and races. The possession of the French tongue with its automatic entry into the riches of French culture constitutes the only sort of passport necessary for a non-French person whatever the colour of his or her skin. It is easier to find a place in a French world than in a British—language determines the fact; yes, if you are black or blue and even with a British passport it is harder to integrate with us.

"This little homily is written in the belief that one day you will visit the temples in that extraordinary valley below the horrid tumble of modern Agrigento's featureless and grubby slums—and suddenly feel quite bewildered by finding yourself in Greece, one hundred per cent in Greece. And you will immediately ask yourself why (given the strong anti-northern and secessionist sentiments of the Sicilians) there has never been a Greek claim to the island. You will smile. But in fact if we judge only by the monuments and the recorded history of the place we are dealing with something as Greek in sinew and marrow as the Argolid or as Attica. How has it escaped? *Because the language is no longer a vital force.* There are a few pockets where a vestigial Greek is still spoken, but pathetically few (luckily for the Italians). There is an odd little Byzantine monastery or two as there is in Calabria. But the gleam of its Greekness has died out, its language has been swamped by Italian. Only the ancient place-names remain to jolt one awake to the realisation that Sicily is just as Greek as Greece is—or never was! The question of Greekness—and the diaspora—is an intriguing one to think about. If we take Athens (that very first olive tree) as the centre from which all Greekness radiates outward . . . Sicily is about like Smyrna is—if we take its pulse today. O please come and see!"

Not very well expressed perhaps, but the sentiments harked back to our long Cyprus arguments in the shade of the old Abbey of Bellapais. The dust raised around the question of Enosis with Greece, which constituted such a genuine puzzle to so many of our compatriots. Their arguments always centred around the relative amenities offered the Cypriots under our unequal, lazy but relatively honest regime. No military service, standards of living etc. . . . all this weighed nothing against a claim which was purely poetic, a longing as ancient as Aphrodite and the crash of the waves on the deserted beaches of Paphos. How to bring this home to London whose sense of values ("common sense") was always based upon the vulgar contingencies of life and not on its inner meaning? You would hear nice-minded civil servants say: "It's astonishing their claim—they have never been Greek, after all." Yet the Doric they spoke had roots as deep as Homer, the whole cultus of their ethnographic state was absolutely contemporary, absolutely living. Was it, then, the language which kept it so? The more we disinterred the past the Greeker the contemporary Cypriot seemed to become.

Through all these considerations, as well as many others—for I had been living in the Mediterranean nearly all my adult life—I had started very tentatively to evolve a theory of human beings living in vital function to their habitats. It was hard to shed the tough little carapace of the national ego and to begin to see them as the bare products of the soil, just like the wild flowers or the wines, just like the crops. Physical and mental types which flowered in beauty or intelligence according to what the ground desired of them and not what they desired of themselves or others. One accepts easily enough the fact that whisky is a product of one region and Côtes du Rhône the product of another; so do language and nationality conspire to evolve ways of expressing Greekness or Italian-ness. Though of course it takes several generations for the physical and mental body to receive the secret imprint of a place. And after all, when all is said and done, countries as frequently overrun and ravaged as Greece cannot have a single "true" Greek, in the blood sense, left.

If indeed the phrase means anything at all. What is left is the most hard wearing, even indestructible part, language whose beauty and suppleness has nourished and still nourishes the poet, philosopher and mathematician. And when I was a poor teacher in Athens striving to learn demotic Greek I found with surprise that my teacher could start me off with the old Attic grammar without batting an eyelash. Much detail had obviously changed, but the basic structure was recognisably the same. I could not repay this debt by starting my own students off with Chaucer, the language had worn itself away too quickly. Even Shakespeare (in whose time no dictionary existed) needed a glossary today. What, then, makes a "Greek"? The whole mystery of human nationality reverberates behind the question. The notion of frontiers, the notion of abstract riches, of thought, of possessions, of customs. . . . It all comes out of the ground, the hallowed ground of Greece—wherever that was!

This train of thought was a fitting one for a baking morning with a slight fresh wind off the sea. The little red bus had doubled back on its tracks and was heading north briefly before turning away into the mountains. Today we would climb up from sea-level into the blue dozing escarpments which stretched away in profile on our left. Mario plied his sweet klaxon to alert the traffic ahead of us—mostly lorries bringing building materials to Syracuse. Roberto hummed a tune over the intercom and told us that it would be nice and cool in the mountains, while tonight we would find ourselves once more at sea-level in a good hotel just outside Agrigento. Deeds felt like reading so I pursued my long argument with Martine's ghost, upon themes some of which had invaded my dreams. I saw her irritating the Governor at dinner by being a trifle trenchant in support of the Greek claim—it made him plaintive for he felt it was rather rude of her, which perhaps it was. What could he do about a situation fabricated by his masters in London?

But in fact these old arguments had a burning topicality for me, for they raised precisely the questions I had come to Sicily to try and answer. What was Sicily, what was a Sicilian? I had already noticed the strongly separatist temper of the inhabitants which had won them (but only recently) a measure of autonomy. The island was too big and too full of vigorously original character to be treated as if it was a backward department of a run-down post-war Italy. In every domain the resemblance to Greece was fairly striking—and Sicily was politically as much a new nation as the Turk-free modern Greece was. Indeed metropolitan Greece was itself still growing—acquiring back places like Rhodes from Italy itself. All this despite the predictable tragedy of the Cyprus issue, envenomed by neglect and the insensitivity and self-seeking of the great powers with their creeping intrigues and fears of influence.

What was the Mediterranean tapestry all about anyway; particularly when it came to extending the frame of reference in the direction of art, architecture, literature? Italy, Spain, Greece, the Midi of France—they all had the same light and the same garden produce. They were all garlic countries, underprivileged in everything but the bounteous sense of spareness and beauty. They were all naïfs, and self-destroyers through every predatory Anglo-Saxon toy or tool from the transistor to the cinema screen. Yet something remained of a basic cultural attitude, however subject to modification. But why wasn't Spain Italy, why wasn't

The temples of Juno Lucina and Concord at Agrigento

Italy Greece, or Greece Turkey? Different attitudes to religion, to love, to the family, to death, to life. . . . Yes, deep differences, yet such striking likenesses as to allow us to think of such a thing as a Mediterranean character. After all, there are many varieties of the olive tree, which for me will always mark the spiritual and physical boundaries of that magical and non-existent land—the Mediterranean. Martine was right. How I regretted not having come here before.

We passed Augusta again—how dismal it looked by daylight with all its rusty refineries and sad clumps of rotting equipment. But oil had come to Sicily, and with it prosperity and of course the death of everything that makes life valuable. They were doomed to become soft, pulpy and dazed people like the Americans so long as it lasted. But in a generation or two, after the land had had its fill of rape and disaster the magnetic fields would reassert their quiet grip once more to reform the place and the people into its own mysterious likeness—the golden mask of the inland sea which is unlike any other. How lucky France was to have one foot in the Mediterranean; it modified the *acerbe* French northern character and made the Midi a sort of filter which admitted the precious influences which stretched back into pre-history. It would not be the first time or the last that a whole culture had plunged to its doom in this land. The long suppurating wars of the past—Etruscan against Italian, Carthaginian against Greek against Roman. After every outburst of hysteria and bloodshed came an era of peace during which the people tried to reform their scattered wits and build for peace. It never lasted. It never would. A spell of years with the promise of human perfection—then collapse. And each succeeding invader if given time brought his own sort of order and beauty.

Such a brief flowering fell to the lot of Sicily when the Arabs came, during their great period of ascendancy, at the invitation of the Byzantine admiral Euphemius. It was a fatal invitation, for the island slipped from the nerveless fingers of Byzance into the nervous and high-spirited fingers of the Arabs who immediately entered the struggle and at last succeeded in mastering the masterless island. Then there was another period of productive peacefulness—just as there had been when Syracuse had enjoyed its first flowering of peace and prosperity. They were astonishingly inventive and sensitive these newcomers from over the water, people with the austere desert as an inheritance. For the Arab knows what water is; it is more precious to him almost than oxygen.

So were rural areas resettled, inheritance laws revised, ancient waterways brought back into use for irrigation. They were planters of skill and choice, they brought in citrus, sugar-cane, flax, the date palm, cotton, the mulberry with its silkworms, melon, papyrus and pistachio. Nor was it only above ground for they were skilful miners and here they found silver, lead, mercury, sulphur, naphtha and vitriol—not to mention alum and antimony. The extensive salt-pans of today date from their inspired creative rule. But they also vanished within the space of a few decades—like water pouring away down a drain; the land took over once more, trying to form again its own obstinate image.

We were entering the throat of a plain which led directly into the mountains, and here I got a premonitory smell of what the valley of Agrigento must be like—it was purely Attic in the dryness, in the dust, and the pale violet haze which swam in the middle distance foxing the outlines of things. To such good effect that we found ourselves negotiating a series of valleys diminishing all the time in width as they mounted, and brimming with harvest wheat not all of which had yet been garnered. It is impossible to describe the degrees of yellow from the most candent cadmium to ochre, from discoloured ivory to lemon bronze. The air was full of wisps of straw and the heat beat upon us as if from some huge oven where the Gods had been baking bread. I expected Argos to come in sight at any moment. What is particularly delicious to me about Attic heat is its perfect dryness—like a very dry champagne. You are hot, yes, you can pant like a dog for water; but you don't sweat, or else sweat so very lightly that it dries at once on your skin. In such heat to plunge into an icy sea is marvellous—you get a sharp pain in the back of the throat as if from an iced wine. But here we were far from the sea, and starting to climb amidst all this glaze of peacock-blue sky and yellow squares of wheat. Underneath that hot heaven the sun rang as if on an anvil and we were glad of Mario's cooling apparatus which sent us little draughts of cool air. Dust devils danced along the plain, and the few lorries we passed were powdered white—they had left the main roads for the country paths. Half-way up Roberto announced a "physiological halt" as he called it, and we pulled into a petrol station in order to fill up and, by the same token, to empty out.

There was a canteen where we had a few moments of quiet conviviality over wine and a strange white aperitif made from almond juice and milk. Like everything in Sicily it was loaded with sugar though a delicious drink when sufficiently iced. The Petremands stood treat and Mrs. Microscope was back in sufficient form to engulf a couple of glasses before Mario honked and we all trooped back to the bus to resume our ascent which was now to become a good deal more steep as we left the plain behind. It was pleasant to look down on it as it receded, for the sinuous roads curved snakewise in and out among the hills and the fine views varied with angle and altitude. We were heading for a Roman villa where quite recently the archaeologists had discovered a magnificent tessellated floor of considerable importance to them—and in consequence to us, the curious sightseers of the Carousel. We would base ourselves at Piazza Armerina in order to see the Villa Imperiale and have lunch before crossing the scarps and descending with the descending sun upon Gela and Agrigento. This gave us our first taste of the mountains and it was most refreshing. In one of the rock-cuttings there were little tortoises clicking about and Mario stopped to allow Deeds to field one smartly and hand it to Miss Lobb who did not know what to do with it. It was an astonishingly active animal and ran all over the bus into all the corners, upsetting all of us and causing a full-scale hunt before it was caught. Finally she freed it. Its little claws were extremely sharp and it fought for dear life, for its freedom. I had always thought of tortoises as such peaceable things which simply turned into stones at the approach of danger. This little brute attacked all along the line and we were glad when at last it clicked off into the bushes.

Piazza Armerina is a pretty and lively little hill town, boasting of more than one baroque church, a cathedral and a castle, and several other sites of note in the immediate environs. But it is quite impossible to convey that elusive quality, charm, in writing —or even in photography which so often deludes one with its faked images and selected angles. The little town had charm, though of course its monuments could not compare in importance to many another Sicilian town. Yes . . . I found myself thinking that it would be pleasant to spend a month there finishing a book. The walking seemed wonderful among these green and flourishing foothills. But the glimpse we had of it was regrettably brief; having signalled our presence to the hotel where we were to have lunch we set off at once to cover the six or so kilometres which separated us from the Imperial Villa—a kind of summer hide-out built for some half-forgotten Roman Emperor. What is intriguing is that almost no ascription ever made about a Sicilian site or monument is ever more than tentative: you would have thought that this important version of Government House. Everywhere would offer one a little firm history. No. "It has been surmised that this hunting lodge could have belonged to the Emperor Maximianus Heraclius who shared his Emperorship with Diocletian." The site they chose for the Imperial Villa is almost oppressively hidden away; it makes one conjecture why in such a landscape one should plank down a large and spacious building in the middle of a network of shallow ravines heavily wooded, and obviously awash in winter with mountain streams. Instead of planting it on a commanding hillock which (always a problem in hill architecture) drained well during the rains. There was something rather unhealthy and secretive in the choice of a site, and it must be infernally hot in August as a place to live in. It buzzed with insects and butterflies. We arrived in a cleared space where, together with a dozen or so other buses, we dropped anchor and traipsed off down the winding walks to the villa, marvelling at the sultriness and the oppressive heat—so different from the Attic valleys we had traversed with all their brilliant cornfields.

We came at last to a clearing where an absolute monstrosity

greeted our eyes—a straggling building in dirty white plastic which suggested the demesne of a mad market gardener who was specialising in asparagus. I could not believe my eyes. None of us could. We stood there mumchance and swallowing, wondering what the devil this construction was. Roberto, blushing and apologetic, told us.

So precious were the recently uncovered mosaics and so great the risk that they would be eaten into by the climate that someone had had the brilliant idea of covering them in this grotesque plastic housing through which a series of carefully arranged plankwalks and duckboards allowed the curious to walk around the villa. It was a groan-making thing to do and only an archaeologist could have thought of it. Moreover the mosaics, so interesting historically that one is glad to have made the effort to see them, are of a dullness extraordinary. But then the sort of people who build villas for Governors are for the most part interior decorators with a sense of grandiose banality, a sense of the expensively commonplace. Of such provenance is the Imperial Villa, though of course the number and clarity of the decorations merit interest despite their poor sense of plastic power. Historians must be interested in these elaborate hunting-scenes, the warfare of Gods, and the faintly lecherous love scene which ends in a rather ordinary aesthetic experience. And all this in a white plastic housing which turned us all the colour of wax. Was this the pleasure dome of an Emperor, or was it perhaps (an intelligent suggestion by Christopher Kininmonth) more the millionaire's hideaway, constructed for the rich man who purveyed animals for the Roman arenas? The frescoes of animals are so numerous and their variety so great that it makes one pause and wonder. But as usual there is no proof of anything.

Dutifully we prowled the duckboards while Beddoes, who had culled a whole lot of Latin words from the Blue Guide, made up a sort of prose poem from fragments of it which he murmured aloud to himself in a vibrant tone of voice. Thus:

And so we enter the Atrium
By its purely polygonal court
To the left lies the Great Latrine
Ladies and Gents, the Great Latrine
For those who are taken short
But the marble seats are lost
Yet ahead of us is the Aediculum
Giving access to the Thermae
The vestibule can be viewed from the Peristyle
Do not smile.
Next comes the frigidarium
With its apodyteria
Leading onwards with increasing hysteria
To the Alepterion
Between tepidarium and calidarium
Whence into a court where the Lesser Latrine
Waits for those who have not yet been
In construction sumptuous
As befitted the Imperial Purple

But here the Muse punished him and he wobbled off a duckboard and all but plunged down upon one of the more precious tessellations, to the intense annoyance of Roberto and the collective disapproval of the Carousel. The dentist's lady seemed particularly shocked and enraged and flounced about to register her disapproval. "That guy is sacrilegious," she told her companion with a venomous look at Beddoes who seemed only a very little repentant. Frescoed bathers massaged by slaves, animal heads bountifully crowned with laurel—yes, but it was a pity that so extensive and such energetic cartoons had not come from more practised or feeling hands. The commonplaceness of the whole thing hung about in the air; I was reminded suddenly of the interior decorations of the Castle of the Knights at Rhodes—which had been hatched by a Fascist Governor of the Dodecanese Islands who tried to echo the pretensions of Mussolini in this seat of government. The same empty banality—and here it was again—an echo from the last throes of the expiring Empire. "In richness and extent the villa can fairly be compared to Hadrian's villa at Tivoli or Diocletian's Palace at Split." I don't agree, but then who am I to say? The site alone militates against this opinion. These idle thoughts passed through my brain as we slowly negotiated the lesser latrine; "whose brick drain, marble hand-basin and pictorial decoration attest to the standards of imperial Roman comfort". Yes, but if it were just the home of the local Onassis of the day all would be clear.

The visit was long, it was thorough, and it explained why when Martine listed the places she wished that I might visit in order to write the "pocket" Sicily for her children, she had quite omitted to mention it. Perhaps she had just forgotten—such is the vast prolixity of memorable monuments in this island that one could be forgiven for simply forgetting one which made no particular mark on one's nervous system. I write these words, of course, subject to caution and with a certain diffidence, for the finds at the Imperial Villa, the most extensive in Europe, have become justly famous and it may well be that I am putting myself down as a hopeless Philistine. But I think not. And I am somewhat comforted by the fact that Deeds gave the place a very tentative marking in his little guide. But this he rather tended to explain away over the lunch table by saying that he was so deeply in love with the little red town of Aedoni which was a few kilometres off—and with the marvellous ancient Greek site of Morgantina—that all this heavy dun Roman stuff did not impress him. Indeed opinions were rather divided generally, and there were one or two of us who rather shared my view of the Villa. The dentist's lady was most unsparing in her open dislike for Beddoes who glimmered about everywhere like a dragonfly peering over people's shoulders and whispering things they didn't want to hear. "That man," she told her dentist at the lunch table, "is a pure desecrator." It was as good a way of viewing Beddoes as any we had invented, and her accent had an envenomed Mid-Western sting in it.

The lunch was toneless but the mountain air was fresh and we drank a good deal of wine with it; one had begun to feel rather fatigued, almost sleepy. We had been on the move for what seemed an age now, though in reality it was only a few days; but we had begun to feel the stress of travelling about, even over perfect roads, and being exposed the whole time to new sights and sounds. We took off languidly in the cool air, replete with wine, and for the most part with the intention of having a short doze as Mario negotiated the hairpins and forest roads on the way down to Agrigento. The very old Italian couple who never spoke but tenderly held hands like newlyweds seemed in the seventh heaven of smiling joy. They sat back, quiet as apples, and smiled peacefully upon the world as it wheeled by. The little red bus chuckled and rippled its partridge-like way among the forests and pretty soon we once more came in view of the distant sea and the black smudges which marked the site of Gela. There was a good deal of fairly purposeful reafforestation among these cliffs and scarps but I was sorry to see to what extent the eucalyptus had been used, not because it isn't very beautiful as a tree—its shimmering spires of poplar-like green are handsome; but the shallow spread of its roots makes its demands for soil immoderate and nothing very interesting can be set beside it. I suppose that it was chosen precisely because the roots hold up the friable and easily washed-away soil. And Sicily has the same problems of reafforestation as Greece has.

And so from Caltanissetta the long downswing began into the plain where Gela lay; the sea-line today as misty and incoherent as only the heats of July can make it. Somewhere away to the left sweet Vittoria (another dream-town of Deeds which we were going to miss) whose smiling baroque remained to this day a suitable monument to the lady who founded the city, Vittoria della Colonna—was she not once Queen of Cyprus? The slopes lead enticingly downwards towards the Bay of Gela, one of the American landing places in 1943. The dust is rich in this long valley intersected by a number of lively rivers which seemed very high for the time of the year. For a long while, half dozing, we descended along the swaying roads through vineyards and clumps of cane, olive groves and extensive plantations of oranges. And at last of course we struck oil—as we neared the town which Aeschylus had chosen to spend his last years in, indeed to die in.

There was probably a hotel named after him—there always is such a fitting memorial of the mercantile age we live in! The last whiff of the open country is soon extinguished at the approaches to this famous town whose great complex of petro-chemical installations seems to girdle it. There is little to see save what the museum has put on view—an extensive and fine historical collection of objects both votive and utilitarian. The bald skull of the Greek dramatist should perhaps have been among the relics? The legend says that an eagle mistook his skull for a stone and dropped a tortoise shell upon it in order to break it.

Now I took this story to be simply one of those literary fables with which we are so familiar until . . . one day in Corfu, long ago, I actually saw a big bird, perhaps a buzzard, doing exactly this, dropping shells from a great height, on to a seagirt rock and then coming down to inspect and peck. I watched it for over an hour and in all it tried out three or four different shells—they seemed to be clams of a sort, and not tortoises. Though a tortoise would be quite a logical animal for an eagle to sweep in its claws and try to crack apart in this fashion. One Doric column is all that is left unless you like a chunk of defensive ancient wall half silted into the sand. Oil rigs off the shore with their ominous message. But the sweep of the bay is in the grand style and even in the mess of modern Gela one sees how sweet a place it must have been, how rich in fruit and vine, and how splendid as horse-country because so well watered and green. Also it lay just back from the coast so that Syracuse and Akragas were in the front line as far as commerce and warfare were concerned; Gela must have been a little démodé, a little second-hand and old-fashioned, a fitting place for Pythagorean thinkers and poets who wanted a quiet life. At any rate that is what one feels even today. How ugly, though, they have allowed this important site to become (ah Demeter, where is your shrine!) with its haphazard modern development.

There was no time to go down to the sea for we were due in Agrigento that evening, so that after Gela we tumbled back into the bus and set off along the coastal road—the section leading us to Agrigento struck me as desolate and full of dirty sand-dunes; even melancholy, if you like, but not melancholy and depressing as some of the later stretches after Marsala. Perhaps it was the anticipation of the Vale of the Temples which lay ahead, or simply the sun made one drowsy and content to feel the ancient pulse-beat of the vanished Gela where now, off the coast, strange steel animals with long legs probed about like herons in a shallow lake. An idea came to me, and I jotted it down in order to chew it over later at leisure. (Before Christianity the sources of power were in magic, after it in money.) What is to be done? Nothing, it is too late.

On a remote country road, in the deep dust, we unexpectedly drew to a halt under a great carob-tree full of fruit, which is known as the locust-bean. There was an enclosure with trees and a wicket-gate behind which one could see a trimly laid-out little cemetery. This little halt had been organised specifically for Deeds by Roberto. It was a war-cemetery which came into his purlieu for inspection. Accordingly he somewhat apologetically took himself off in the direction of the British and Canadian graves, lighting a cigarette and promising us not to be long. Roberto turned us loose in the road and we straggled about for a while like lost sheep. I walked a little way and entered a vineyard where I found a patch of grass, almost burned brown by the summer heat. Here I lay down in its warm crackling cradle, dislodging swarms of crickets which hardly ceased their whirring as they retreated. The earth smelt delicious, baked to a cinder. Ants crawled over my face. In my heat-hazed mind dim thoughts and dreams and half-remembered conversations jumbled themselves together as a background to this throbbing summer afternoon with the cicadas fiddling away like mad in the trees. Every time a light patch of high cloud covered the sun the whole of nature fell silent—or at least the crickets did. Did they think that winter had suddenly returned? And when the heat was turned on again was I wrong to detect in their fervour a tremendous relief that such was not the case? I hovered on the edge of sleep and then called myself to attention, for the others did not know where I was and it would not do to miss the bus or keep poor Mario fretting and scowling by being late.

I hoisted myself sleepily to my feet and crossed the field back to the road where Roberto, who had been trying to explain something about the carob-tree to the rest of the party, had run into vocabulary trouble. Here I could help a little, for these great strong carob-trees were a handsome feature of Cyprus with their long curving bean. When wind or lightning broke a branch of the tree one was always surprised to see that the wood revealed was the colour of human flesh. The locust-bean, Roberto was trying to explain, was highly nutritious. He was picking a few—they were dry and snapped between his teeth—and handing them round for the party to try. We had often done this on picnics in the past and I was pleased once more to make the acquaintance of this noble tree whose produce is "kibbled" (an absurd word) very extensively in Cyprus for animal fodder. By now Deeds had sauntered back to us in time to take the long seed in his fingers and try it with his teeth. "Can I bore you with a story?" he asked diffidently. "Some of the boys in that cemetery came from a commando I trained in Cyprus. Now among our training tips was to keep an eye wide open for carobs if short of food. You can live almost indefinitely on carob-seed and water, and for a commando in this theatre it was most essential gen. In fact several of those men were lost between the lines during the first assault for about ten days, without rations of any sort. But they found fresh springs and they found locust-beans and lived to tell the tale. Alas, they were killed later in a counter-attack. But if we had been training a commando in the U.K. we would have forgotten about the nutritive qualities of the carob. I always think of Cyprus in those days when I inspect this little cemetery." He had been quite a time and seemed a trifle sad, and somewhat glad to pile back into the bus with us and start off again down the long roads which led onwards to Agrigento and the Temples which for Martine (and not ruling out Taormina) had been the great Sicilian experience. So on we sped now, eating carobs.

The land had gone yellower and more ochreous, the valleys had become longer and more spacious. It had a feel of wildness. But there were strings of lorries loaded with dust-producing chemicals which floated off into the air and powdered the bus until Mario swore and shook his fist at them. Somewhere some

Herculean constructions were being mounted—I hoped it was not Agrigento which had come under the scourge of urbanisation. On one of these long declines we slowed down for an accident involving a lorry and a large sports car. A very definitive accident for the sports car with its occupant still in it had been pushed right into the ditch on one side, while the lorry responsible for the push had itself subsided like an old camel into the ditch on the opposite side. As in all scenes of terror and dismay everything seemed to have settled into a sort of timeless tableau. The police had not yet arrived. Someone had covered the form of the lorry driver with a strip of sacking—just a bare foot sticking out.

But the occupant of the sports car was a handsome blond youth, and he was lying back in his seat as if replete with content, with sunlight, with wine. The expression on his face was one of benign calm, of beatitude. He wore a blue shirt open at the throat. There was no disorder in his dress, nor was he marked by the collision; he seemed as if asleep. The light wind ruffled a strand of blond hair on his forehead to complete the illusion of life, but the little man whose stethoscope was planted inside his blue shirt over the heart, was shaking his head and making the traditional grimace of doctors the world over. The front of the sports car, the whole engine, was crumpled up like a paper bag. Yet there was no blood, no disorder; the young man had simply ceded to the demands of fate. It was a death by pure concussion. He lay, as if in his coffin, while around him stood a group of half a dozen peasants who might have been chosen by a dramatist to give point and resonance to this classical accident in which so unexpectedly death had asserted itself. No one cried or beat his breast; the women had drawn the corner of their headshawls into their mouths and held them between white firm teeth—as if by this gesture to allay the possibility of tears. Two peasants, with mattocks held lightly in hands wrinkled as ancient tortoises, stared at the young man and his sumptuous car as one might stare (the operative phrase is perhaps "drink in") at a holy painting above an altar. Their black eyes brimmed with incomprehension. They did not try to understand this phenomenon—a dead boy in a brilliantly coloured car with yellow suede upholstery. But there was no sorrow, no breast beating, no frantic curiosity such as there would have been in the north or in Greece. Nobody crossed themselves. They simply stared, without curiosity, indeed with a kind of stern bravado. You felt that they and death were equals. It was simply that the island had struck home once more. This was Sicily! And one realised that even death had a different, a particularly Sicilian resonance. The groups of black eyes remained fixed and unwinking whereas the Greek or Italian eye is forever darting about, restless as a fly. In the background there was an older man with a mane of white hair, who stared as hard as the others—indeed with such concentration that his little pink tongue-tip stuck out and gave him an absurdly childish expression. But no fear.

It was we in the bus who felt the fear—you could see gloom and dismay on every visage as Mario drew up in a swirl of whiteness and leaned out to inform himself of the circumstances. Was there anything we could do? Nothing. An ambulance was on the way from Agrigento, also the police. The doctor with his open shirt looked more like a youthful vet. He had managed to edge his tiny Fiat right off the road into a nook while he examined the young man in the car. Nobody used the word for death either: the fact was conveyed with gestures of the fingers or the head. The whole thing was amazingly studied; it was as if all of us, even us in the bus, had been chosen by a dramatist to fill a part in this tableau.

The Bishop had put on an expression which read as: I told you so. He seemed rather like the chief cashier of a great Bank (Death Inc.) who had a good deal of inside knowledge. The old Italian apple-people stayed quietly smiling; perhaps they did not understand or remained locked in their dream of Eden. Renata, the German girl, closed her eyes and turned her head away. Miss Lobb looked severe, as if it reflected discredit on the tourist company to let people who had paid good money suddenly come up against this kind of thing. Beddoes straightened an imaginary tie furtively; you could see that death was for him a headmaster in Dungeness. How did I look? I caught sight of my reflection in the dusty glass and thought I looked a trifle sick—I certainly felt it; it was so unexpected on that brilliant afternoon with the sun sliding down into the mist-blue waters of the Underworld. Would we arrive before dark? We had gathered speed now, and had at last cleared the long file of lorries which were causing all the dust. The air was dry and hot; the limestone configuration of the land spoke of water and green, of spring and rivers and friendly nightingales. Deeds seemed rather remote and preoccupied by his own thoughts and I did not subject him to mine which as usual were rather incoherent and muddled—across the screens of memory old recollections of Athens and the islands came up like friendly animals to be recognised and stroked. Yes, we were in Attica, there was no doubt about it; just north of the capital, say in Psychico or perhaps east near Porto Rafti. . . . I must not hurt Roberto's patriotic feelings by all my Greek chatter. Sicily after all belonged to neither Greece nor to Italy now (geographical frontiers mean nothing) but strictly to itself, to its most ancient and indestructible self. On we sped, skimming the hills like a swallow.

It came in sight slowly, the famous city; at first as a series of suggestive shapes against the evening sky, then as half dissolved forms which wobbled in the heat haze to settle at last firmly into the cubist boxes of a modern city—and with at least two small skyscrapers to mark the ancient (I supposed) Acropolis. But as we approached, a black cloud of a particularly heavy and menacing weight began to obscure the sun. It was very strange—the whole of heaven was, apart from this cloud, serene, void and blue. It was as if the thing had got left over from some old thunderstorm and lay there undissolved, drifting about the sky. It was not to be regretted as it was obviously going to cause a dramatic sunset, threshing out the sun's rays, making it seem like the lidless dark eye of a whale from which stray beams escaped. If I make a point of this little departure from the norm of things it is because as we journeyed along we saw to our left a small cottage perched on a headland with two wind-bent pines outside it—the whole hanging there over the sea, as if outside the whole of the rest of nature. There was no other sign of human habitation save this desolate and memorable little cottage. With the black sunlight it looked deeply tragically significant, as if it were the backdrop for a play. Hardly anybody paid attention to the little scene, but Roberto with an air of sadness, announced over the speaker: "The birthplace of Pirandello. A little hamlet called Chaos!" He looked at his watch. The museum would be shut he thought. Perhaps one might just stop for a moment? If the idea was tentative it was because he knew that hardly anyone in the bus knew or cared much about this great man, this great original poet of Agrigento. We risked, by a detour, to arrive a trifle late and perhaps prejudice a trip to the valley of the Temples which were floodlit at night. Would anybody care to . . . but only three or four hands were raised so it was decided to press on.

Meanwhile, staring across the dusty *bled* on my left I saw the sunbeams lengthen and sink, like stage-lights being lowered for a play, while suddenly from the beaches behind the silhouette came a stream of grinding labouring lorries, like a string of ants upon a leaf. I suppose they were doing nothing more sinister than bringing up sea sand from the beaches, but the clouds of whiteness they sent swirling heavenwards contained so many tones of pearl, yellow, amber that the whole display, with the sunlight shining through it, was worthy of a nervous breakdown by Turner. It made my heart beat faster, it was memorable and at the same time a little ominous—as if by it we were warned not to take the famous city we were about to visit too lightly. To bring to it our real selves. Yet it was all over in a matter of half a minute, but it had a sort of finalising effect on our decision, for we turned our backs upon this vision and set about climbing into the sky, towards the town whose shabby outlines and haphazard building became slowly more and more evident as we advanced. Roberto uttered its name with a small sigh of fatigue.

I had not conveyed my impressions to Deeds believing him to be otherwise occupied, but the all-seeing eye had taken in the headland and he said now: "Pity about Pirandello. The little museum is very touching. But what a strange light. And the small scale is striking—like the humbleness of Anne Hathaway's cottage." It was an apt comment on the origins of greatness.

But by now the cloud had mysteriously vanished backstage and all was serene, a transparent, cloudless dusk with no trace of wind; and as we followed the curves and slants of the road up to the town it became slowly obvious that what was being unfolded before us and below us was a most remarkable site. Successive roundels led in a slow spiral up to the top of the steep hillock upon which once an Acropolis had perched, and where now two parvenu skyscrapers stood and an ignoble huddle of unwarranted housing did duty for the old city's centre. We had reached by now the commercial nexus of the new town which lies a bit below the city, makeshift and ugly. But the light was of pure opalescent honey, and the setting (I am sorry to labour the point) was Hymettus at evening with the violet city of Athens sinking into the cocoon of night. I tremble also to insist on the fact that from the point of view of natural beauty and elegance of site Agrigento is easily a match for Athens on its hills. Just as the ocean throws up roundels of sand to form pools, so the successive ages of geological time had thrown up successive rounds of limestone, rising in tiers like a wedding-cake to the Acropolis. From the top one looks down as if into a pie-dish with two levels, inner and outer ridges. It is down there, at the entrance to the city, that all the Temples are situated, like a protective screen, tricked out with fruit orchards, with sweeps of silver olives, and with ubiquitous almond trees whose spring flowering has become as famous as the legendary town itself.

We climbed down into the twilight with a strange feeling of indecision, not knowing exactly what was in store for us. It was only after a brief walk across a square, when we found ourselves looking down into the tenebrous mauve bowl where the Temples awaited us that we realised that our arrival at that precise time was an act of thoughtful good sense on the part of Roberto. "Before the city lights go on you may see more or less how the classical city looked at sunset." The air was so still up here that one could catch the distant sounds of someone singing and the noise perhaps of a mattock on the dry clay a mile below us. At our back the streets were beginning to fill up for the evening Corso, the tiny coffee-shops to brim over with lights which seemed, by contagion, to set fire at last to the street-lamps behind our backs and set off the snarling radios and juke-boxes and traffic noise. Ahead of us the darkness rose slowly to engulf us, like ink being poured into a well; but it was a light darkness, slightly rosy, as if from a hidden harvest moon. But we belonged to the scattered disoriented city now with its stridulations of juke.

We were about to turn away from this slowly overwhelming darkness and back into the raucous streets when Roberto, who still peered keenly down the valley, implored a moment's patience of us, for what reason I could not tell. He seemed as keyed up as if we were to expect something like a firework display. But it was better than that; presently there came the swift wingbeats of a church-bell which sounded like a signal and soundlessly the temples sprang to floodlit life all together, as if by a miracle. This was aerial geography with a vengeance, for they were to be our after-dinner treat tonight! But there were signs of raggedness and fatigue in the party and I could see that some of us might prefer to stay in the hotel and sleep. The Count's wife looked really ill with weariness and I wondered why they had embarked her on such a journey. Mrs. Microscope too looked crusty though we had had no more news of her spleen. But there was to be a bit of delay as yet for our schedule called for half an hour's shopping halt in the town, to enable us to buy curios and generally take a look round. Not all set off for this treat; many stayed in the bus. While, rather cowardly, I took myself off with Deeds to a *bistro* where I anticipated dinner and the fatigues of temple-haunting by a couple of touches of *grappa* which was like drinking fumed oak in liquid form. Heartening stuff. Deeds fell into conversation with a eunuchoid youth who brought us coffee with a kindly but disenchanted air.

In the far corner, however, there was a small group of middle-aged to elderly men who attracted my instant attention by their hunched-up look and their black clothes and battered boots. They were gnarled and leathered by their avocation—could they have been coal-miners, I wondered? Dressed awkwardly in their Sunday best with heavy dark suits and improbable felt hats which looked as if very seldom worn. Or perhaps they were mourners attending the funeral of some local dignitary? They spoke in low gruff tones and in a dialect Italian. The sister of the eunuch served them exclusively and with such obvious nervousness that

I finally concluded that they must be a group of Mafia leaders on a Sunday outing. Their little circle exuded a kind of horrid Protestant gloom, and most of their faces were baneful, ugly. They were drinking Strega as far as I could make out, but the massive sugar content was not making them any sweeter. It was a strange little group and all the other customers of the place beside ourselves shot curious glances at them, wondering I suppose like ourselves, what and from where. . . . The mystery was only cleared up when Roberto appeared in search of a quick coffee and caught sight of us. He seemed not unprepared for the question and it was clear from his way of looking at them when Deeds pointed them out that they did seem singular, almost like another race. But no, that was not the case. They were simply sulphur-miners on a night out in town.

"They are Zolfataioi," said Roberto with a smile. "We have been shielding you from the uglier side of Sicily, but we have our own black country here like you have; only it's not black, it's yellow. The sulphur-workers live a sort of grim separate life except for their occasional excursions like this—though it's usually to Caltanissetta that they go. It's the headquarters of the trade." The men looked as if they were waiting anxiously for transport and those at the two tables playing cards were doing so abstractedly, as if marking time. They were as impressively different from the other Italians as would have been, say, a little group of Bushmen, or Japanese. But they drank with precision. One of the elder ones with a leather face and expressionless eyes had the knack of tilting and emptying his glass in a single gesture, without swallowing. He looked like Father Time himself, drinking a whole hourglass of time at each quaff. I watched them curiously.

At that moment there came a diversion in the form of a large grey sports car which drew up outside the café. From it descended a couple of extremely well-dressed and sophisticated youths of a vaguely Roman allure—I put them down as big-city pederasts having a holiday here. But their manner was offensively superior and they acted as if they owned the place. They were fashionably clad in smart coloured summer wear and open collars, while their hair was handsomely styled and curled. They wanted to leave a message for some local boy and they engaged the flustered eunuch in conversation. Meanwhile, and the touch had a somewhat special insolence, they had left the car's engine running so that the exhaust was belching noisome fumes on to the terrace and into the café itself. One felt resentful; it was as if they were deliberately flaunting not only their classical proclivities but their superiority as well. Their tones were shrill and their Italian of the cultivated sort.

Their arrival produced a little ripple of interest in the circle of sulphur-miners, though the general tone was apathetic and not resentful. They eyed these two butterflies in their expressionless way and then looked at one another with a kindly irony. It was not malicious at all. Then the old man set down his tiny Strega glass and, wiping his moustache, said in a firm audible tone, "*Ah*! *pederastici*!" It was not offensive, simply an observation which classified the two, who must have overheard for they shrugged their shoulders and turned back to the eunuch with more questions about their friend Giovanni. Moreover the word fell upon the silence with a fine classical limpidity—five lapidary syllables. It was perfectly summed up and forgotten—the whole incident. The one eloquent word was enough. No further comment was needed, and the miners turned back to their inner preoccupations and sank ever deeper into their corporate reserve while the two turkeys gobbled on.

A Greek root with
A Latin suffix
A Grecian vice
A Latin name

But at last it was time to take ourselves off to the gaunt restaurant where a single long dinner-table had been prepared for us. There were to be some casualties among us, and about six of the wearier, as predicted, decided on an early night. We were anyway to have another look at the Temples by daylight on the morrow so that they were not to lose very much. It was only annoying for Mario, for the hotel was in the valley, some way off, and he would have to ferry them and then come back and ferry us to the Temples, going without dinner in the process. But he took it all with grave good humour and that undemonstrative courtesy that I was beginning to recognise as a thoroughly Sicilian trait. The weary therefore moved off, content to eat a sandwich in bed, while we doubled up our ranks and did our best to look joyfully surprised by yet another choice between spaghetti and rice. But the wine was good in its modest way. And we did full justice to it telling ourselves that we owed it to our fatigue, though Roberto warned us that we were only going to have a sniff at the Temples and not attempt to "do" them thoroughly until tomorrow. It was to see them floodlit, that was all. But how grateful one finally was for the glimpse, however brief, and how sorry one felt for the absentees.

We had hardly finished dinner when impassive Mario appeared with the bus and we were on the way down the hill, curving away upon the so-called *passegiata archeologica*, a beautiful modern road which winds in and out of the temple circles; one by one these great landmarks came out of the night to meet us, while a thousand night insects danced in the hot light of the floods. The bare ground—yes, it smelt of Attica again. The whiffs of thyme and sage, and the very soil with its light marls and fawn-coloured tones made the island itself seem like some huge abstract terra-cotta which by some freak of time might give birth to vases, amphorae, plates, craters. An ancient Athenian must have walked here with the sympathetic feeling of being back in Athens. And it was extraordinary to realise that this huge expanse of temples represented only a tiny fraction of what exists here in reality, and which remains to be unearthed. The archaeologists have only scratched the surface of Agrigento; stretching away on every side, hidden in the soft deciduous chalk through which the twin rivers have carved their beds, there lie hidden necropolises, aqueducts, houses and temples and statues as yet quite unknown to us; and all the wealth inside them of ceramics and jewellery and weapons. It seems so complete as it is, this long sparkling ridge with its tremendous exhibits. Yet Agrigento has hardly begun to yield up all its treasures, and in coming generations what is unearthed might well modify all our present ideas about it. Long shadows criss-crossed the night. Leaving the glare of the floods one was at once plunged into dense patches of fragrant darkness. There was another busload of dark figures round the Temple of Concord, all down on their knees. Were they praying? It seemed so.

In the circumstances, with the massive and blinding whiteness of the floodlights, the magical temple looking down upon us from some unimaginable height of centuries, the activity of the group of persons clustering about the stylobate, kneeling, bending, crawling, seemed to suggest that they were engaged in some strange archaic rite. Was it a propitiatory dance of some sort, an invocation to the God of the site? But no, the explanation was more prosaic. Yet before it was given to us the strangeness of the scene was increased by the fact that, as we approached upon the winding paths, punctuated by lanterns, we saw that they were Asiatics—Chinese I thought. Their faces were white in the white light, and their eyes had disappeared with the intensity of their concentration upon the ground. Our groups mingled for a moment to wander about on this extraordinary headland over the brimming darkness of the valley. Their guide was an acquaintance of Roberto's and provided a clue as to the mysterious behaviour of his group. Two of the more ardent photographers had lost their lens caps and everyone was trying to help them recover these valuable items. It was extremely hard. The floods were pouring up into the sky with such power that unless one was directly in their ray one could see nothing, one became a one-dimensional figure, a silhouette. They cast an absolutely definitive black shadow.

Even if you held out your hand in the light the underneath, the shadowy side, was plunged into total blackness. Thus to pick up something small from the ground just outside the arc of white light presented extraordinary difficulties. Which explained all the crouching stooping peering people. Standing off a little from them, feeling the velvety warmth of the night upon my cheek, I felt grateful to have outgrown the desire to photograph things; I had once been a keen photographer and had even sold my work. Now I preferred to try and use my eyes, at first hand, so to speak, and to make my memory do some work. In a little schoolchild's exercise book I occasionally made a note or two for the pleasure of trying to draw; and then later I might embark on a watercolour which, by intention, would try to capture the mood or emotion of a particular place or incident. It was a more satisfactory way of going about things, more suitable to my present age and preoccupations. The photograph was always a slightly distorted version of the subject; whereas the painting made no pretensions to being anything more than a slightly distorted version of one's feelings at a given moment in time.

Our Japanese couple seemed disposed to exchange a word with the Chinese, but the attempt made no headway and they retired into their shell once more, having pronounced the other group to be North Koreans. Some of us, with simulated good will, tried to join in the search for a moment, but it did not last long for we were now a little tired. Indeed we were glad to regain the bus, and after one more brilliant glimpse to coast quietly down the sloping roads towards the hotel where doubtless the others were already fast asleep. Fatigue lengthens distance mentally—we felt now as if we had been to the moon and back. And yet, despite it, a queer sense of elation and of freshness co-existed with the fatigue. The darkness was sort of translucent, the air absolutely warm and still; the hotel was rather a grand affair pitched at a main cross roads and obviously laid out for tourism. There was a huge swimming pool, and its lights were still on. A few people still lounged by it in deck-chairs or swam; and so warm was it that several of our party, notably the German girl and her boy friend, elected to have a dip before going to bed. I hesitated but finally decided upon a whisky on the balcony before turning in; Deeds had retired sleepily, and I did not fancy the company of Beddoes who had doubtless been peering through keyholes already.

In the little file there were no letters actually written from Agrigento though she had had plenty to say about the place which she had visited on numerous occasions with her little car. "In early February it is pure wedding-cake with the almond blossom of three tones and the fabulous later flowering of an occasional Judas. That is the real time to come, though of course it will be still too cold to swim." I had missed it, but I already had the configurations of the Temple hills clearly in mind and could visualise easily how they must look—like a series of flowered panels, Chinese water-colours, with the mist-mauve sea behind. From my balcony I could sit in the warmth of the scented night and see the distant moth-soft dazzle of the temples crowning the lower slopes of Agrigento; immediately underneath me in loops of artificial light swam the fish-white bodies of northern bathers who as yet had not become nut-brown with Sicilian sunlight. A slight splashing and the murmur of voices was rather agreeable from the second storey of this comfortable if nondescript building. I read for a little while, dipping here and there among the letters to recover references to the temples, and listening with half an ear to the voices in the pool. "Whole conversations at Bellapais in Cyprus came back to me when I visited the Temples at night—they have only just started to floodlight them, and the result is marvellous—the whole of nature takes part; every insect in creation, every moth and butterfly comes rushing to this great kermess of light, like people impelled to go to war, only to perish in the arcs. In the morning they are swabbed off with cloths. I picked up a most beautifully marked moth which looked as if it came from India specially to see Pythagoras or the other one—who is it? The one you find so great with his two-stroke universe, operating like a motor-bike on the Love and Hate principle? O and yes, when I saw the ring of the temples, the so obviously defensive ring of them here on the outer slopes of the town I thought of your notions of ancient banking."

It was not simply banking, though we had canvassed pretty thoroughly the notion of the temple as a safe-deposit of values, both sacred and profane. I had been trying to sort out some muddy notions about the idea of Beauty, and its origins in history and myth. You could not well take on a more intractable field to hoe—for we cannot even establish a working notion which defines excellence ("purity of function?" "congruence?") let alone something as absolute as an aesthetic ideal of Beauty. Greece was an appropriate place to chew such an idea to death, since it was in Greece that all these unanswerable questions had first been ventilated. But riffling a large book of ancient Greek sites drawn and described for architects I had been struck by the frequency with which the temple or the sacred fane had found its place, not in the interior of the city or fortress, but along its defensive walls. The temples with their magical properties were a more efficacious defence against piracy in a world of superstition than bolts and bars and moats even. And thinking over the theory of value as another mystery of our time (unless you accept the Freudian or Marxian notions which oppose each other) it seemed to me that in ancient times the whole notion of sacred and profane had not been separated; the riches of the temple were protective; and a site protected by the magic of its temples and its Gods would encourage investment in the form of artisanship—workers in metal and precious stones and furs. The numen would protect them and let them work in peace, while in their turn they would render the city rich and notable with their products. There was an underground connection between the Bank and the Temple and it has cropped up over and over again. In the Middle Ages the Order of Templars, themselves vowed to frugality and poverty, became the bankers of kings, and their temples the actual banks where treasure was deposited for safety.

The Greek temple implicated the whole of nature in its magical scheme—the world of animals as well as Gods. The notion of value was twofold, namely, material gain and also a degree of beauty which enslaved and ennobled, which enchanted and enriched on the spiritual plane. But how inadequate words were when it came to trying to point up the difference between these two degrees of excellence. There was, however, a continuity between the Greek temple with its ex-votoes and the modern Christian or Orthodox Church with its same pathetic objects of gratitude or propitiation. And the notion of beauty worshipped in icons, in paintings, in holy relics. One thinks of the golden statue that Cicero found "beslubbered by the kisses of the faithful who loved its unique beauty"; today the icon is still kissed, but not for its beauty. For its power.

Martine took the idea and played with it for a while, making fun of my woolliness and vagueness—it is impossible to be too precise, for so many fragments of the jigsaw are missing. Everything is supposition.

But we have had enough experience now of the thought-schemes of savages to be thoroughly on our guard when it comes to trying to imagine how primitive peoples think, how they associate. Were the ancient Greeks, with their highly organised and, to them, very logical superstitious systems, any different? I don't think so. Why, the notion of gold being valuable may well have come from the first golden Aryan head which the Greeks saw, with its marvellous buttercup sheen. The men went mad over this hypothetical girl—Circassian or Scythian or British perhaps? Gentlemen preferred blondes even then, so it became necessary to manufacture golden wigs, or tresses of beaten filigree gold as a head ornament. We know that prostitutes in ancient Athens were forbidden by law to imitate the blandishments of respectable married women by wearing rich gold ornaments, fillets or clips, in their hair. That is probably why they set about finding cheap dyes in order to effect a transformation that was legitimate. They tried saffron and, like the modern Egyptian of the poorer classes, common soap with its strong bleaching agent. The story of Goldilocks. A theory of how beauty came to be evaluated. But where, then, did the metal come into this scheme of things? These matters we used to argue to the point of sheer irritation with each other. In one of her letters she records our violent disagreements.

"I couldn't help thinking of you and your wretched relativity notions the other evening when I went to see Loftus Adam who now lives here, just down the coast from me. He too said how irritated you made him by trying to subject everything to the merely provisional: and all truth as subject to scale. Yet he himself at last admitted that if you selected your co-ordinates you could prove anything from any evidence; he wants to write a modern history of Europe based on three co-ordinates, namely the moustaches of Hitler, Marinetti and Chaplin, which have formed our unhappy age. They were all the same little smudge moustache which must prove something. And between them the new European sensibility was forged and founded. It sounds highly fanciful but why not? He is going to call the book *THE MOUSTACHE; and why*".

I went to sleep quite late that night and had a dream in which I recovered the name of the philosopher which had escaped her—the great Empedocles who was a native of the town and around whose name and memory gathered so many tales of necromancy and witchcraft as to almost obscure his real fame as a philosopher as eminent and as fruitful as any of the great men of his time. Is it nothing to have won the respect of Aristotle, or to have influenced Lucretius? Moreover enough of his system remains extant today for our scholars to evaluate and describe. Why has he been written off as a mythomane? In the case of Bertrand Russell the reason is plain; great as Russell is, he was, in the affective and intuitional sense, colour-blind. He is no poet but a geometer. And it was inevitable, given the type of temperament that was his, that he should be as unfair to Plato as he was to Empedocles. Then one recalls the gibes and sneers of Epicurus when he referred to Plato's attempts to systematise reality and to comprehend nature. To him everything that Plato beheld was the purest illusion, the purest self-deceit. He believed in a world which held no mysteries and in consequence no great dangers. Temperamentally Empedocles lies on a tangent between the absolute behaviourism of one and the pure subjective vision of the other. To each his truth, and *qui verra vivra* to adapt the phrase to suit philosophers who are also visionaries (charlatans to the Russells of this world and the last). The two functions, however, the two arts of deduction and of intuitive vision must be complementary at some remove. Plato to Aristotle, Freud to Jung. . . . In this sharp diversity is born the marriage of true minds.

For Empedocles also the world was arranged in not too mysterious a fashion, though it was far from an impulse-inhibition machine run by invisible and soulless engineers. One could best comprehend it as a sphere ceaselessly agitated by two primordial impulses or dispositions which in turn acted upon four primary roots of all being—fire, air, water, earth. This joining and separating motor (the Love and Strife machine) in its quite involuntary convulsions manipulated matter and shook it out in a million differentiated patterns and mixtures like a kaleidoscope shakes out pictures at the slightest jog. The arch-movers of all process were Love and Hate—the joining and separating impulses. The domination of one or the other produced quite recognisable effects in nature, alloys of the four basic elements. It seems fair enough.

The original condition of matter was to be envisaged as a sphere in which Love played the dominant role and where the four basic elements were perfectly accorded and mixed. Into this primordial harmony entered the principle of Strife which set off the whole dance of process and foxed up the original harmony of things. First air became separated, then fire, then earth—the motion acted like a milk-separator, forging unexpected unities and dissonances; and the effects of these changes were reflected in every department of man's life and thoughts. Quantity was all-important—a hint perhaps of a Pythagorean influence? The present world—the world he knew and which has not noticeably changed since his time—is a theatre where Love is being everywhere assailed by Strife; and where Strife becomes dominant species and sexes become separated, lose their coherence and identity—it is matter in a state of hysteria. But at the other end of the cosmic seesaw—for the gain of one element turns to loss by overplus and gives ground to its opposite—the overwhelming force of undiluted love could bring about bizarre physiological changes in nature. Empedocles, in his vision of the disorder brought about by the mixture of unequal quantities of the four elements, speaks about separate limbs being begotten, arising and walking around, as in the canvases of Dali; hands without shoulders and necks, bodies without hands. And all sorts of singular combinations, like oxen with human heads, fishes with breasts, lions with hands, birds with ears. . . . A chaos of undifferentiated forms ruled.

But nature aspired to the functioning rule of the sphere, and only the sphere mixed the elements rightly, in the proper proportion and harmony. Yet the slightest push from one side or the other and one got an imbalance in nature which only hazard could redress. This then was the reality of things as we were living it, for we were part and parcel of the whole convulsion, our thoughts and feelings were all influenced by it. As for thought, Empedocles was convinced that we think with our blood, and more especially with the blood around the heart, because in the blood here all the elements are more correctly fused than in other sectors of the body. What is endearing, and indeed peculiarly modern, is his interest in embryology and in the growth-systems of plants; whenever possible he drew his analogies from this department of knowledge. For him thought and perception were materially functions of our bodily constitution. All this was down to earth, was perfectly functional, was the fruit of sweet reason and not of fantasy; somewhere at heart he was temperamentally akin to Epicurus.

Yet in spite of this rational disposition the visions kept intervening—Nature kept unfolding itself before his eyes, delivering its secrets to his curious and poetic mind. By some strange alchemy, too, he somehow managed to include a purely Orphic notion about the transmigration of souls into his system, where it sits somehow awkwardly. But so much of his work is missing that it is really a miracle that the extant remnants present as coherent a view of things as they do. It is rather like trying to reassemble a beautiful vase from a few recovered bits and pieces of it—the task which faces the archaeologist. Inevitably there will be here and there a shard which does not fit. In the case of this great man I was always struck by the fact that he felt that he himself had forfeited the final happiness; he describes himself as an "exile from a possible Bliss", because he had put his trust in "senseless strife". Was there any way to escape from such spiritual contamination? Apparently there was—by fasting, abstention from animal flesh, and the performance of certain mystical rites. . . .

For him also the first completely realised forms to grow on earth were trees in whom male and female sexuality were so perfectly conjoined. And so on. Apparently the intoxication of these high thoughts was matched by a brilliant fuliginous style which made Aristotle christen him the first of rhetoricians or the father of rhetoric.

Yes, it is not hard to see why the notions of magic, of necromancy, clung to the name of old Empedocles—one thinks of his final leap into the maw of Etna. A suitable way for a great magician to take his leave of his fellow Sicilians. But the truth appears to be that he actually died far away, in the Peloponnesus. He must have been a very dramatic figure, this great rhetor, poet, visionary. In my mind's eye I see always someone of the aspect of the modern Greek poet Sikelianos, who so charmed and bewildered us all with his strange mixture of greatness and histrionic absurdity. He became as much beloved for his aberrations and exaggerations as for his truly great verse which he insisted on declaiming at gale force and with gestures—which so often all but disguised its real merits. He too chose "big" subjects like his contemporary Kazantzakis—St. Paul, Buddha, Socrates. . . . They were grist to his poetic mill. I remember how Martine used to adore anecdotes about the Greek poets of our time—she was fully aware of their European stature in a period when Greece had yet to find its immortal echo outside Athens and Alexandria. Sikelianos at that time was already a walking re-incarnation of an ancient God. He had founded the Delphic festival not as a piece of tourist folklore but, in true Empedoclean fashion, because he believed that the spirit of place was ever present, and that Delphi despite its silenced shrine of the Pythea was still pregnant with life. The meeting of great European minds at this sacred spot could have an incalculable effect on the poetic destiny of Europe—so he thought. He did not lack detractors, as may be imagined; but the incontestable greatness of his poetry silenced them. But sometimes he got so carried away by his vatic role that people thought of him as a mountebank. Yet the peasants at Delphi saw him as a sort of magician of today.

He was a strange mixture of vagueness and gentleness; and his great unassuming physical beauty made one sit up, as if in the presence of the Marashi. Nor was he foreign to the most endearing absurdities. One hopes that there will soon be a biography to enshrine the many anecdotes born of his flamboyant life and thought. One that Martine particularly enjoyed was concerned with death, for old Sikelianos believed so firmly in the absolute-ness of poetic power that he went so far as to declare that a great poet could do anything, even bring a dead man to life by the power of his mind and vision. He was rather belabouring this theme while sitting in a little taverna, having dinner with Kazantzakis and, I think, Seferis, when the waiter, who had been listening to him with sardonic disgust stepped forward and informed him that someone had just died on the second floor, and if he wished to prove his point he had a subject right under his hand. Everyone smiled at this but Sikelianos appeared enchanted with the chance to show, not his own greatness, for he was a modest man, but the greatness which resides in poetry. Moreover he believed in what he said, he could bring the dead man back to life as he had promised. They did not ask how he proposed to do such a thing. But anyway, the poet rose and asked to be taken to the room where the corpse lay. In a resigned mood the others continued their dinner; they were not entirely unconvinced that the old poet might, by some feat of magic, actually be as good as his word and make the dead man breathe again. But he was a long time gone. They listened but there was no sound of poetic declamation. He must have chosen some other method of raising the dead. Well, after quite a time a crestfallen Sikelianos made his appearance once more, deeply disappointed. Pouring himself a glass of wine he said: "Never have I seen such sheer obstinacy!" He was very sad about the failure of the Muse to come to his aid.

This was the delightful man whom once Seferis brought to meet me—indeed it was to chide me for a bad translation of one of his great poems. I was terrified, but he rapidly put me at my ease by his gentleness. He had just come from the doctor where he had been informed that he was in danger of a thrombosis. A vein in the brain. . . . But far from being despondent he was wild with elation. "Think of it," he said to Seferis, "a little gleaming swelling in there, shining like a *ruby*!" And he placed his long index finger upon the supposed place in his skull where the swollen vein was situated. He should have disappeared into Etna like Empedocles, or have been found half-eaten by the Minotaur in Crete, or suffocated by the Pythean fumes at Delphi. But his death was the more tragic for being so banal. He suffered from a chronic sore throat and to soothe it drank quantities of a glycerine mixture the name of which differed by one letter from that of

Lysol. He sent a boy out to the pharmacy for a bottle of his medicine and by a tragic mishearing the boy bought instead a bottle of the poisonous detergent. Without thinking the poet raised the bottle as he had always done with his throat mixture and half drained it before he realised the full horror of what he had done. By then it was too late.

I could not sleep, with all these thoughts fluttering about in my mind. I lay for a while on the balcony quietly breathing in the warm unmoving night air; it was strangely light, too, as if from somewhere offstage there was a bronze moon filtering its light through the vapours of the night. But before I realised it the dawn had suddenly started to come up, the distant sea-lines to separate from the earth like yolk from white of the cosmic egg. The hills with their soft chalk tones rose slowly, tier upon tier, to where the city stood once more revealed with its two baleful skyscrapers. But an infinity of pink and fawn light softened every outline, even the huge boxlike structures looked well. I slipped down and coaxed the night porter to open the changing-room door; the pool was delicious, not a tremor of coolness. I was swimming in something the temperature of mammals' blood.

Yes, Sikelianos belonged to that old assured classical world where only great men wrote great poetry—there was an assumed connection between the power to write and orate great verse and the power to be morally and psychically superior to one's fellow men. Greatness, though thrust upon one by the Muse, did not absolve one from being a great example to one's fellows. An epic grandeur of style was believed to match an epic grandeur of insight and thought. They were another race these men—they were bards, whose sensibilities worked in every register, from uplift to outrage. The poet was not cursed, but blessed in his insight; and his themes must be equal to his mighty line. It is probably a fallacy to imagine that with the Symbolistes, with Baudelaire, there comes a break and the poet becomes a passive object of suffering, a sick man, a morally defective man like Rimbaud, like Leopardi. His work comes out of sickness rather than an overplus of health. Swinburne, Verlaine. . . . No, this is donnish thinking, for Sikelianos existed side by side with Cavafy, just as Mistral lived in the epoch of Apollinaire. But we should avoid these neat ruled lines between men and periods. The distances are much vaster than that and the poetic constellations move much more slowly across the sky. I betook myself to the coffee-room where the majority of my fellow-travellers were hard at work on breakfast, and where Deeds had emerged in some magical fashion with a brand new *Times*. This always made him vague, and over his coffee he was repeating "Sixty-three for five—I can't believe it." It seemed that a disaster had overtaken Yorkshire, and that Hampshire. . . .

It was by far the hottest day yet, and brilliantly invigorating; there was no wind, the sea had settled into long calms like a succession of soft veils. Agrigento glimmered up there on the sky and Mario in some mysterious fashion had succeeded in giving the bus a wash and brush-up for the floors were still moist from his mop.

The temples were bathed in an early morning calm and light, and there were no other tourists at the site, which gave us the pleasant sense of propriety, the consciousness that we could take them at our ease. Drink them in is the operative tourist phrase—and it wasn't inapposite, for the atmosphere on this limestone escarpment with its sweeps of olive and almond, and its occasional flash of Judas was quite eminently drinkable. The air was so still one was conscious that one was breathing, as if in yoga. The stolid little temples—how to convey the sense of intimacy they conveyed except by little-ising them? They were in fact large and grand, but they felt intimate and lifesize. Maybe the more ancient style of column, stubby and stolid, conveys this sense of childishness. It was not they but the site as a whole which conveyed a sense of awe; the ancients must have walked in a veritable forest of temples up here, over the sea. But one slight reservation was concerned with the type of light tufa used in the Sicilian temples; it was the only suitable material available to the architect, and of course all these columns were originally faced with a kind of marble dust composition to give the illusion of real marble. In consequence now when they are seen from close to the impression is rather of teeth which have lost their glittering dentine.

They are fawnish in tone, and matt of surface; while embedded in the stone lie thousands of infinitesimally small shells, tiny worm-casts left by animalcules in the quarries from which the stone was taken. This is not apparent at night during the floodlighting unless one looks really closely. But by day they strike a somewhat second-hand note which forces one to recall that originally all these temples were glossy—fluted as to their columns while their friezes and cornices were painted in crude primary colours. It is something too easy to forget—the riot of crude and clumsy colour in which the temple was embedded. Statues painted. . . . It is my private opinion that the Greeks had, for this reason, little of what we would call plastic sense in our present-day terms. I speak of our lust for volume and our respect for the parent matter out of which our sculptures are shaped. Obviously for them wholly different criteria obtained; it is intriguing to try and imagine whether we would not have been shocked rather than moved by these sites if they had been today in their ancient state of repair, bright with colour-washes. It might have seemed to our contemporary eyes as garish but as refreshingly childish as the painted sideboards of the little Sicilian carts which from time to time we passed in the streets of the towns. I thought back to the Pausanian description of the Holy of Holies on the Acropolis; perhaps one should make the mental effort to compare our impressions of, say, Lourdes (horrible!) or St. Peter's or the Cathedral of Tinos. . . .

So we slowly passed down at a walking pace in that pleasant sunshine following the sweet enfilade of the temples as they curved down towards the one to the Dioscuri—like a descending chromatic scale. One by one these huge mythological beasts came up to us, as if they were grazing, and allowed us to pat them. The image had got muddled up in my mind with another thought about temples as magical defensive banks; and by the same token with the thought that all religious architecture carries the same sort of feeling. In America the most deeply religious architecture (in the anthropological sense) is the banks, and some are watched over by precisely the same mythical animals as watched over the temples here, animals staring down from a frieze—lions or boars, bulls or bears. Just as in the Midi, added Deeds jokingly, the deeply religious architecture of the wine co-operatives betrays the inmost religious preoccupations of the inhabitants. He thinks this a *boutade* but has in fact made an observation of great perspicacity and truth. They are indeed very much alike, and quite religious in their style, like stout laic churches.

The Bishop now elected to fall into a shaft, gracefully and without damage, and for a moment a terrible beauty was born. One touch of music-hall makes the whole world kin. All we heard at first was a kind of buzzing and booming. It was his voice from the depths giving his rescuers instructions as to how to help him clamber back into the daylight. Beddoes at once suggested that Hades had mistaken him for Persephone and had made an unsuccessful snatch at his coat-tails, almost dragging him into the Underworld. He would have been disappointed one supposes. At any rate a pretty scene was enacted not unworthy of its ancient Greek echoes, for his saviour turned out to be none other than Miss Lobb who (like Venus on a similar occasion) undid her plaited goat-skin belt and extended the end of it to the upraised hands of the holy man. The idea was simple and efficacious. We all formed up, myself with my arms round Miss Lobb and the rest linked on as in a childish game and with a tug or two we raised the Bishop into the daylight, where he seemed none the worse for this brief adventure. The one who was really pale with anxiety was of course Roberto who at once realised that his charge could have broken an ankle. The shaft was not profound, however; the sides had subsided, that was all; and as for the Bishop he was only wounded in his *amour propre*.

The theory of Hades snatching at him was all the more plausible as down here there had once been a shrine to the chthonic deities —another bewilderment of contradictory ascriptions—and it was just the place where a Protestant Bishop might expect to run foul of a pagan God. Anyway, this accident put us all in a very good humour and we felt a little touch of pride in the classical aspect of the whole affair. Though we were mere tourists we had a touch of the right instinct. As for poor Persephone, that is another story. But I could feel no trace of her sad spirit calling from its earthen tomb—the sunlight made such fictions too improbably cruel to contemplate. The chthonic deities had little reality for us on that sunny morning. It was hard to admit that one so beautiful had, as one of her attributes, the title of "bringer of destruction".

But what was a real knockout on this extensive and rather chaotic site was the enormous figure of the recumbent telamon—that gigantic figure whose severed fragments have been approximately assembled on the ground to give an indication of his enormous height and posture. This temple of Zeus is the most extraordinary in conception and has a strangeness which makes one wonder if it was not really constructed by some strange Asiatic race and left here. It feels somehow unlike anything else one may think of in the Greek world of temples, and particularly here in Sicily. I found the thing as barbaric and perplexing (despite its finish) as an Easter Island statue, or a corner of Baalbek. Who the devil executed this extraordinary Bank—which could have been the City National Bank in Swan Lake City, Idaho, or that of Bonga Bonga in Brazil? My elated puzzlement communicated itself to Deeds who raided his battered hold-all and finally found a copy of Margaret Guido's admirable book on the archaeological sites of the island. He used no other, it seemed. From it he read me a bit, sitting on a fragment of pediment to do so. The great temple had, like so much else, been toppled by an earthquake; but the fragments had fallen more or less in order and some notion of its construction could be deciphered. With this lucky factor, and with the description of Diodorus Siculus who had seen it standing, it was possible to work out its shape. But the real mystery begins at this point for the wretched thing is unlike anything else in the island—it is overgrown and vainglorious and, if one must be absolutely truthful, overbearing and grim. It makes you uneasy when you look at the architectural reconstruction.

The whole thing, to begin with, stands on a huge platform about 350 feet long, reposing on foundations nearly 20 feet deep. Around this chunk had been strung a series of Doric half columns of staggering size. Their diameter is 13 feet. The top of this wall was surmounted by a sort of frieze of enormous stone men—the telamones. They supported the architrave with the help of an invisible steel beam linking column to column. Each of these giant men was over 25 feet tall, male figures, alternately bearded and beardless. Feet together and arms raised to support the architrave they must have been really awe-inspiring. Some of this feeling actually leaks into the dry-as-dust description of Diodorus who notes with wonder that the simple flutings of the columns were broad enough to contain a man standing upright in them. "The porticos," he writes, "were of tremendous size and height and on the eastern pediment they portrayed the battle between the Gods and the Giants in sculptures which excelled in size and beauty, while in the west they portrayed the Capture of Troy in which each one of the heroes may be seen depicted in a manner appropriate to his role."

Nothing but ruins and conjectures remain of all this. Mutilated fragments of statues and coins and walls marked by fires. But here to my astonishment the Japanese couple suddenly began to behave strangely, overwhelmed I suppose by the giant stone figure on the ground. They screamed with laughter and pointed at it. They started to talk one hundred to the dozen and to nod and giggle. They climbed on it and photographed each other sitting on it. They clucked and beamed. They behaved like children with a new toy. And climbing about its defenceless body they reminded me of illustrations of *Gulliver's Travels*. It was an intriguing reaction and I would have given a good deal to ask them what had provoked such an expression of feeling, but the limitations of language made it impossible. We walked thoughtfully around the recumbent warrior, wondering at the coarseness of the workmanship yet aware that in terms of imaginative pictorial originality the temple marked an important point in the architectural history of Sicily. There was only one other construction which in style resembled it—and that we had not seen as yet; but I made a mental note to watch out for the Temple labelled F at Selinunte, and was struck by the suggestion that perhaps this heavy treatment of the building may have come here via Egypt—where of course they worked in heavy and recalcitrant stones for their religious buildings.

But what earthquakes and weather began was more often than not finished off by the marauders—not necessarily foreign invaders, but simply lazy local builders who picked these choice bones of history and culture simply because they lay to hand and saved transport costs. Every architect will tell you what a godsend it is to find your building materials on the site, instead of being forced to transport them.

The party had spread out to visit the further corners of the site but Deeds, who knew from old not to waste time, headed me away across the meadows towards a pleasant little bar where we celebrated the Bishop's narrow escape from Hades with a glass of beer and a roundel of salami. "It was a very singular sound he made," said Deeds. "Like a bumble bee in a bottle. I heard it from quite a distance. It sounded like the bees in Agamemnon's tomb." It was another reference which carried a small built-in pang—for a whole generation had heard and remembered those bees at Mycenae; but an unlucky spraying with insecticide had silenced them and the great tomb has sunk back into its original sinister anonymity.

But the mystery of the Japanese behaviour was absolute; we could not evolve a theory to account for this little wave of hysteria. Unless, as Beddoes suggested, they were suddenly filled with the conviction that this gorgon-like figure was a sort of carnival joke, placed there to evoke innocent merriment.

Miss Lobb walked about with a pleasant air of having done her duty. The two old apple-people sat down in a clump of bushes and began to eat fruit which the old man peeled with a small pocket knife. They were radiant, obviously without fear of the Underworld. The Bishop had recovered his composure and was once more pacing out the temples and behaving as if he were suspicious about being overcharged for them. If they were not of the stipulated size he would report them to the agency. Roberto, still shaken, drank Coca Cola. Mario blew his sudden horn at last and we awoke to action once more.

Selinunte

Selinunte

Down the curving roads we went now, among the almond groves, to where the little port of Empedocles lay glittering in the sun; but not quite. Just before we reach it the main coastal road turns sharply to the right and begins to head away towards the next objective—another cluster of temples in a different situation but set in a countryside which presents a complete contrast to the smiling hillsides we were just leaving. "In about half an hour," said Deeds, "there will be a sudden deterioration of morale and general good humour. People will get out of sorts and start contradicting one another. Roberto says that it is always along this strip, and he thinks it is due to fatigue and a rather late lunch. I have only experienced it twice, but he says that it happens every time. Just watch." In his own view this strange surge of bad humour was due to the sudden conviction that this journey was not only fatiguing but also morally indefensible; nobody should treat Agrigento like that. "We should have given it more time and more thought, not have been rushed through it like marauding Visigoths. Two weeks or two months—that is what it deserves. And then there is also the feeling of surfeit; people suddenly realise just how thick with old monuments of every period the island is. So they get grumpy."

The astonishing thing is that it fell out exactly as stated. The Bishop's wife crossed swords with the German girl about an open window which allowed the dust to blow in; the Count complained about the shag that Beddoes smoked. While the parent Microscopes said that the lavatories in the café had left much to be desired and they would report the matter to the responsible authorities. I was frankly hungry for something better than a box lunch and touched with the Deedsian misgivings about having been a traitor to Agrigento. This is the whole trouble about package travel. Yes, we were all put out, and in Mario's driving mirror we looked like a gaggle of wattle-wagging turkeys. The shadow of the imperfectly grasped Agrigento lay over us.

Nor was the country through which we passed reassuring because of the heat and the dust streaming up from the lorries we passed. Then came a bundle of package-like valleys of green parched smallholdings and so at last came Selinunte. Mario nosed along the valley towards the sea-headland upon which the main part stood, going so very slowly that I felt we were advancing almost on tip-toe. The bone structure of the assembled headlands and valleys was thus revealed to us in a slow sweep and we climbed until at last the bus came out in a clearing of olives over the hazy sea. What a contrast to Agrigento—all sunlit glitter and blueness. Selinunte is stuck in a criss-cross of grubby sand-dunes crammed into the mouth of a small mosquito-ridden river. A little hardy scrub was all that had managed to surface in these dunes. And yet it was becoming obvious that the array of temples and vestiges was far richer than Agrigento and their disposition more complex and intriguing than anything else we had seen in Sicily. To be hot and in a bad temper was no help, however, and I wondered whether the best time for such a visit would not be at sundown on a full moon. There was in fact a whole city of temples dotted about among the smashed altars and statues. It was as if some had got bored and just wandered off for a stroll among the surrounding dunes only to be silted up and fixed by the sand—this bilious looking tired sand. The landscape was made out of darkish felt. The sky hazed in. The river choked.

Needless to say here the ascriptions are even more hazy than anywhere else—one could hardly spell out the identity of a single one of these monuments to a heroic past. They stood there in the echoless sand, glinting with mica, and they gave off a melancholy which was heart-wrenching. It was worldless, out of time. Moreover the heat was quite blistering and there was no scrap of wind to cool the traveller's fevered brow. All this, one felt, was Roberto's fault. . . . The party took refuge in the diffuse shade of a thorn tree, and Miss Lobb almost went so far as to "have words" with Mario because the Chianti was a bit too warm. So the prophetic words of Deeds came true. But worst of all was the fact that we were now conscious that if we were really going to appreciate this site properly and redeem our casual philistinism at Agrigento it would entail a circuit of about two miles in the burning dunes, the blackish dunes. We betook ourselves to lunch, sitting upon various bits of marble, edged together to stay in the shade. Then the Microscopes went to look at a broken column and were startled by the appearance of a huge snake—probably harmless. They behaved as if Roberto had personally put it there to frighten them.

I decided, however, to shake off both the apathy and the ill-temper, and make use at once of Deeds' knowledge of the site and of his stout binoculars. We climbed in the hot sunlight up to the nearest eminence, a sort of Acropolis from which the surrounding country could be studied through the glasses, thus obviating a long walk. I was still acting under advice, for on Selinunte Martine had been fairly explicit, and I had re-read her letters the night before.

"Your first impression is one of great loneliness and melancholy; but in a moment you will reflect that what is really wrong with the site is the fact that the headland is not really high enough over the sea, and then that the blocked mouth of the river is responsible for the tatty vegetation and the flies which abound everywhere and the mosquitoes. But this said, the wretched place grows on you as you walk about it.

"I came twice, the first time with the children and we wisely waited for evening before embarking on the shuffling scramble to reach the temples, which for want of any clear evidence of their origins are simply labelled by letters of the alphabet, or like the description of a sonnet sequence. Dust and lizards and prickly heat were our portion, and we were glad for straw hats and a thermos with something cold. But as the effort increased so their beauty grew on one, though they obstinately spoke of places much further away like Leptis Magna or Troy. Straggles of prickly pear made a kind of guiding channel. Huge lizards and in one temple a hole full of bats. I had looked them up carefully before setting out but what with the heat they all swam together in a glad haze of dun whiteness. The heat throbbed, it was the pulse of the ancient world still beating somewhere, far away. Even after dark they were still blazing, for we stayed until sunset on the little promontory just to watch the mithraic animal plunge hissing into the sea.

"But I want to recount an incident which happened in a desolate place just near Temple E, which was one of the happier in style and feel. Nevertheless as we approached, from a kind of gully in the sand came the clank of chains and the whistling and straining of breath, as if a human being were wrestling with the Minotaur and having all his bones crushed with the embrace. We advanced, looking around with trepidation, and saw that it was a fox caught in a steel trap. It was half mad with pain and fright and its bloodshot eyes were almost bursting from their sockets. There in the wilderness this poor creature was wrestling with this steel instrument; and of course our approach only increased its terror, which multiplied the terror and dismay of the children. We would have given anything to free it, but at every approach it showed its fierce teeth and hissed at us. The heavy steel trap would not, by the look of it, yield to any but a savage peasant hand, or possibly even a steel bar. It would have been a mercy to despatch it but we had nothing to hand. And though we examined the whole site there was no trace of a guardian to whom we might report this death-struggle. It was a barbaric interlude and it shook us all; after that the heat and the oppressive silence which succeeded the groans of the poor red fox weighed a ton. And when we returned to the acropolis we were all on the point of tears with vexation and sadness."

I thought of this incident as with the help of the glasses I identified Temple E where it had occurred and admired its stylishness, though it looked from the west rather shorn of its head-trimmings—the marble decorations and cornices which Deeds informed me had been carried off to grace the museum in Palermo—a most irritating habit this, common to the archaeologists of all nations.

But apart from cherished details made more vivid by the incidents recorded by Martine the glasses revealed along the sloping hills a really extravagant assemblage of ruins of all kinds, whole sections in tumbled heaps with only one column or two standing. A whole city of confused remains. Only juniper and thorn and lentisk managed to pierce the sand, and of course the prickly pear. We stood for a long time on the quiet grass-covered acropolis trying to feel our way into the meaning of this strangely anonymous town. On each side the crooked profiles of temples and columns stretched away, and there did not seem to be any central marshalling point, a central shrine or acropolis from which they radiated. There must of course have been a heart to the great city but unlike Agrigento we could not map it out by eye—even with probability. Selinunte . . . the very name is like a sigh. It is derived from the wild celery stalk which must once have been abundant here.

And as for the question of a centre the guides inform us that there was indeed a central acropolis, very strongly walled and containing many of the temples still extant today. It stood on a low hill as on a platform between two rivers at their point of confluence, and at the point where they flowed into the sea; moreover the mouth of each river formed a lip with a small but serviceable harbour sheltered in it. "When you know that you can at once feel the fresh air rush into the landscape," said Deeds folding away his glasses carefully. We crept and crawled our way back to join those of the others who had remained obstinately in the shadow of the thorn tree. Having braved the heat we had a somewhat virtuous air as we poured out a little more warmish wine. Deeds, who had done his homework and was clearly quite at home here, proved to me that the archaeologists had really managed to plot out the growth of the town; but our feeling about the lack of a centre had also been right in a way for Selinunte started in a scattered and spattered fashion with two main groups of religious buildings. To the west the Sanctuary of Demeter Malophoros—a resonant name indeed. Gradually with increasing prosperity and time the ring broadened and spread itself over the adjoining hills.

At this point Roberto pulled himself up and proposed a visit to the temple of Apollo, unique both for its size and for the fact that it took so long to build that fashions in building outran the architectural plans. "The total effect is a curious one, for the temple is archaic in style on the east side and classical on the west. It must have reached a height of a hundred feet or more and dominated the other temples, and indeed the whole surrounding area." Alas! There is nothing left upright, and on the ground just this awkward medley of smashed stones and columns. The prospect of crawling about among them like flies had the effect of unmanning the party and Roberto got no takers for his gallant cultural proposal. I asked how far the Malophoros sanctuary was but was disappointed to discover that it was a full half-hour's walk to the west along a footpath leading from the Acropolis. Roberto made a vaguely thoughtful offer to accompany me there, but I rapidly made an excuse that I did not want to hold up the others in the heat; so we straggled in rather ungainly fashion back to the entrance to the ruins where Mario had backed the bus under a tall fig-tree—an authentic piece of shade this. Here he had fallen asleep, and so deeply, that the noise of our arrival did not wake him. We formed an affectionate circle round him watching him sleep with admiration. It is rare to see someone so thoroughly asleep. He lay with a hand across his eyes, his mouth open, very slightly snoring. It was somehow most encouraging and invigorating. All our ill-humour slipped from us as we watched this noble man taking his ease. But the noise of a foot upon gravel—or was it perhaps the sheer force of our gaze upon him?—did the trick at last and he woke, blushing deeply to be thus caught napping. Hazily we climbed aboard and implored him to turn on the fresh-air vane of the bus. The seats were hot. We started up and nosed our way down into the boiling valley and along to the coast road.

I don't think there was one of us who could have given a coherent account of the next hour's voyaging—we all fell into a leaden sleep, only very vaguely conscious of the wheels of our little bus rubbing along the tarmac. There was sea, and a fresh wind, and there were scattered villages here and there when the horn did its warning work. But the transition in time to a vast and cavernous warehouse in Marsala happened like a piece of *avant-*

garde film-cutting. The jolt of stopping in the middle of a sort of impromptu cocktail party shocked us awake; for Mario had edged the whole bus into the echoing dark *cave* where, disposed along two vast trestle tables, was a constellation of beautiful bottles of every size and colour. We were to take part in a promotional *dégustation* for the famous product of the island. Moreover our hosts, the packers and shippers, were a large and beaming crowd of big-moustached elderly men who were obviously half-mad with impatience to get at the bottles and were only held back by the laws of etiquette from anticipating our arrival. A united huzza went up as we swung into the cool of the great barn. "My goodness the whole darn Mafia," said Beddoes with approval; and out we all got to shake their hands and pat them on the back. A great show of amity followed and it was not long before we were beautifully implicated in studying the varying merits of the wines —one went up and down as if on a keyboard, testing and criticising the wine. For each of us was to be offered a sample bottle as a present. Beddoes spared no effort to get to the bottom of the matter and played the half-filled sample tumblers as if they were a xylophone.

One of the directors of this partly promotional yet wholly life-enhancing operation, a whiskered gentleman who looked like the giant panda off duty, made a short emotionally charged speech to give us a brief historical glimpse of the Marsala trade. A speech which, said Beddoes, "was calculated to make the patriotic Briton's blood course in his veins." British shippers had played a great part in the production and development of Marsala. "Indeed," said Beddoes, warming to his theme under the influence of his third sample, "it was not a case of trade following the flag but simply a question of the flag following the drink. In this matter we lead, I think." He became knowledgeable now about Canary and Sack and Sherry, while Deeds waxed primly tedious about China tea and Indian. Altogether we were in a lather of British self-congratulation when a little patch of acrimony developed in another corner of the barn owing to some unfortunate reference to the Mafia by one of the Microscopes. It was rapidly smoothed over by politeness and Roberto explained somewhat plaintively. "It's all adverse propaganda. The Mafia doesn't exist. Long ago it was certainly a fact. But it was not unlike England. We sent one son to the Navy, one to the Army, one to the Church and one . . . to the Mafia." If it was a joke—I think it was—it did not help to heal the breach. "Our Mafia today is called The Trade Unions," said Beddoes forcefully. And so forth.

I said under my breath in demotic Greek: "I abjure the foul fiend!" an incantation which keeps one safe from all harm, and then turned my back on them all to watch the deep vibrant light sifting through a rainbow of sunbeams and striking their faces with marvellously liquid shadow, dense with oil and varnish. It was so very much an oil-painting that I could almost smell it. But if the tragic truth must be told the wine-tasting was not a great event for me, for my palate had long since been utterly corrupted by French wine; and even among the heavy artillery these Italian syrups did not measure up against, say, the muscat of Frontignan, to mention but one sweet wine which grew near me. I had had the same bellywearying experience in Cyprus with Commanderia, which has at least the literary merit of being brewed from the original Malvoisie grape. No. I artfully contrived to give my little case of complimentary samples to Miss Lobb, who being a Londoner had probably been brought up on port flip.

So gradually the party drew to an end and our hosts, bedewed with warm feeling and alcohol, found it hard to part from people so marvellously charming as we—if that is good English; profound expressions of brotherly love flew about, followed by an exchange of visiting cards and expressions of regard and esteem. Mario ground his teeth with impatience and mistrust at all this facile amiability. He was dying to hit the road again. One had forgotten that he sternly refused all drinks while on duty. Roberto had begun by being pious and ended up a tiny bit soaked.

At last we were away. As we swung about in the dusty streets, seeking out the coast road, Miss Lobb, borne upon a wave of sympathy and gratitude for the little gift I had made her, found her way to the back of the coach and engaged us in conversation on the subject (unexpectedly) of astrology. "I believe in the stars," she said firmly. "If you believe in them they are usually right and never let you down." Well, this was really arguable, but somehow whatever Miss Lobb did was all right with us. She had been following with the closest attention our vague arguments about landscapes and climates and atmospheres, and had wondered why the stars never figured in these deliberations. The reason was simple. Neither Deeds nor I were at all astrology-prone; but we were open-minded about it. I was sure that one could use the astrological map to "skry" just as one used a crystal ball. The quality of the vision . . . that was another matter. But what Miss Lobb now produced was a sort of little handbook of horoscopes devoted not to people but to places.

I was at a loss to know how one established the sign of a country or a town, but some of the findings which she now read out to us, working slowly round the heavens, were interesting and suggestive, though obviously highly empirical. Among the places which figured in our discussions about Greece and Greater Greece we found that Greece was Taurus while Sicily was in the sign of the Lion. Would this explain their likenesses and differences? There was not enough detail to judge. But there was many a surprise—such as finding that Germany, England, Japan, Israel and Poland were all in the same sign, Aries. I was naturally more interested in the places which had played a part in my own life and it was interesting to see that Cyprus was in Taurus—so incidentally were Dublin, Palermo, Parma, Leipzig, Persia, Georgia and Asia Minor for good measure. Meanwhile Marseilles, Florence, Naples, Padua and Birmingham were all clustered together in Aries. "Well I'm dashed if I know what to think," said Deeds, which was a polite way of voicing his innate scepticism. But Miss Lobb was serious and her face had become round and schoolgirlish. But "If you think it too silly I won't go on," she said; no, we assured her of our devoted attention and agnosticism and she plunged deeper into her little volume.

London, Melbourne and San Francisco were all in the Twins; so were America, Belgium, Wales and Lower Egypt.

The sign of Cancer harboured Holland, New Zealand, Rhodesia, Paraguay, and among the towns Amsterdam, Algiers, Venice, Berne, Constantinople, Genoa and New York.

In the Lion together with Sicily were France, all Italy, Northern Roumania, also Rome, Prague, Ravenna, Damascus, Chicago, Bombay, Bristol, Cremona.

We were so engrossed in this witchcraft that we got quite a start when Mario drew rein on the coast road in a clump of trees and Roberto sang out for Deeds. It was another little war-cemetery.

Deeds obediently but reluctantly got down to do his little tour of inspection and he was instantly replaced by Beddoes and the German girl whose boy friend was also mad about astrology. Alas, we failed to find any trace of Dungeness in the manual, to the great disappointment of Beddoes who said that it must be an evilly aspected place with a swingeing Saturn in the ascendant. But there was plenty of other material at hand, and almost everyone was keen to know the ruling sign of his or her country or home town. Switzerland, Brazil and Turkey were Virgin, as were Virginia and Croatia. Of the capitals under the influence of Virgo were Jerusalem, Paris, Lyon, Heidelberg, Boston, Los Angeles, Babylon and Baghdad!

This led to a good deal of argument and counter-argument; the Microscopes were a bit irritated to be bracketed with heathen towns and asked me to register their scepticism translating from the French and to convey the same to Miss Lobb; but she simply pursed her lips and said, quite firmly, "Nevertheless!" Whatever that meant.

By the time Deeds came back to his seat we were deep in the penetralia of this strange system, without, however, being able to determine how the maps had been established—how could a town have a birthday? Nevertheless once stuck into this business the public interest forced us to continue. We forthwith announced: in the sign of the Balance, or the Scales in English, were grouped China, Tibet, Argentina, Upper Egypt, and Indochina; while the cities in the same sign numbered Frankfurt, Copenhagen, Vienna, Nottingham and Amiens.

"I think the whole thing is highly questionable," said the Bishop, forever guardian of the nation's conscience. "It depends how much one can bring oneself to believe." Beddoes shot back

"What about the Thirty-nine Articles?" and Deeds pacified the contestants by asking what their birth sign was. The Bishop had a troublesome Saturn and Beddoes a badly aspected Mars which explained, though it did not excuse, everything. Miss Lobb pursued her quietly triumphant way with the air of an early Christian with faith enough to snuff out the stake.

But of course like everyone else I was really only profoundly interested in my own sign—the wretched Fishes, with their coiling uncertainties and fugues; I obtained no comfort from the knowledge that Portugal and Normandy came under this sign, and also Nubia, the Sahara and Galicia; but it certainly did give me a start to find that among the towns which found themselves under the fishy influence were both Alexandria and Bournemouth—though what they had in common with Seville, Compostella, Ratisbon and Lancaster I could not tell. . . . Anyway, after this instructive session Miss Lobb put away her book and resumed her seat with a quiet air of self-approbation, as if she had done her duty. A discursive argument now broke out around the general theme of astrology. The Bishop was conciliatory and Beddoes was snarly. I think the remark about the Thirty-nine Articles had made a hole in the Bishop's intellectual lining; at any rate he kept hull down and did not provoke any more grape-shot. On we went.

I dropped into a doze and saw the dunes of Selinunte rise in my memory with a sort of concentrated melancholy. What was interesting to notice was that at this point in the journey a new rhythm had set in, a rhythm based on fatigue and fresh air. We had started to cat-nap at all times of the day like bedouin. Quarter of an hour was enough to restore good humour and extinguish heat-weariness. We had also learned to double up a bit—it is no use pretending that travelling in a bus does not gradually begin to feel cramping, restricting. Thus when we passed a series of caravans with highly decorated sideboards it was no surprise to see that the gipsies (for they were gipsies and not villagers) who occupied them, were blissfully asleep, lying anyhow on the jogging bottom, like a litter of puppies, dead to the world. It was the rhythm of the open road. And I think we poor tourists felt a subconscious tug towards the freedom and adventure of the Romany life—it contrasted so radically with our own. Some of the fatigue had leaked into my dream, and I yawned as I saw the string of temples rising one after another on the dunes. Then other vaguer thoughts and visions came to intrigue me. I remembered Martine writing, "Then somewhere before Trapani everything changes and becomes—not to exaggerate—ominous; or at least *fraught with moment*. It is the spirit of Erice advancing to meet you. I was terrified. I expected *It* to happen when I reached Erice. What? I don't know what. Just *It*."

A large bird smashed itself against our windshield and was dashed aside into death—leaving a large smear of blood on the glass. Mario swore and wiped the spot clean with a cloth.

The thump of the collision woke me up.

Erice

Birdsong: Erice

Rock-lavender full of small pious birds
On precipices torn from old sky,
Promiscuous as the goddess of the grove.
No wonder the wise men listening pondered why
If speech be an involuntary response to stress,
How about song then? Soft verbs, hard nouns
Confess the voice's submission to desire.
A theology of insight going a-begging.

This Aphrodite heard but cared not,
The unstudied mating-call of birds was one
With everything in the mind's choir.
Someone sobbing at night or coughing to hide it.
The percussion of the sand-leopard's concave roar
A vocabulary hanging lightly in viper's fangs.

All this she knew, and more: that words
Releasing in the nerves their grand fatigue
Inject the counter-poison of love's alphabet.

Erice

At Erice one feels that all the options of ordinary life are reversed. I do not know how else to put it. We steer our lives by certain beliefs which are perhaps fables but which give us the courage to continue living. But what happens even before you reach the "sickle" of Trapani is that you lose your inner bearings, become insecure. It's as if the giant of the mountain up there, riding its mists, had kicked away your crutches. History begins to stammer; the most famous and most privileged temple to Aphrodite in the whole of the Mediterranean has vanished without leaving a trace. The one late head of Aphrodite is nothing to write home about. The holy shrine of Eryx has been blown out like a light, yet as at Delphi, one can still smell the sulphur in the air. You feel it in the burning sun like a cold touch on the back of the neck. But I am going too fast for we are still approaching Trapani, that deceptively happy and unremarkable town so beautifully perched upon its seagirt headland. The old part of the town, rather as in the case of Syracuse, occupies a firm promontory thrust out into the sea like a pier; the town has developed on the landward side. Salt-pans and windmills, yes, and the view from the so-called Ligny Tower is a fine one; but what is really fine is the fresh sea-wind, frisky as a fox-terrier, which patters the awnings and bends the trees and sends old sailors' caps scuttering along the cobbles of the port. Westward a fine expanse of the Tyrrhenian Sea, smouldering in the sinking sun; two of the Egadi Isles with the choice names of Levanzo and Favignana glow with a kind of mysterious malevolence.

We were tired, we were really in no mood for further sightseeing, and Roberto let us off easily with a short visit to an indifferent church and a glimpse of the stern battlements constructed by Charles V. But the main thing was the frolicking wind whose playfulness allayed somewhat the curious feeling of tension and misgiving which I felt when I gazed upwards towards the ramps of Monte Giuliano and saw the sharp butt of Erice buried in the mountain like a flint axehead which had broken off with the impact. There was a short administrative pause while Mario made some growling remarks to the world at large and some adjustments to his brakes. Somewhere in the town a small municipal band had slunk into a square and started to play fragments of old waltzes and tangos. The sudden gusts of wind offered the musicians a fortuitous nautical syncopation—the music fading and reviving, full of an old-world charm. The Petremands ate a vividly coloured ice-cream and bought one for Mario. The Bishop had broken a shoelace. The old pre-Adamic couple were fast asleep in their seats, arm in arm, smile in smile, so to speak. It is pleasant when sleeping people smile and obviously enjoy their dreaming; they looked like representations of the smiling Buddha—though he is very far from asleep, sunk rather in smiling meditation. At last we began the ascent.

The sun was over the border now, rapidly westering, apparently increasing speed in its long slide into the ocean. Our little red bus swung itself clear of the crooked streets of Trapani and then started its tough climb up the dark prow of Eryx. Adieu Via Fardella, Via Pepoli! The road now began to mount in short spans on a steepening gradient, swinging about first to the right, then to the left; and there came a gradually increasing sobriety of spirit, a premonition perhaps of the Erycinean Aphrodite whose territory we were approaching. I am not romancing, for several of my fellow-travellers expressed a sharpened sense of excitement in their several ways. Mario varied his engine speeds with great skill and the little motor had us valiantly swarming up the steep cliffs in good order.

The vegetation gradually thinned away, or made room for hardier and perhaps more ancient plants to cling to the crevices and caves in the rock. The precipices hereabouts were bathed in the condensations of cloud, as if a rich dew had settled on them; or as if the whole of nature had burst into a cold sweat. Yes, there were clouds above us, hanging lower and lower as we climbed, but they seemed to part as we reached them to offer us passage. At each turn—for we were still tacking up the cliffs like a sailboat—the view increased in grandeur and scope until the whole province of Trapani lay below us bathed in golden light and bounded by the motionless sea. Far off twinkled the Egadi, with Marettimo printed in black-letter—the island which Samuel Butler so surprisingly decided must be the historical Ithaca in his weird book about the supposed female author of the *Odyssey*. I love wrong-headed books. But a short residence in modern Greece would have made Butler somewhat uncertain about the main theme of his book. Only a man, only a Greek could have written the poem—at least so think I.

We worked our way with elephantine determination round the north-eastern flank of our two-thousand-metre odd mountain. There was only one little village to traverse, Parparella, perched up in solitude like a nest and empty of inhabitants at that hour. Bare rock now, with sudden ferns, cistus, caper and an occasional asphodel to surprise one. And the views below us went on steadily unwinding like a scroll. The air had become purer, colder, as if filtered by the passing clouds. Once or twice our engine sneezed and Mario cocked an alert ear; but there was no trouble and on one of the penultimate loops we called a halt designed to let the amateur photographers in the party record the scene below. But while they clicked happily away at Trapani I found myself craning upwards to gaze at the crest of Eryx, printed on the unfaltering blue of the evening sky, still touched by the sun's rays. You could see a dabble of ancient wall and some higgledy-piggledy towers and minarets just below the summit. They must mark the site of the now vanished temple of Aphrodite. From the rugged Cyclopean bases the walls mounted in a faltering and somewhat ramshackle fashion—improvised in layers, in tiers, in afterthoughts and false starts—Phoenician, Greek, Roman and Norman.

Once we had broken the back of the ascent the road spanned pleasant but lonely pinewoods which scented the still air and led us in mysterious hesitant fashion to the gates of the little town, the Porte Trapani, where Roberto got down for a long confabulation with a clerk from the Mairie while the rest of us set about digging into our luggage for pullovers. The dusk was about us now though the higher heavens were still lit by the sun, and up there the swifts darted and rolled, feasting on insects. A chill struck suddenly and the Bishop shivered.

There had been a hitch, said Roberto, and we had been switched to an older hotel; this was irritating. Like all guides he decried the old-fashioned and only respected modernity. But in this case there was no need for apologies; the hotel was a fine old-fashioned tumbledown sort of place but with all the right amenities. Mario turned the bus round and conducted us steeply downhill upon a forest road; but it was not far, for we emerged upon a sort of ledge like an amphitheatre above the sea. It was a spacious site and belonged to spacious times when they built hotels with comfortable billiard-rooms and lounges and terracotta swimming pools. It was fine to be thus perched over the sea in the middle of a pine forest. The wooden floors creaked under our feet in comfortable fashion. There were several dusty bars full of dusty half-full liqueur bottles. But at the back underneath the dining-room there came a short stretch of forest followed by an astonishing vertical drop—a sheer drop to the bottom of the world as represented now in diagrammatic fashion by a Trapani with its salt-pans and harbour picked out in lights. We were a bit below the castle here and the little town was not visible. A heavy mist from the precipice rose and dispersed, rose and dispersed. "It's all very well, but I have got cold feet and I want my money back," said Beddoes to the distress of Roberto who took everything he said seriously. Despite the season the mountain chill and the fatigue had chastened us and we were glad to settle for a drink and dinner and early bed.

The Count walked about in the dark for a while before turning in—I saw the glow of his cigar. Deeds found a crossword in an ancient paper while Miss Lobb replaced her book and appropriated another. I retired to my narrow wooden chamber which reminded me a bit of a ship's cabin, or a room in a ski-chalet. The wood smelt lovely and it was not too cold to step out upon the balcony with its great view. All along the horizon line there was a tremulous flickering of an electrical storm, soundless from this great distance. It reminded me of the only naval engagement I have ever witnessed—if that is the correct word; the ships were all out of sight and only this steady flicker (followed centuries later by the thunder of guns) was to be seen. It went back and forth regular as a scythe-stroke.

I watched, straining to hear the following thunder, but none came for ages. It was up here, perhaps in this very room that Martine had spent a night of "intense nervous expectation". It was so intense that she could not sleep, and it was at last with weary elation that she had watched the dawn break over the exhausted sea. She felt as if she had escaped whatever it was that had been haunting her subconscious in the form of vague premonitions of something doom-laden which she would encounter here at Erice. Nor was she completely wrong. Nor had she escaped, for months afterwards she realised that it was here, and more especially on that sleepless night, that she had felt the first twinges in the joints, the first stiffness of the neck and backbone which were only to declare their meaning long months afterwards. "I recognise now in retrospect just what I went to Erice to find. It was a rendezvous which would finally lead me towards death—one must not fuss too much since it is everyone's lot. Only now I know what I did not at Erice—I know roughly when. Yes, I am going into a decline in a year or two. Or so they say, the professors in Rome. I like the Victorian phrase, don't you? It has pride and reserve—though I was never a woman of ice, was I?"

But all this was at another season, and the hotel had been deserted, and the rock-levels of Venus' temple had been smothered in tiny spring flowers she could not identify. Now I had followed her, not with quite such an acute apprehension of momentous happenings, but with something nevertheless which troubled and disturbed me and made me expectant. During that first night (I could hear the desultory click of billiard balls, where Beddoes was still up. Floors creaked.), during the long vigil she had spent some time "scratching about among the bewildering debris of legend and conjecture which makes everything Greek in

Sicily such a puzzle. It is as if everything has been smashed into dust by a giant trip-hammer; one can reach nothing coherent among these shattered shards; just the tantalising hints and glints of vanished people and their myths. So finally one says, to hell with Daedalus the engineer, and first labyrinth-maker—what did he find to do here in Sicily? Head of public works for old King Cocalos? Why did he assent to the murder of Minos his old patron? One becomes so weary of the oft-repeated tales which make up the historic pattern. It is hopeless! And then what about the ultra-famous temple of Venus—Astarte-Aphrodite-Venus—the goddess had diverse roots and multiple attributes? Everything, woman, wife, nurse, mother, Muse, as well as ritual prostitute. . . . There was no aspect she did not rule over. In this grim temple there was ritual prostitution, as well as fertility rites—while for the sailor the place was a notable navigational seamark to guide him to Trapani; and just as today the sailor asks for weather reports, so his ancestor took the omens for the voyage from the temple and acted according to whether they were fair or foul.

"But how could it have disappeared so completely from sight, this world-famous place? Nothing but a tiny bit of stone ramp remains to mark the site of the temple. Nothing? Well, only this intangible feeling of dread, of something momentous preparing itself. And the empty sockets mock one in the one late banal head of Aphrodite."

Youth, beauty, death—the three co-ordinates of the ancient world. Martine wrote: "I told myself that in Sufism and Taoism (it would take too long to convince you that the original Astarte of Erice was much older than Greek) they do not have any truck with the notion of disease as we see it. They do not talk of getting cured but simply of modifying conduct. It is presumed that your wrong action has procured a disharmony with the universe which manifests itself in disease. I believe this with all my heart, but I also believe in destiny, as well as in just wearing out like a pot. Then there is another aspect of things—I hate the Christian notion of prayer as an act of propitiation. But I like the old Byzantine notion of turning it into a sort of heart-beat—each man his own prayer-wheel so to speak. Everything you feel in

Erice goes way back beyond any notion which the monkey mind or tongue can formulate. Into the darkness where those great vegetable forms, tuberose creatures, wait in order to munch your flesh when you are once in the ground. The chthonic gods and goddesses as they are so strangely called. . . ."

The light went out—the hotel generator packed up at midnight. It was still very light—a white milky light as if of moonlight diffused through a silk screen. I was weary now and I set down my papers and slept—but it was a light, nervous sort of sleep without great density.

At about three I woke with a start and sat up to look at the forest. I thought at first what I had heard was muffled sobbing somewhere in the building. I am still not sure. But what had happened was that a powerful surge of wind had sailed upon the promontory and bent the pines. It made a sudden rich hum, like a sweep of strings long drawn out but slowly dying away. Then the quivering silence returned. But one felt excited, on the *qui vive*. It was exactly as if one woke in the middle of the night on the African veldt slowly to realise that the noise which had wakened one was the breathing of a lion. The forest stirred and shook and resettled itself. A kind of breath of music had passed over it—like breath passing over embers. No, there was nothing particularly disquieting or singular about it, but waking, I felt the need to get up and drink some water. It was icy. I went to the balcony and looked down at the necklace of lights etching in their diagram of Trapani. It was some time off dawn yet but I felt completely rested and wondered if I would get to sleep again. Hesitating there I suddenly caught sight of a figure advancing towards the hotel through the pines. It was the German girl and she was naked.

The light, though diffused, was extremely bright and I saw quite clearly that she had no clothes on. I wondered if she could be sleep-walking but it did not seem so for she looked about her, turning her head now this way and now that. She carried her hands before her, palms turned up, but lightly and without emphasis. And her walk was slow and calm.

Perhaps the sweep of wind in the pines had woken her also, or else the forest had evoked in her her native Bavarian landscapes? Or more simply still, she felt the incoherent stirrings of a primeval inheritance—suppose she were, without realising it, some Nordic goddess who had come on an accidental visit to a remote cousin called Aphrodite of Eryx? She walked slowly and calmly under my balcony and disappeared round the corner of the house. And that was all. I dwelt a little while on the spectacle, wondering about it. Then I turned in again and at once fell into the profound sleep which up to now had been lacking. The sun was up when I awoke. And the disquiet had been replaced by a calm elation. Yet in a sort of way I felt that it was a relief to have traversed the night without incident.

Breakfast was very welcome on that fine sunny day; and we had been promised a look at the castle before being spirited away to Segesta and thence Palermo. Our trip was soon going to be at an end, and the consciousness of it provoked a new sense of friendliness. Conversations became warmer and more animated. A Microscope helped the Japanese girl change a film. I looked curiously at Renata the German girl when she came down but she seemed perfectly normal and assured, and of course one could not question her about her nudist escapade. I wondered if her boy friend knew of it. They were both very obviously much in love and went to no pains to hide it—which crucified poor Roberto as he watched, biting his nails.

It was necessary to set the red bus to rights this morning, for the little town of Erice was only going to be a brief stop on the road to Segesta whence we would face a long haul into Palermo.

I rather feared the ardours of this journey but in fact the calculations of Roberto were fairly exact and we arrived at night not too late and not too fatigued. But Erice in that bright blue morning was something for a glider-pilot's eye or an eagle's. The drops, the views, the melting sea. Light clouds frolicked way below us. The little town had tucked itself into the nape of the mountain while the successive fortresses had been squarely planked down on the site of the ancient temple, thus obliterating it. But the rock promontory, sticking out like a stone thumb, was a perfect emplacement for a place of worship. "It makes me wonder," said Deeds, "since all the ancient shrines have served as Christian foundations for our churches, whether there isn't always a little bit of the pagan devil leaking into the stonework of our Christian edifices. I would like to think there was; we seem such a rigid and unfunny lot. But I don't think I dare ask the parson."

The little town stumbled up and down its net of cobbled streets below the fortress garden. The architecture was all that one finds in the Aegean—houses built round a courtyard tesselated with coloured pebbles and decorated with old corned-beef tins full of sprouting basil and other sweet-smelling plants. It was Samos, it was Tinos all over again. We were warmly bidden to enter several courtyards to admire the arrangements of the house; these dark-eyed smiling people might have been Corfiots. The snug little courtyards bounded-in their lives, and one felt that here, when once night fell and the mists began to climb up from the valley below, people did not hesitate to lock their courtyard-gates. After midnight one could knock a long time on a door without getting an answer, for their world was both ancient and also one of contemporary goblins and fays. And with the temple site brooding up there. . . . But the domestic organisation of their houses was that of birds' nests, and they had all the human force which comes from living on top of one another in a small place; making room for children, for livestock, for everything important to life—and not less for the sacred icons which ensure that the dark spirits shall be kept at bay.

Roberto had a small chore to do and it was quite a compliment that he should ask Deeds and myself if we would like to accompany him. He had to visit the ancient grandmother of a friend and give her some messages of congratulation for her eighty-sixth birthday plus various assorted messages. We found the house without much difficulty and when the portals opened to us we saw that quite a number of people were there on the same errand. It was rather a spacious house on its own courtyard, and a short flight of steps led up to the upper room and gallery where the old lady lay in state to receive her visitors, in a great bed like a galleon with carved headboards. It looked, as Deeds said afterwards, as if one could have hitched a horse to it and just ridden off into the sky, there were so many cherubs and saints carved upon it, all *con furioso*. She wore an old-fashioned shawl of fine black lace with a white fichu and her long witch-like white hands with their filbert nails were spread on the sheet before her, while her clever old eyes accepted the compliments of her visitors with grace and no weariness. Her fine room was furnished with graceful Sicilian earthenware plates beautifully painted, and flowers in bloom. Two small children played with a sailboat upon a handsome carved trunk under the window. She must have been a person of great consequence for several of her visitors were local dignitaries, as Roberto explained later—the barber, the chemist, the *podesta* and *medico condotto*. It all went off with great style and ease, but the appearance of Roberto was a thrilling surprise and his presence evoked questions and answers which took a good twenty minutes. She had questions to ask involving several generations and several families and I had the impression that nobody was passed over—she checked up on the whole lot of them, for who knows when she might have another chance? The peasant memory and the peasant sense of life is a tenacious and determined thing—it draws its strength from this sense of a corporate life, shared by all, and to which all contribute a share of their sap. Moreover I think the old lady felt that she was not long for this world and that she must make the most of things, such as this surprise visit which had brought her all the gossip of a far corner of the island.

Duty thus done, Roberto kissed the long patrician fingers of the old lady and we made our way back into the sunshine to negotiate the little curling streets back to the main square where by now the rest of the party must be sitting under awnings and writing postcards or drinking lemonade. The day was bright and hot, and it was quite a contrast to think back to the evening before with its mists and murmurs of another world, another order of life. Nothing could be more ordinary in its beauty than Erice by day, with all the little shops functioning—post office, bank, gendarmerie. The minute main square was built upon a slope—

indeed such an acute tilt that everything tended to slide about and run down to the bottom. Tables at this angle were in danger of falling over, as were chairs; as one wrote one's postcards or drank one's beer, one found one was insensibly sliding downhill. People who came out of the café had to brake sharply in order not to find themselves rolling about like dice.

A very fat policeman made something of an act of this natural attribute of Erice's Piazza Nationale by allowing himself to slide helplessly downhill until he ended up on the lap of a friend who was trying to eat ice-cream at an angle of fifty degrees. Just how the poor café owner managed to dispose his tables and chairs was something of a mystery—it would have seemed necessary to wedge them in place. Over the lintel of the butcher's hung a peeled and dry little kid which bore a label reading "*Castrato*" and giving a price per pound. This intrigued Beddoes who said: "It's a rum word, I thought it meant something frightful that Monteverdi did to his choirboys to enable them to hit high C." The kid was so neatly cut in half that it looked rather like a violin hanging up there; the rest of the meat on display was pretty indifferent-looking stuff; of course, like all Mediterranean islands Sicily is a lamb country.

Our little visit had cost us a bit of time and by now the others had already done the cathedral and the Church of St. John as well as the public gardens, so full of yellow broom; but the real heart of the place was the restored towers and the old castle standing grimly on its sacred site, sweating with every gush of mists from the lowlands. What a farewell sweep the eye takes in up there—the whole sweep of western Sicily exposed in a single slice, as if from an aeroplane! Roberto was disposed to be knowledgeable about the *Aeneid* with its famous cruise along this coast which is described in poetic detail—but to my shame I have never read it, and I rather doubted whether anyone else had either. But the few lines he quoted from memory sounded sinewy and musical on that fine silent air and I made a mental note to repair this grave omission as soon as I could happen upon a version of the poem in parallel text. We were leaving and suddenly as we entered the bus I had a sudden reversion to the mood of the night before—a sudden atmosphere of unreality in which some momentous happening lay embedded, encysted, waiting to flower. But the faces of my fellow-travellers did not seem to express any untoward emotion and it was perhaps my own imagination. But whatever they were, these small preoccupations, they were swept away like cobwebs by the fine speed of our descent, for Mario was in a particularly expansive humour and swung the little bus about with a professional dexterity that was marvellous—in the sense that it caused us no alarm, so confident were we in his ability. And the land swept about with him on this turntable of a road, swinging like a cradle this way and that. At one corner he slowed for the Japanese girl and her camera and I caught a glimpse of a couple of appropriate eagles sitting motionless in the mid-heaven, staring down at the vanished altars of Erice.

Segesta

Segesta

We were on the Palermo run at last, once we had arrived at sea-level, but we hoped to take a running look at Segesta—a temple and a site hardly less important than the others, for it had had a full share in the ancient politics and the wars, even though its position lay some little way inland. Running along the sea-roads the bays opened in all their blueness, and the gentle limestone valleys seemed awash with yellow wheat. But goodness it was hot. In half an hour of this we felt the full power of the sun's rays on our roof and were glad of the air-cooling devices. Roberto had an unexpected sneezing fit, the first manifestation of which got into the loudspeaker and shook us all up. But he was happy, there was little to describe, and so he decided to sing us a couple of Sicilian folk-songs, which he did in a remarkably true and robust tenor, while we tried to help him out with the choruses. Then with courtesy he asked us each to sing a song of our country, and this threw a sudden shyness over us all. Yet after much giggling and persuading Miss Lobb went forwards and sang to us of the Foggy Foggy Dew, which was very warmly applauded. Surprisingly the Japanese girl took her place at the microphone but it was only to sing "Parlez Moi d'Amour". There were of course numerous abstentions due to shyness.

Deeds and I had not brought our music, nor had the Bishop. But Beddoes sang a surprisingly discreet version of Colonel Bogey, to the chorus of which we all joined in heartily, though the soldier next to me rather avoided my eye, doubtless because he remembered the ribald Eighth Army version of the song. But it was a stirring melody and had been made world famous by the film of the famous Bridge on the River Kwai, so nobody could feel left out. What with the heat and the dust, however, this song-contest left us rather weary and it was very pleasant when, after curling through the soft green hills, we came into a smiling and verdant valley where the old temple stood—the general atmosphere of the place reminding one not of Mycenae this time but of gracious quiet Olympia. There were no strange atmospheres and no bogies; just the exceptional heat and the quiet density of the old temple sitting there with some of the assurance of a country town hall. Under a fine tree there was a rather handsome tavern where we were to have lunch, I surmised.

The smooth hills were densely thicketed with holm-oak and laurel and rosemary and buzzing with crickets. A picturesque place with noble and romantic associations, though Deeds for the first time swore under his breath at people who could shove a motor road right through such a place, without blushing. They were simply unaware of anything but tourist gold. Just like the Greeks of today, and the Italians of yesterday. The only consolation is that it will all fall apart again and vanish into dust—for our civilisation seems to be far less solid than those which have already vanished and left us these vestiges of lost greatness. But no, Deeds would not be consoled. "Here God is definitely mocked," he asserted, "though thank God Segesta's position is still fairly remote and one rarely finds it crowded—you can still sit in the theatre and drowse, which is something." It was true; ours was the only bus at the site, and by now, to my astonishment, we did not get on each other's nerves any more. If we had not become friends we had become in a sense partners and ready to make allowances. Even the dentist's lady had started to take a liking to Beddoes, who had swept her into a tango during a moment in the bar in Agrigento where a juke-box churned out jazz. As for the dentist he had assuaged a tiresome toothache which afflicted the child Microscope after he had been eating too many sweets. Even the Bishop had taken a hand at pontoon during a halt. Deeds had done tricks with string which fascinated and awed. In short we had all shaken down.

The place, the temple . . . how impossible it is to convey the charm of atmosphere in a travel folder or a photo. One is forced to fake, and the result is always a false emphasis. This place, even if there had been no temple, would have radiated a quiet magnetism and well-being, just like an Aesculapium—like Cos or like Epidaurus. I have spent half a lifetime trying to analyse why and the only result has been to decide that it has something to do with fresh water and green in a limestone context. The sanatoria of the ancient world were chosen for their seclusion and the purity of their air; in our age also, but we tend to place too much emphasis on mountains, most likely because for so long the most popular of human diseases has been tuberculosis, which nowadays has all but disappeared. As for Segesta, so far nothing has been found to indicate that it was a spa unless the presence of sulphur springs near Calatafimi might hint at it. But of course here again nothing about it is known with any real exactitude—everything is conjecture. The people claimed to come from Troy though some say that they were Italians from the north; but the stamp of their Greekness remains, for their coinage bore a Greek legend, and their architects were Athenian in mind and scope. It did not need the learned dissertations of guide books to tell one about the splendour of this particular temple, standing there so quietly in the vale, wise as an elephant bearing the world on its back. What was missing was the context simply, the vanished town which would have put everything in its place and reduced the sense of strangeness and alienation which I must say I personally found exciting and stimulating. But the feeling of deep composure and calm was conveyed not only by the temple and theatre but by the whole site. "I slept here in the grass once without a blanket," said Deeds with a gesture, "by starlight in summer—what a huge display of jewels. And so silent." The gesture he sketched suggested someone who just spontaneously sinks to the ground, rendered completely defenceless by the beauty and silence of the place. Of course he had seen it all years ago, hence his irritation. He must have intuited my thought for he said: "Twenty years I suppose; we came up on it by muleback from the direction of Calatafimi. It came to us valley by valley, in little sips so to speak, appearing and disappearing; each time from a different angle and a different light. At first it was tiny, like a little dice floodlit by the sun. Then it grew. Then at last you arrived with your tongue cleaving to your palate with thirst, but with the feeling of moral grandeur that must come to people who complete an arduous pilgrimage. It was unfenced then and one could put a sleeping bag down anywhere inside the temple. No road, you see, no access. Nowadays of course one drives straight up to these places by bus and so one doesn't get the pleasure of the effort. One just rapes them."

I think his little homily must have sounded a trifle reproachful for all at once everyone—almost everyone—decided to get out and walk a bit, as if to atone for our slack philistinism. However morally worthy as a gesture it was somewhat intrepid because of the heat beating down from the rocks and vales. We were far from the sea here and the valley gathered up the rays of sunlight like a green burning glass. Nevertheless we set off in a straggle, I with Deeds and Roberto; we were shortly joined by the Count who was a good amateur botanist and was collecting wild flowers and leaves to press in the pages of his Goethe. "You know," he said, "I am very sceptical about our attitude to the past; I don't believe that we have a shadow of an inkling about how a Greek thought. Understanding and sympathy need a common culture. We are so different that it is idle to pretend that we can for a moment appreciate what their attitude to life and death was. I think we fake the whole thing. Fake reverence. Fake understanding. No, it has all disappeared once and for all, there is no way of recovering such a remote past by the imagination. Do I depress you?" We assured him stoutly that he did not, but in fact he did. I felt suddenly the fatigue of this journey growing upon me—the fatigue of the *speed* which did not give time to take in enough. A brilliant butterfly sat on a leaf. And suddenly I felt nothing but pure hate for the Carousel.

On we pressed in the heat, bursting with vainglory and good intentions, anxious to do the honest thing by one of the most beautiful ancient Greek theatres in existence when there came an encounter so hubris-punishing as to be worthy of some ancient Greek fable. Beside the road, upon a large rock, sat a couple of very fragile and very ancient people, obviously a man and his wife, both older than the rock upon which they perched. The man was of an incomparable distinction from every point of view—

Grecian temple at Segesta

worn but excellent light tweeds, gillie's hat, light cape, solid gold-handled walking stick. . . . He looked like a senior Druid. His wife was beautiful and silver and fragile, a fitting mate for a man so handsome, whose silver hair spoke of age and serenity, but whose old eyes spoke of culture. Moreover, a lunch-basket lay open between them, and she was in the act of reading from a book—it sounded like ancient Greek in an Erasmic pronunciation.

Suddenly we appeared round the corner, puffing our noble way uphill; the reading stopped and the couple gazed at us with a quiet aristocratic commiseration. Scrutiny would be the word—a long cold scrutiny which made us aware of the extent to which we were disturbing the peace of this honeyed place. That wasn't all. As we passed the old man spoke to his wife in a low clear voice, not intended to be overheard, and what he said was: "*Poor tourist scum.*" It was like machine-gun fire—the whole front line wavered. We had been assailed in our poor fragile corporate identity; we had been weighed and found wanting. We could look at ourselves now with the proper misgiving and see just what a scruffy raggle-taggle mob we were, ill assorted and self-assertive with our little red bus. We felt suddenly terribly ashamed and full of self-pity. And here were these damned British aristocrats sniffing their contempt down their long aquiline supercilious noses. They had doubtless done things the right way—they had probably walked the last hundred miles, sleeping in the trees, and pausing from time to time to read select chunks of Theocritus or Thucydides to each other. Here they were, professionally appreciating the place in the right way while we, a sweaty mob of people of all shapes and sizes were galloping about destroying the peace. . . . I was furious, we were all furious, we were hopping mad. Hopping mad. Hopping.

Scum!

I did a fictive brood in the theatre like everyone else, but this sudden criticism had disarmed and annihilated my composure. "How foolish to let a trifling barb like that irritate one." (The theatre was everything they said it was, and I resolved to come back and camp in the region next time.) But while only the English speakers of the party could have been winged by the smallshot of the old British couple, there was a general sense of strain setting in, which could only have been due to travel fatigue. We were feeling the need to lie up in one place for a few days, to get everything into perspective. This much-needed breather would, of course, come when we reached Taormina. But as yet we had to face Palermo, and a long coastal stint as far as Messina before the end, the parting of the ways. But as if to taunt us for our lack of moral fibre the drive, when we once embarked on it, was one of the most beautiful yet, across rolling valleys, through sleeping-beauty towns. Skies domed and blue, fragile as pigeons' eggs, liquid horizons where the sea clung to the edge of the world like a drop of silver. I dozed fitfully while the Microscopes had a bitter argument about something. The Count's wife was really feeling pretty bad and there was some question as to whether they would not stay on a night or two in Palermo to recover enough strength for the rest of the journey. He had sat beside me in the theatre and expressed some of his apprehension about his wife. "Since we lost our son she has been unable to regain an interest in life. She began to smoke and take tranquillisers and sleeping pills. She has ruined her health and now she can't break the habit. I only came on this trip in the hope that it might shake her up and enable her to regain her health."

Palermo

Palazzi

Cool vegetation, ageless functionaries,
Winter palaces on slimy canals
Folded on green conservatories starred
With time, and all their forlorn flora,
Big dusty plants without their mistresses.
No challenge in the acres of dumb carpet
Sarcophagus of reception-rooms groaning
"Who goes there?" You may well ask aloud.

Further on an artificial lake, forgetfulness.
Neither anguish nor joy obtains on it.

The ancient servant trembles as he points,
A corpse-propelling ninny with bad Parkinson's
Croaks "Questa la casa" and the silence falls
Touched by the silver chime of clocks,
While soft as graphite or mauve plum-pudding
The recent hills frame cities of the dead, Palermo.

Palermo

And Palermo, despite the fine presence of a colourful capital, exuded simply stress. It was everything that we had come to Sicily to get away from! Yes, the physical amenities were there, the hotel was large and comfortable; but there had been a strike of personnel and the beds were not made, while the meals had to be on the self-service pattern and luggage had to be man-hauled into lifts. Inevitably there was a bit of irritation and Roberto, always sensitive, began to feel once more that everything was his fault. It was late evening when we got in and we were offered a chance to see a few of the night spots, such as Mentobello Beach, and while this was pleasant it was touched very heavily with the brush of Palm Beach or Torquay and for that reason did not specially enchant us. The lighting in the hotel was precarious and early in the evening, due to some unspecified contingency, the bath water gave out and an official communiqué assured that it would not be restored until the following morning. It may be imagined that this did not lead to rejoicing, and the more acrimonious among us (the French take the first prize for selfishness and bad-temper in moments of crisis) became very angry with Roberto who had the bar specially opened (there was no barman) in order to try and mollify them. Mario offered us a short bus tour of the town but there were few takers—specially when it was discovered that this extramural trip would cost a small supplementary sum. The sniffs of the French could have been heard a mile off. What was one to do?

I walked a bit and ate in a trattoria and then went straight to bed with a couple of paperbacks I had found in a kiosk. I was surprised to find how well Sartre came over in English and what an accomplished novelist he was. But I slept ill. I resorted to Mogadon to help—breaking my promise to myself.

Meanwhile Beddoes, who never seemed to go to bed, played his eternal pool in the bar and Deeds drank a quiet whisky and pondered the cricket scores in a brand-new *Times* he had found in a waterfront kiosk. It was now the turn of Miss Lobb to produce an unusual reaction to circumstance. She had been very quiet all day, indeed rather sleepy. Now, seated in a dark corner of the bar not too far from Deeds she began to drink in a slow but extremely purposeful way—gin and soda, one following hard upon another. Gradually her quiet concentration forced itself upon the attention of Deeds who saw, to his astonishment, that Miss Lobb was showing signs of getting steadily drunker as glass succeeded glass. He felt alarm and concern, but after all her life was as much her own as her bank balance. What could he do, after all? Perhaps she had, in the course of a long bar life, contracted a touch of that blissful alcoholism which makes all the difference between despair and muddled indifference? Perhaps there was some past experience which ached her? Deeds felt sympathy and deep respect for Miss Lobb—who did not? But on she went.

He continued his careful analysis of the psychological weaknesses of the Hampshire eleven, and it was about eleven when he looked up to see that Miss Lobb's eyes were swimming in tears. She was not actually sobbing or sniffing but, as if from some invisible fountain inside her, tears just welled out and rolled down her cheeks. Deeds felt acute embarrassment, which was succeeded by anxiety as he saw her rise and slowly cross the hall towards the front door of the hotel. Surely she was not going out into the streets like that? She walked with a certain slow majesty which some people would say was the authentic Dublin glide—just a hint of being on castors, propelled by dark interior forces. It was rather a dilemma for a quixotic Englishman; after all, if the girl had trotted off in search of adventure surely he could not intervene. On the other hand if she got into trouble. . . . A perplexed Deeds pocketed his *Times* and set off in tactful pursuit of the lady, keeping a fair distance behind her and not in any way trying to bring himself to her attention. It was rather like following a sleep-walker about. But he felt his position acutely—after all he did not know her very well. She was simply a travelling companion. But on the other hand he could not bear the thought that she might by some accident of hazard find herself in a situation where she needed help. He followed.

Miss Lobb walked absently along the sea front for a while, apparently having decided to let the sea wind sober her up a little; but from the occasional glimpse Deeds caught of her face it seemed that her tears still flowed. She turned into the side streets and walked along the sides of a rectangle in order to emerge once more on the sea front which was not completely empty of life at that hour. There were a few rather undesirable-looking youths about and Miss Lobb appeared to wake up to the fact for she suddenly turned round, as if to return to the hotel, and found herself face to face with Deeds. She smiled at him and said: "O I am so glad to see you," which at once set Deeds' doubts at rest concerning his appropriateness on the scene. She now relaxed and settled upon a bench with an air of sleepy devoutness, and after a moment's hesitation he sat beside her and put his arm through hers, a gesture which she appeared to find reassuring. "It's this damned old anniversary of my mother's death," she explained at last, drying her tears in a pocket handkerchief. "It always catches me, and I get the migraine." She was in a sodden depression but not drunk and Deeds after showing an appropriate sympathy which was not unfeigned—and which contained a good portion of relief that she was in her right mind—suggested the only sort of therapy suitable for such cases, such circumstances, such moods. "We must walk it off," he said briskly, glad to have such a simple solution at hand. So walk they did.

All this of course he described to me on the morrow over a late breakfast, and I envied him the experience. They had walked half the night, in fact, and in fairyland. The sea front was more or less folded up and deserted but as they advanced upon the interior of the town they came to the margins of the darkness, and saw everywhere lights budding and springing up. It was an inferno of activity, and they realised that they were intruding upon the preparations for a great fête—in fact the name day of Palermo's patron saint, Saint Rosalie. Half the great city was still alive and awake, for apart from the numerous artisans who were busy arranging the decorations the streets were full of wide-eyed onlookers and curious children. The crowds walked up and down in this atmosphere of impromptu kermess, watching the coloured awnings going up, the electric-light fixtures being set and tried out, watching the Catherine-wheels and other fireworks being settled on their pinions. And tall as giraffes moved the three-storey trollies normally used to change the municipal electric-light bulbs but now pressed into service to string out rolls and rolls of coloured bunting across the streets. Children were bathing in the fountains, infected by all this blazing light and excitement. A whole market garden of flowers had sprung up in one quarter which they doused down with water every few minutes. It gave off a smell of wet earth like paradise. No wonder the hotels were short of bath-water! Livestock too was coming into town in lorries and being planked down beneath the booths and stalls; pigeons, ducks, quail and chickens, and morbidly sensitive rabbits! Miss Lobb thought herself in Paradise, and she was sad to think that she could not at that late hour buy a rabbit or a pot of basil. But the stress of the alcohol was diminishing now, and it was clear that by the time they regained the hotel she would be all right again. Deeds, combining therapy with culture, told her the story of Saint Rosalie.

Walking lightly thus, arm in friendly arm, they joined themselves to the dense groups of curious promenaders, who had turned the principal streets into an impromptu midnight Corso. The crowd swayed and swelled, ebbed this way and that, just like batches of seaweed in a sea-grotto. It was quite simply bliss, and the history of Rosalie gave a kind of folklorique colour to all that was going on round them. Deeds, who had had a lot of practice telling stories to his own children, found no difficulty in enlisting Miss Lobb's tenderest feelings on behalf of this little fifteen-year-old niece of William the Good who was so overcome by feelings of sanctity that she disappeared from the face of the earth—translated, some say, by angels direct to heaven. In fact, she had retired to a hermit's cave on Monte Pellegrino, there to pass a long life of anonymity, and finally there to die without letting anybody know what she had done. This was in 1159. The long

Palermo, the cathedral

silence fell and she was forgotten, all trace of her was lost. Then in 1624 while the town was in the dread grip of the plague, a holy man was troubled by a dream of her. He dreamed her history, and quite clearly saw in a vision that her remains lay buried in a mountain cave—he could indicate the exact spot. He suggested to the proper authorities that if these relics, which had in the interval acquired great magical powers of healing, were reverently gathered and carried in triumphal procession round the walls of the city, there was a sporting chance that the plague would abate.

This was duly done and Saint Rosalie saved the city and became its patron. The relics of the little saint were placed in a silver coffer and duly housed in the main cathedral of Palermo while her festival (July 15) leads off several days of rejoicing and present-giving, with brilliant and extravagant firework displays and religious services. It was the dress rehearsal to this event that Deeds had so luckily attended with Miss Lobb. They were so thrilled with all there was to see that they did not get back to the hotel for several hours. By then Miss Lobb was completely sobered and went to bed with expressions of rapturous gratitude. Deeds felt ennobled, if a bit exhausted, or at any rate so he admitted. But it was while he was embarking on an account of his wild night out with Miss Lobb that Saint Rosalie intruded on our sunlit breakfast in person, so to speak. Maroons started going off all over the town and for those not in the know there was a moment of pardonable anxiety. I thought the strikers had blown up the hotel. The Bishop, who was in the pool, almost gave signs of cardiac failure—he thought for a moment that the Catholics had struck home. But after the first smoke had cleared a smiling Roberto came to explain the noise, and suddenly we all noticed that everything was all right again, the stress and fatigue. We were all friends again and full of joy abundant—a new mood had set in, though there was no real reason for it unless it be a change of wind in the night. Or the soothing effect of little Rosalie's sanctity.

Good humour, like the bath water, had all of a sudden returned to the company and breakfast in the bright sunlight of a Palerman summer morning was almost a convivial affair. After the onslaught of the maroons had been explained away, that is. But this morning we were to bend our mind to sterner cultural things than the processions which had already started forming in the streets of the capital. We were going to visit the Archaeological Museum in order to see the sculptural treasures which the wretched archaeologists had carefully removed from Selinunte. It was distasteful to be forced to replace them mentally in order to admire them—I was reminded of my youth when I used to traipse round the Elgin Marbles in the British Museum, trying in a dispirited fashion to replace them upon the Acropolis which I had not as yet seen, with the help of photographs. It did not work, context is everything; besides, these were decorative additions to structure not independent art works.

Nevertheless the Sala de Selinunte contains real treasures like the famous Zeus and Hera on their wedding day, Heracles strangling an Amazon; they brought back memories of the deserted dunes, melting away in the sunlight above the lonely blue sea. There were other fine things too, from Himera and from Agrigento—indeed the museum is apparently the largest Greek Classical Museum outside metropolitan Greece itself. But something stuck, some subtle change of key, of rhythm; it was like a grain of sand in a Thermos flask. One somehow couldn't receive the full impact of these disembodied objects, however beautiful they were. Something that Deeds said made me realise that the reason was, of course, Saint Rosalie. What had happened was that we had stepped out of the Greek and Roman world, the historical Sicily of ancient times; and we had entered a new Sicily, the Arab, Norman, Spanish Sicily with its own notions of temporal beauty. The arrival of Saint Rosalie had been timely—together with her uncle William the Good—she symbolised this sudden change of axis and emphasis which was the message that Palermo held for us. We were now in modern times, and the effect of the Greek spirit had become distant, diluted, all but lost under the waves of cultures more recent if just as agitated. That was why these precious Greek relics seemed to lose their density and weight. Yes, objectively one realised that they must be seen, for even as fragments many of them were superb. Nor do I really know if the other members of the party shared this queer feeling that they were somehow dispossessed of their birthright in being put on view in this spacious and beautifully lit museum. But altogether it was an hour agreeably spent in a cool cavern of sculpture and nobody could pretend to be the worse for the experience.

It was a pleasant walk too to rejoin the little bus which waited for us in a small piazza nearby. Of course I realised that we would hardly see a tithe of the treasures available in Palermo, for we were leaving for Messina in the early afternoon. Nevertheless when I actually stood in the hushed shadow of the cathedral in Monreale and waited my turn to enter its august portals, I knew what it was. It was as if we had turned a page in the story-book which was Sicilian history and emerged into a period which echoed the most unusual juxtaposition of styles imaginable. This pure Palermo Sicilian is an extraordinary thing, the most beautifully realised merging of the grave and lofty Norman shapes with riotous and intricate Byzantine and Moorish decorative motifs, a brilliant syncopation of the grave central theme. It was my first taste of Sicilian baroque-Moorish—I think there is no established designation for this weird Gaudi–Arabian–Gothic. But it comes off in a magnificently innocent and playful way. The central religious solemnity of the impulse has been rendered childish, naïve and touching as a child's view of the Garden of Eden. Most of this work belongs to the period of Norman rule. Indeed the cathedral was the work of William the Good, while in its precincts lay the tombs of the other Williams, Good, Bad and Downright Indifferent, but no tomb for Rosalie who had first brought us this inkling of a sea change.

A whole town has grown round the cathedral but it draws its life from this great munificent work, one of the wonders of Christendom today. The marble rood screen, the sparkling mosaics and the gorgeous Byzantino–Moorish decoration make the whole thing feel as vibrant in colour as the heart of a pomegranate. Yet quickened and excited as one was by the novelty of this style one could not help asking oneself who actually worshipped here: or did all the denominations regard it as their own altar of worship? "You have a point," said Deeds who had read all the relevant books on the subject. "The dons seem to think that the style grew up as a kind of political accident; the Normans wanted to create an all-inclusive style for political reasons—they wanted a home-grown Sicilian style to emphasise the separateness of the island, its political uniqueness. With all the many races and religions it was very necessary to seek some kind of unifying motif. Maybe so. Myself I think that it was even simpler—giving work to the local artisan, creating jobs for the locals in order to keep them happy. It was completely unplanned; it just happened that the mix was a godsend, and worked. Genius in fact but quite accidental. And the jobs kept the chaps quiet and silenced criticism. These blood-thirsty northern invaders were sometimes relatively peaceful people and longed for a quiet life; why not mollify local resentments and satisfy local needs? Unless you prefer to believe that old William was an architectural genius and had the whole thing built to specification. I don't myself."

And there we had to leave the matter for I was determined to spend a few moments loitering in the cool and water-sounding colonnades which stretched away tenebrously from one side of the main building. Deeds left me for a moment to buy a few postcards in order to illustrate his remarks with views of the Cefalu Cathedral.

Yes, it was a new world with a different world-style and attitude. The various elements of this Norman–Oriental thing had no right to fuse so happily together and form something which was downright cheeky-exuberant but without archness. After all, when one thought of the relative gravity and staticness of the two differing styles—Norman architecture reaching to high heaven like a grave bear, and the Oriental feeling for intaglio, for marquetry, for the involuted forms of the Arabic script. No, it should not have worked so marvellously well as to constitute something pre-eminently Sicilian. One thinks of a place where the marriage did not work—Cyprus, where the Turks knocked off the towers of medieval cathedrals to add minarets; and of course the pictures one has seen of the Acropolis transformed into a mosque. . . . Here the whole thing is a triumphant success—

would that something similarly fond and creative had emerged on the political scale after the long suppurating Crusades. I made my way slowly back to the huge doors and looked for traces of my friend. He was busy postcard-hunting in the veritable tourist bazaar that had grown up in the little square outside the cathedral. What mountains of rubbish in bad taste the poor tourist is obliged to buy, for want of something pretty to spend his souvenir-money on. Or have they gauged our taste aright? It would seem so. One wonders what the old Greek equivalent would have been —in the time of Pausanias say. Sellers of magic herbs, snake-oil (still used in Cyprus against the sting of scorpions), spells. . . . "Nothing ever changes," said Deeds comfortably when I broached the idea to him. "Any Greek cathedral or Italian has always been like that; first of all it was a place of pilgrimage, you came from far away, you bought a candle, you left a thank-you gift or an *ex voto*. Now in order to mark the event you felt you ought to buy a medal or a trinket which would prove to your pals back at home that you had actually done the trip—you had been to Mecca."

"And that would give you a right to call yourself Hadji-Deeds or Hadji-Durrell?"

"Exactly. And you would sport a green turban."

"It would be simpler than buying all this trash."

There was a yellow-eyed man, a gipsy, leaning against a wall and playing monotonously upon a jew's harp, its dull twang rising above the chatter and turmoil of the market. His wife was circulating in the crowd touting for fortunes. Mario was oozing his bus through the crowd with the slowness of oil in order to place it square before the entrance. I suddenly realised that it was crazy—to leave Palermo with so much unseen, and with the prospect of a night of carnival to witness. But our itinerary had been fixed by other hands, elsewhere, and with another part of me I felt I ought to stick with my fellow-travellers. Anyway it was not for long—the Carousel would come to an end at Messina, whence we would be scattered all over Taormina for the "supplementary free week", but in different hotels. Nevertheless . . . "It seems mad not to stay longer," I said, and Deeds agreed but added, "You can come back in your free week, just rent a little car. This trip is only a spot reconnaissance." It was the right way to look at it. Superficial as it was I felt that the admiring recognition of the force of the new architecture was really the key to this end of Sicily. I had grasped the language of its later invaders. Moreover I had bitten off a sufficiently large chunk of the Norman Oriental aesthetic to chew on for the present; a glimpse of Cefalu Cathedral would help, of course, and that was scheduled for the late afternoon. We regained our places and moved slowly off down the long glades towards the capital, whence the roads led outwards again along a grim stretch of coast, towards Cefalu.

The pace had become smarter for we had ambled away a bit too much of our allotted time in the museum; Mario even skipped on to a motorway for a few miles to take in the slack. Then back along a rather grim sea coast, with monotonous outcrops of black cliff covered in sea holly, and black beaches presumably of volcanic ash. Our lunch tables had been set out on a fine shady terrace with a marvellous view but the little beach below was disappointingly rocky and pebbled. Nevertheless a few of our braver members ventured upon a quick dip before lunch over which Roberto presided in an expensive scarlet bathing costume. He was obviously dying to save a life, but nobody gave him the chance. The lunch was banal but the fine setting made it feel almost sumptuous. The Germans held hands in a purposeful way. Beddoes, to everyone's surprise, took a piece of knitting out of his pocket and started to work his way round the heel of a sock. The dentist's lady was so amused by this that she offered to darn the hole for him, an offer which he accepted with grace. Roberto, wounded by the signs of German intimacy, played with the cutlery and went hot and cold by turns.

Today despite the superb sunlight one felt a certain heat heaviness which made one think of earthquakes—and what more appropriate since we were heading for Messina. I gathered that normally the Carousel spent the last week together in a Taormina hotel with all excursions optional; but this year there had been trouble with strikes and all European bookings had become problematical. Hence the rather *ad hoc* arrangements for Taormina where each of us found himself alone in a separate lodging. I was surprised to verify Deeds' earlier opinion about being sorry to part with my fellow-travellers. It was true that I felt a twinge of regret; but I also felt a twinge of relief—for it would have been unthinkable to extend this mode of travel over a longer space of time without coming to dislike, even to hate, it. Had the distances been greater and the stresses more intense we should all now be life-enemies instead of friends.

A wind off the sea had got up and on the coast road tugged at our tyres like a puppy, making the task of Mario rather more difficult since he wanted to put on a bit of speed. The sea rose. Roberto made a short apologia through the microphone about the wicked way we were just about to treat Cefalu. "You will begin to complain and say it is a scandal to rush into the cathedral and then rush away again. But please try to be charitable. What would you have felt about the Agency if we had cut out Cefalu altogether, saying that there wasn't enough time, which there isn't?" It was marvellous the way he found his way among the English tenses; it proved that he always felt called upon to make this statement at this particular place, so that the little speech was well-rehearsed. Indeed it was not long before one of the sharper loops of the coast road brought us up on a wooded knoll from which we saw the characteristic profile of Cefalu facing us across a blue bay. I found it astonishingly like the headland of Paleocastrizza in Corfu. It looked like a great whale basking in the blueness—a mythological ruminant of a fish, dreaming of some lost oceanic Eden, its eyes shut. The town clustered close about it. It was very beautiful and Roberto was right really—it was no place to treat with tourist disrespect. But on the other hand, was he right to bring the matter up at all? The Microscopes, for example, would have noticed nothing untoward in our haste, whereas this little speech only tended to make them feel that they ought to ask for their money back. But the Bishop felt the full cultural enormity of the thing for he sunk his chin on his breast bone and gave out the impression of seething like hot milk.

We nosed into this most atmospheric of little towns on a low throttle, for the streets were crowded with holiday-makers in different stages of undress; Mario had by now convinced us that he could put our bus through the eye of a needle if he wished. But Cefalu was quite a trial with its narrow and encumbered medieval streets, and the cathedral lay right at the end of a loop of one-way streets which did not seem to correspond to the traffic realities of the little spa, where ten bicycles might block all the traffic for days, it would seem. But what was good was that the unafraid pedestrian had taken possession of the place and everything conformed to his walking pace. This at once made things harmonious and pleasant—at this speed you could lean out and buy an ice, for the French ladies did, or a clutch of gaudy postcards, for the old Count did, or a charm against the evil eye, for Roberto did. This he handed to Beddoes to preserve him from harm. In a way it sort of accredited us to the townspeople of Cefalu and made us feel at home straight off. But owing to the fool one-way street we had to do that last hundred yards on foot, a pleasant martyrdom for the square in which the church stands is a handsome one.

Once again we had the place more or less to ourselves, and once more Miss Lobb took the opportunity to say a short and comforting prayer to her creator—or was she just praying for the death of Beddoes, as Deeds rather wickedly suggested? Not Miss Lobb, the spirit of London town. Deeds, who knew the place well, elected to spend his time in the lofty porch while the rest of us perambulated the shadowy interior of the building. He was unwilling to snuff out his pipe which was drawing particularly well that day. One of the French ladies had beautiful teeth and was most conscious of the fact, for she showed them frequently in a large smile. It had become somewhat automatic as a gesture and it was interesting to see her giving this warm alert smile of recognition to inanimate objects, even to the saints in the frescoes. But Roberto was right about Cefalu—the church of Roger II was too important to miss out. It was a wonderful example of the same Norman–Byzantine–Spanish–baroque which had been such a singularly new experience in the island. The building was started in 1131, but took over a century to complete, so that it reflects more than one cycle of historic changes in forms and materials. But William had vowed to have a cathedral built in this place after he nearly suffered shipwreck on the headland. It was the customary way to express gratitude at that epoch, and we have been the ones to benefit from it.

Half an hour was soon spent and once more we sailed out from the crags of Cefalu and up on to the snaky coastal road which would carry us from headland to headland, past Himera with its Doric temple, towards Messina which would be our penultimate port of call. Tomorrow Mario would distribute us all over Taormina to continue our Sicilian adventure alone. Alone!

It was dusk when we arrived at Messina—sunset is an ideal time to take in the marvellous views of the harbour, subject of so many Victorian water-colours. But the earthquake which devastated Messina still rumbles on historically—it is a black date which has permanently marked the historical calendar of modern Sicily, grim and cruel, as if in contrast to the sweet Theocritan landscapes of this part of the island. The words have a kind of density, an echo, like the date of the Fall of Constantinople. We did several of the standard views of the town—the whole island seems to be one extraordinary belvedere—and then disembarked at the hotel in rather a sober mood. The only cultural fixture was a glimpse of the cathedral on the morrow. Tonight we were free to visit the town with Roberto or dine and go to bed. No one was in the mood to go out, it seemed. So in a shuffling unpremeditated fashion we congregated in the bar to exchange visiting cards and addresses against the parting tomorrow. Someone offered a drink all round in honour of the German engagement and this was loyally drunk.

It was a little sad.

I went for a trot round the town to do a little bit of shopping, and to gather what impressions I could of its relative newness, its rawness—for it had been laboriously put together again after the cataclysm. I found it atmospherically most appealing, perhaps the town in Sicily where life would be the most delightful. In trying to analyse why I discovered that it was once more the question of scale. Since the earthquake the houses had been limited to two or three storeys, so that it had all the spacious charm of somewhere like the Athens Plaka under the Acropolis, or like Santa Barbara in California. The minute your architecture dwarfs people, shows disrespect for the purely human scale, you start to stunt their minds and chill their spirits. Messina was a fine proof of this notion of human relevance to architecture—a model in fact. And on the morrow these views were underlined in the most overwhelming way by the qualities of the cathedral.

At the hotel our identities were looked into by a couple of suspicious looking carabinieri to the intense annoyance of Roberto who felt it was a slur on the good name of the Company. Did they think he was ferrying carloads of criminals all over Sicily? But I missed this visitation.

Italy of course was in the grip of an inflation far worse than anything we had seen back in France; but one singular aspect of it was the sudden disappearance of small change. It had just happened in Messina. Nothing under a thousand-lira note seemed to exist and in order that business should continue as usual one was forced to accept change in kind so to speak. For example, in order to buy some toothpaste, aspirin and tissues, which I did need, I was forced to accept as "change" a pair of silk stockings, a surgical bandage for sprains, and a pair of nail-scissors. This sort of thing was going on in all the shops with the result that people were being loaded down like Christmas trees with things they didn't want. I even got a telephone tally of nickle as part of my change in a tobacconist's shop. It represented the price of a local phone call. Of course we were obliged to carry over this strange kind of primitive barter into our own lives—I tipped the hall porter with the telephone tally and an unwanted Tampax which had strayed into my chemist's bundle. It was quite childish and chaotic. But the staff of the hotel seemed used to accepting these strange collections of objects instead of money tips. And finally one got quite used to going out to buy one orange and coming back with a bunch of grapes and a pound of figs as well. In a couple of days we had accumulated dozens of unwanted objects like this.

The evening was a trifle saddening; we all hung about a little, rather feeling that perhaps the situation called for a little speech from Roberto, or a more formal farewell to each other. But timidity and lack of organisation held us imprisoned in the mood until it was too late.

Messina was a calm and tranquil place to spend a night, but we slept badly; afflicted by a woebegone sense of anti-climax. Even breakfast was an unusually subdued affair. We packed and loaded our gear automatically like the experienced tourists we had by now become. Then we swung off in the bright sunshine to have one glance at the cathedral before taking the long coastal road to Taormina. Here again was a fascinating aesthetic experience for me, and one which I had not expected. I knew that, like the rest of the town, the cathedral had been shattered to bits by the famous earthquake, and had been more or less shoved together. I had little hopes that this forced restoration of the great building would be a success. It is a quite fantastic success; it has been done so simply and without pretensions, executed with a bright spontaneity of a Zen water-colour. Whatever they found left was run into the new structure which itself was graced with an anti-earthquake armature. The result is simply marvellous; the huge building is among the most satisfying and gorgeous to be enjoyed in the island; and one is moved by the almost accidental simplicity with which it has all been brought off. Deeds was touched by my enthusiasm, and was glad, he said, that he had not overpraised the thing.

And so off along the coast road in the fine sunlight towards the last port of call. On the last headland Roberto called a halt and we made a few colour photographs of the Carousel which I knew I would never see. Somewhere, in discarded photograph albums, they would lie, melting away year by year.

And soon we ran in on Taormina and the melancholy distribution began; the French ladies and the Count with his wife were put down on the road to Naxos, the Japs disappeared, Beddoes was dropped at a pension which looked like the headquarters of the Black Hand. It was indeed like the casualty list of a battalion, men dropping away one by one. "So long!" "Bye-bye!" "See you again I hope." "Ring me in London!" "Come to

Geneva, but let me know." Mario had become sulky with sadness and Roberto was a little bit on edge too it seemed. We sorted out baggage and shook hands. Deeds disappeared into an orange-grove with his bags, promising that we should meet again for a drink somewhere in the island. He had a few more visits to make as yet. The pre-Adamic couple walked away into the sunlight with an air of speechless ecstasy. I was the last one—the higher we went the fewer we became; my little pension was in the heart of Taormina—which is built up in layers like a wedding cake. But at last my turn came. I embraced Mario and Roberto and thanked them for their kindness and good humour. I meant it. They had done nobly by us.

Taormina

Taormina

We three men sit all evening
In the rose-garden drinking and waiting
For the moon to turn our roses black,
Crawling across the sky. We mention
Our absent friend from time to time.
Some chessmen have tumbled over,
They also die who only sit and wait,
For the new moon before this open gate.

What further travel can we wish on friends
To coax their absence with our memory—
One who followed the flying fish beyond the
Remote Americas, one to die in battle, one
To live in Persia and never write again.
She loved them all according to their need
Now they are small dust waiting in perfect heed,
In someone's memory for a cue.
Thus and thus we shall remember you.

The smoke of pipes rises in pure content
The roses stretch their necks, and there
She rides at last to lend
A form and fiction to our loving wish.
The legions of the silent all attend.

Taormina

"Taormina, the old Bull Mountain—I'm so glad I followed my instinct and saved it up for the last. It was like a kind of summation of all that went before, all the journeys and flavours this extraordinary island had to offer. Like a fool, I loped up it with Loftus in an old racing-car at full moon; but something made me aware of the sacrilege and next day I walked humbly down to the bottom where I left a propitiatory candle in the little Christian shrine of St. Barnabus (isn't it?) and retraced my way up again. Of course it must have once been a sort of sacred way, laid out against the breast of this steep little mountain so that one could approach it step by step, loop by loop. The long steep zigzags of the road must have been punctuated significantly with statues and flowering shrubs and little fanes to take an offering of the first fruits. One arrived, slowly and breathlessly, watching the scene widen out around one, and deepen into a screen of mountain and sea and volcano."

Thus Martine. In the garden of the Villa Rosalie to which I had been assigned, two white-haired men played chess amidst dense flowering shrubbery which suggested rather the cultivation of a spa like Nice than the wild precincts of Sicily; I had come back to Europe really. I left my bags and walked the length of the main street with its astonishing views. It was so good that it aroused indignation: one almost suspected it to be spurious; but no, it simply outstripped language, that was all. And a wonderful sense of intimacy and well-being suffused the whole place. Yes, it was sophisticated as well—and as if to match the idea I found a small visiting card from Loftus waiting in my box inscribed in that fine old-fashioned lace hand which he had cultivated in order to write ancient Greek. A message of greeting, giving me his phone number. But tonight I was in a mood to be alone, to enjoy and to regret being alone. It was a strange new feeling, not unconnected with fatigue. But the sinking sunset which one drank out of one's glass of Campari, so to speak, was as extraordinary as any that Greece or Italy has to offer. And Etna did her stuff on the skyline. "However blasé one is, however much one has been prepared for the aerial splendours of the little town, its freshness is perennial, it rises in one like sap, it beguiles and charms as the eye turns in its astonishment to take in crags and clouds and mountains and the blue coastline. Here one could sit in a deck-chair gazing out into the night and thinking about Greek flair and Roman prescience—they married here in this place; but why was it a failure at last, why did it fall apart?"

Because everything does I suppose. And now after so long, here come I with my valedictory admiration, inhabitant of yet another culture which is falling apart, which is doomed to the same decline and fall, perhaps even more suddenly. . . . How marvellous to read a book at dinner. I had chosen that fussy but touching civil servant Pliny; his pages tell one all one wants to know and admire about Rome.

And how pleasant, too, to dawdle the length of that main street—like walking the bridge of a Zeppelin. And how astonishingly still the air is at this great height. It is what constitutes the original feature of Taormina, I think; one's thoughts naturally turn to places like Villefranche or Cassis (as they must have been a hundred years ago); and then, quite naturally, to Capri and Paleocastrizza. The difference is not only in variety and prolixity of classical views—the whole thing has been anchored in mid-heaven, at a thousand feet, and up here the air is still and calm. The white curtains in my hotel-room breathed softly in and out, like the lungs of the universe itself. There were cafés of Roman and Venetian excellence, and there were the traditional hordes of tourists perambulating up and down the long main street. Its narrowness grew on one after the sixth or seventh turn upon it.

And in the little side streets there were unforgotten corners of the real Italy—by which I mean the peasant Italy with its firmly anchored values and purity of heart. At dusk next day I walked up to have a look at the villa Lawrence occupied for three years.

It was modest and quite fitting to the poems he wrote here in this pure high tower of silence which is Taormina at night. But at the first corner of the road there stood a tattered trattoria with a dirty cloth across the door to keep the flies at bay. In the street, under a faded-looking tree, stood a rickety table and two chairs. Just that and nothing more. A tin table which had been racked with smallpox and perhaps some hunter's smallshot. A slip of broom was suspended from the lintel. And here I was served a harsh black wine by a matron with a wall-eye and hairy brown arms. She was like Demeter herself and she talked to me quietly and simply about the wines of the island. Hers was Etna, volcanic wine, and it tasted of iron; but it was not sugary and I bought a demijohn as a present for Loftus when I should decide to take up his invitation. If I hesitated, it was for a rather obscure reason; I wanted, so to speak, to let the Carousel experience evaporate before I changed the whole key. For I knew that encountering Loftus and his life here meant that I would find myself back in the Capri of the twenties; in the world of Norman Douglas—a world very dear to me precisely because it was a trifle precious. Martine had had one foot in this world, to be sure, but what I had personally shared with her had not belonged to this aspect of our islomania. Capri had long since sunk below the horizon when Cyprus became a reality. Yet she had loved Douglas as much as I, and Compton Mackenzie as well, while the silent empty villa of Lawrence up the hill also carried the echoes of that Nepenthean period where *Twilight in Italy* matched *South Wind.*

But Taormina is so small that it was inevitable that from time to time I would bump into other members of the Carousel. I saw the Microscopes in the distance once or twice, and the American dentist waved from the April café as I passed. I also saw the Bishop—he had taken up a stance in order to "appreciate" a piece of architecture, while his wife sat on a stone and fanned herself with her straw hat. But that was all. There was no sign of Deeds. After two days of this delicious privacy in my little pension where I knew nobody, I visited the bookshop and bought a guide to the island, intending to spend my last few days filling in the lacunae in my knowledge. I could not leave without bracing Etna for example, or standing on the great "belvedere of all Sicily", Enna; then Tyndarus . . . and so on. I thought I would rent a small car to finish off the visit in a style more reminiscent of the past than by having any truck with trains and buses. It would be interesting to see what Loftus thought.

I rang him, and was amused and pleased to recognise his characteristic drawl, and the slight slurring of the r's which had always characterised his speech. He had a little car he could lend me, which was promising, and so I agreed to dine at his villa the following evening. In a way it was reassuring that nothing much had changed for Loftus; he had ruined a promising diplomatic career by openly living with his chauffeur, an ex-jailbird, and then, as if that were not enough, winning notoriety by writing a novel called *Le Baiser* in French which had a *succès de scandale*. Someone in the Foreign Office must have known that the word "baiser" didn't only mean "kiss" (though it is difficult to think who) and Loftus was invited to abstract himself from decent society. This he did with good grace—he had a large private income—and retired to Taormina where he grew roses and translated the classics. He had been one of the most brilliant scholars of his time, though an incurable dilettante. About Sicily he knew all that there was to be known. But of course now he was getting on, like the rest of us, and hardly ever moved from the Villa Ariadne —a delightful old house built on a little headland over the sea, and buried in roses. He too was a relic of the Capri epoch, a silver-age man.

I hardly recognised the chauffeur-lover after such a long lapse of time—he had grown fat and hairy, and spindle-shanked. But he panted with pleasure like a bull-terrier at meeting me again and ushered me into the car with a good deal of friendly ceremony. I was glad that I had been fetched when he started to negotiate the steep descent from the mountain to the coast where the villa was. It was a labyrinth of criss-crossing roads, with snatches of motor road to be crossed. But at last we arrived in that cool garden full of olives and oleanders and the smell of rushing water in dusty fountains—the house had been designed by water-loving Romans. And there was Loftus frail and smart as always, though a little greyer, waiting for me.

Terraces led down to the sea; there were candles already burning on a white tablecloth; wide divans with stained cretonne covers were laid out under the olives. The parrot Victor had gone to bed, his cage was covered in a green baize cloth. Smell of Turkish tobacco. "Dear boy," said Loftus, "I can't rise to greet you as is fitting. I had a small ski-mishap." His crutches lay beside him. The tone and temper of his conversation was reassuringly the same as ever, and I was glad to feel that now it would never change. It belonged to an epoch, it marched with the language of the eighteenth century whose artists (like Stendhal?) discovered how to raise social gossip to the level of an art. The trivia of Loftus had the same fine merit—even though he had not much at present to recount. Various film nabobs from Beverley Hills had come and gone. Then Cramp the publisher from London. There were two amusing local scandals which might lead to a knife-fight. "All this is simply to situate you, dear boy. You are in Taormina now which has its own ethos and manners. It is very degenerate in comparison to the rest of Sicily which is rather strait-laced."

In this easy and languid style the conversation led him closer and closer to the last days of Martine. She had spent a lot of time with him; she would bring over her two children and a picnic and spend the day on his little beach, reading or writing. She had never been happier, she said, than during that last summer. She had spoken of me with affection, and indeed had rung me up once or twice for advice about a book she was planning to write about Sicily. I surmised it must have been the "pocket Sicily" for her children—Loftus agreed that it was. "Finally she gave up and said she would make you do it. She found that in Sicily there is no sense of time; her children inhabited a history in which Caesar, Pompey, and Timoleon were replaced, without any lapse of time, by Field-Marshal Kesserling and the Hermann Goering division—the one the Irish knocked about." He smiled. "It's difficult to know how you would have dealt with that sort of Mediterranean amnesia. Everything seems simultaneous." By the same token Martine seemed as ever-present as Loftus himself—the mere intervention of death seemed somehow unreal, untruthful. "She took everything calmly, gaily, lightly. Her husband was marvellous, too, and made it easy. Also she wasn't encumbered by any heavy intellectual equipment like a theological attitude. She wasn't Christian, was she?" As far as I knew she wasn't anything, though she observed the outward forms for fear of wounding people—but that was just part of a social code. What Loftus really meant was that she was a Mediterranean, by which he meant a pagan; she belonged to the Astarte–Aphrodite of Erice rather than to Holy Mary of Rome. I did not elaborate on all this, it was not our business.

At any rate she had satisfactorily managed to answer the question I had put to her in the Latomie at Syracuse; the word "yes" had been exactly where I had asked her to arrange for it to be. But about the question, it went something like this: "Do you remember all our studies and arguments over the Pali texts and all the advice you got from your Indian princeling? Well, before you finally died did you manage to experience that state, however briefly, which the texts promised us and which was rendered no doubt very inadequately in English as 'form without identity'?" Rather long-winded, but it is hard to express these abstract notions. Yet I was delighted to think that perhaps she might have experienced the precious moment of pure apprehension which had so far eluded me—which I could intuit but not provoke: poems are inadequate substitutes for it.

Loftus said: "After dinner I must put you on a tape-recording of a dinner party we had once here; she wanted to ask me some questions about Theocritos and Pindar, and then she forgot to take the tape. I found it long afterwards. It's pleasant to hear her voice again."

So it was, and the setting was not the less pleasant, this warm olive grove steepening towards the sea. The chink of plates and the little rushes of laughter or the clash of people all talking together. Martine's swift Italian. Somewhere she said that she had given instructions to her lawyers to let her lie in state one whole night on the beach at Naxos, close to the sea, so that like a seashell she could absorb the sighing of the sea and take it with her wherever she was going. "I don't know if she did," said Loftus, "but the idea struck me as typical of her and I dreamed about it for several nights. Martine, all dressed in white, lying in her beautiful coffin which was like a Rolls, lying on the beach almost within reach of the waves, under the stars."

It was late when the chauffeur finally dropped me back in Taormina, but despite the lateness of the hour there were cafés open and I felt sufficiently elated by my evening to want to prolong it for a while; to have a quiet drink and think before turning in with my Pliny. I had, in a manner of speaking, recovered contact with Martine. It was reassuring to feel that she was, in a sense, still there, still bright in the memory of her friends. On the morrow I had promised to return and lunch with Loftus, bathe, and work out an itinerary for my last few days in Sicily. He on his part would have the little Morris serviced and fixed up for my journey on which he would have accompanied me had it not been for his ankle. I must say I was glad, for though he was good company, I still felt a little bit as if I was on a pilgrimage and wanted to spend the time alone before I took off once more for France.

I sat long over my drink, tasting the cool balm of the midnight air and listening to the occasional chaffering voices in the dark street. Taormina had fallen asleep like a rooks' nest; occasionally there was a little movement, a few voices—as if a dream had troubled the communal sleep. Then everything subsided once more into a hush. My waiter was almost asleep on his feet. I must really finish up, I thought, and have pity on him. Yet I lingered, and if I reflected upon Martine the thoughts were relatively down to earth and free from all the nostalgias which tend to lie in wait for one when the mysterious matter of death comes to the front of the stage. I was still very conscious of that tiny chuckle with which my friend had always demolished anything slack or sentimental, anything sloppy in style or insipid. Truth to tell, I hardly dared to mourn the girl so much did I dread the memory of that chuckle. For her even death had its own rationale, its strictness and inevitability. It was thus. It was so. And it must be accepted with good nature, good grace, good humour.

Even Loftus, *homo beatus* as he used to call himself (sitting in the garden in a deck-chair looking out to sea through an old brass telescope)—even he could not speak of her without a smile, as if of recognition. "You know," he said, during our dinner, and apropos of the tape-recording of her voice, "the English can be disappointing in so many ways, but in friendship they have no peers." Due, I think, to this quality of smiling good sense which made it easy to confront life and death without a false Roman stoicism.

I spared the waiter at last and walked slowly back to my lodgings, savouring the soft airs of the invisible dawn with delectation. I did not feel a bit sleepy, and indeed it was almost too late to go to bed. I was sorry not to be on the beach at Naxos, for I should have bathed and waited for the light to break before making myself some breakfast. I compromised with a tepid shower and a lie-down of an hour which was interrupted by the breakfast-gong.

That morning I had some shopping to do, and a suit to get cleaned. At the post office I ran into the two French ladies. They had had a great shock, and they gobbled like turkeys as they told me about it. As usual they had been sending off clutches of post-cards to their friends and relations in France—they seemed to have no other occupation or thought in mind. But peering through the grille after posting a batch they distinctly saw the clerk sweep the contents of the box into the lap of his overall and walk into the yard in order to throw all the mail on to a bonfire which was burning merrily on the concrete, apparently fed by all the correspondence of Taormina. They were aghast and shouted out to him—as a matter of fact they could hardly believe their eyes at first. They thought they had to do with a madman—but no, it was only a striker. He was burning mail as fast as it was posted. When they protested he said "*Niente Niente* . . . questo e tourismo . . ."

I transcribe phonetically, and consequently inaccurately—but that is what they said he said; and I took him to be telling them something like "It's nothing at all, my little ladies, just a clutch of tourist junk."

But the links of our friendship had, I observed, begun to

weaken already for I had forgotten their names. I racked my brains to recall them. Anyway they were leaving in the morning and were half nostalgic and half irritated by the high price of things and the general slipshodness and insolence of the small shop-keepers. But it is ever thus in tourist centres.

Soon I was to begin my solitary journeys in the little borrowed car, trying, in the days which were left me, to fill in the jigsaw of names and strike up a nodding acquaintance with so many of the places mentioned in the letters of Martine and in the guide. It was rather a breathless performance. I realised then that Sicily is not just an island, it is a sub-continent whose variegated history and variety of landscapes simply overwhelms the traveller who has not set aside at least three months to deal with it and its over-lapping cultures and civilisations. But such a certainty rendered me in the event rather irresponsible and light-hearted. I took what I could get so to speak, bit deeply into places like Tyndarus, revisited Segesta, crossed the hairy spine of the island for another look at Syracuse; but this time on different roads, deserted ones. In some obscure quarry I came upon half-carved temple drums which had not yet been extracted from the rock. I had a look at the baby volcanoes in their charred and stenchy lands. Islands whose names I did not know came up out of the mist like dogs to watch me having a solitary bathe among the sea-lavender and squill of deserted estuaries near Agrigento. But everywhere there came the striking experience of the island—not just the impact of the folklorique or the sensational. Impossible to describe the moth-soft little town of Besaquino with its deserted presbytery where once there had been live hermits in residence. Centuripe with its jutting jaw and bronzed limestone—an immense calm necropolis where the rock for hundreds of yards was pitted like a lung with excavated tombs. Pantalica I think it was called.

But time was running out. I had decided, after a chance meeting with Roberto in the tavern of the Three Springs, to keep Etna for my last night—the appropriate send-off. He had promised to escort me to the top to watch the sun come up, and thence down to the airport to catch the plane.

I burnt Martine's letters on a deserted beach near Messina—she had asked me to do so; and I scattered the ashes. I regretted it rather, but people have a right to dispose of their own productions as they wish.

It was the end of a whole epoch; and appropriately enough I spent a dawn in the most beautiful theatre in the world—an act of which Etna itself appeared to approve because once, just to show me that the world was rightside up, she spat out a mouthful of hot coals, and then dribbled a small string of blazing diamonds down her chin. Roberto had been a little wistfully drunk in the tavern; he was recovering from his heart attack over the girl Renata, but he was rather bitter about tourism in general and tourists in particular—there was a new Carousel expected in a few days. I wondered about Deeds, what he was doing with himself; and then I had the queer dissolving feeling that perhaps he had never existed or that I had imagined him. Roberto was saying: "Travelling isn't honest. Everyone is trying to get away from something or else they would stay at home. The old get panicky because they can't make love any more, and they feel death in the air. The others, well, I bet you have your own reasons too. In the case of the officer Deeds you know his young brother is buried in that little cemetery where he told us about the locust-beans—one of the commandos he mentioned. Much younger than him I gather." He went on a while in a desultory fashion, while we drank off a bit of blue-black iron-tasting wine—I wondered if our insides would rust. I had done my packing, I had bought my postcards and guides. I wondered vaguely what Pausanias had been trying to get away from as he trudged round Athens taking notes. A Roman villa on the Black Sea, a nagging wife, the solitary consular life to which he had, as an untalented man, doomed himself?

We walked slowly back to my hotel in the fine afternoon light; and there another surprise awaited me. In my bedroom sat an extraordinary figure which I had, to the best of my knowledge, never seen before. A bald man with a blazing, glazed-looking cranium which was so white that it must have been newly cropped. It was when he removed his dark glasses and grinned that I recognised, with sinking heart, my old travelling companion

Beddoes. "Old boy," he said, with a kind of fine elation, "they are on my trail, the carabinieri. Interpol must have lit a beacon. So I had to leave my hotel for a while." I did not know what to say. "But I am sneaking off tonight on the Messina ferry and Roberto has arranged to have me cremated, so to speak."

"Cremated?"

"Tonight, old boy, I jump into Etna like old Empedocles, with a piercing eldrich shriek. And you and Roberto at dawn scatter some of my belongings round the brink, and the Carousel announces my death to the press."

"You take my breath away. Roberto said nothing to me. And I have just left him."

"You can't be too discreet in these matters. Anyway it is just Sicilian courtesy. They often let people disappear like that."

"Beddoes, are you serious?"

It sounded like the sudden intrusion of an *opera bouffe* upon the humdrum existence of innocent tourists. And then that amazing glazed dome, glittering and resplendent. It looked sufficiently new to attract curiosity and I was relieved to see that he covered it up with a dirty ski-eap. Clad thus he looked like a madly determined Swiss concierge. "Roberto asked me to leave my belongings here with you. When he calls for you at midnight just carry them along; he will know what to do. And it's quite a neat parcel."

"Very well," I said reluctantly, and he beamed and shook my hand as he said goodbye. Then, turning at the door, he said: "By the way, old scout, I forgot to ask you if you could loan me a few quid. I am awfully pushed for lolly. I had to buy a spare pair of boots and an overcoat to complete my disguise. Cost the earth." I obliged with pardonable reluctance and he took himself off, whistling "Giovanezza" under his breath.

His belongings consisted of a sleeping-bag and a mackintosh, plus a pair of shapeless navvy's boots. The suitcase was empty save of a copy of a novel entitled *The Naked Truth*.

Roberto was punctual and accepted full responsibility for the plot concerning Beddoes' disappearance. Apparently the authorities often turned a blind eye to the disappearance of people into

Etna. He said: "There's only one other volcano where one can arrange that sort of thing for hopeless lovers or bankrupts or schoolmasters on the run like Beddoes. It's in Japan."

The car drummed and whined its way into the mountains and I began to feel the long sleep of this hectic fortnight creep upon me. I had a drink and pulled myself together for we had to envisage a good walk at the other end, from the last point before the crater, the observatory. It became cooler and cooler. Then lights and mountain air with spaces of warmth, and the smell of acid and sulphur as we walked up the slopes of the crater. Somewhere near the top we lit a bonfire and carefully singed Beddoes' affairs before consigning them to the care of a carabinieri friend who would declare that he had found them on the morrow. The boots burned like an effigy of wax—he must have greased them with something. Poor old Beddoes!

Then the long wait by a strange watery moonlight until an oven lid started to open in the east and the "old shield-bearer" stuck its nose over the silent sea. "There it is," said Roberto, as if he had personally arranged the matter for me. I thanked him. I reflected how lucky I was to have spent so much of my life in the Mediterranean—to have so frequently seen these incomparable dawns, to have so often had sun and moon both in the sky together.

Autumn Lady: Naxos

Under spiteful skies go sailing on and on,
All canvas soaking and all iron rusty,
Frail as a gnat, but peerless in her sadness,
My poor ship christened by an ocean blackness,
Locked into cloud or planet-sharing night.

The primacy of longing she established.
They called her Autumn Lady, with two wide
Aegean eyes beneath the given name,
Sea-stressed, complete, a living wife.

She'll sink at moorings like my life did once,
In a night of piercing squalls, go swaying down,
In an island without gulls, wells, walls,
In a time of need, all stations fading, fading.

She will lie there in the calm cathedrals
Of the blood's sleep, not speaking of love,
Or the last graphic journeys of the mind.
Let tides drum on those unawakened flanks
Whom all the soft analysis of sleep will find.

Besaquino

No stars to guide. Death is that quiet cartouche,
A nun-besought preserve of praying-time,
That like a great lion silence hunts,
At noon, at ease, and all because he must.
His scenery is so old,
His sacred pawtouch cold.

A lupercal of girls remember him
In nights defunct from lack of sleep
Tossing on iron beds awaiting dawn . . .
He wound up his death each evening like a clock,
Walked to obscure cafés to criticise
The fires that blush upon the crown of Etna.
Leopardi in the ticking mind,
Lay unknown like an exiled king,
Printing his dreams among the olive glades
In orchards of discontent the fruitful word.

Index